I0562709

Pawns

of

Heaven

Justin Phillips

ABSOLUTELY AMAZING eBOOKS

ABSOLUTELY AMAZING eBOOKS

Published by Whiz Bang LLC, 926 Truman Avenue, Key West, Florida 33040, USA.

Pawns of Heaven copyright © 2016 by Justin Phillips. Electronic compilation/ paperback edition copyright © 2016 by Whiz Bang LLC.

All rights reserved. No part of this book may be reproduced, scanned, or transmitted in any form or by any means, electronic or mechanical, including photocopying, recording, or any information storage and retrieval system, without permission in writing from the publisher. Please do not participate in or encourage piracy of copyrighted materials in violation of the author's rights. Purchase only authorized ebook editions.

This is a work of fiction. Names, characters, places, and incidents either are the product of the author's imagination or are used fictitiously, and any resemblance to actual persons, living or dead, businesses, companies, events, or locales is entirely coincidental. While the author has made every effort to provide accurate information at the time of publication, neither the publisher nor the author assumes any responsibility for errors, or for changes that occur after publication. Further, the publisher does not have any control over and does not assume any responsibility for author or third-party websites or their contents. How the ebook displays on a given reader is beyond the publisher's control.

For information contact:
Publisher@AbsolutelyAmazingEbooks.com

ISBN-13:978-1945772146 (Absolutely Amazing Ebooks)
ISBN-10:194577214X

For my mom, who has offered more support than I can say, and has waited a very long time to see these words in print.

1

ONCE CRAFTER could have crossed the entire world in the twinkling of an eye, but since the Fall and the Second Great Flood such magics were both too costly and too visible. Instead he'd lost three days crossing the Great Waters. The time was an inconvenience, but his real concern was the storm that had been dogging his heels since morning. At first the storm had appeared normal enough, a low bulwark of clouds that huddled down across the horizon and stirred up a harsh and briny wind. Around mid-day the lightning had started, slowly at first but quickly gaining momentum until by early afternoon the clouds were pouring rivers of fire into the sea below. He had watched the lightning for a long time, the stark blue bolts reflecting like dried blood in his crimson eyes. The strikes had been too regular, too perfectly repetitive to be completely natural.

He had pushed Aleister, his strider for as much speed as it could muster, but with three days of open sea behind them it was already tired. The wide, flat body of the craft rocked and bucked as it skimmed a few feet above the cresting waves. The swept, manta-like wings almost touched the salty swells, and a few of the taller crests would break over its rounded prow to leave a mist of water settling into the symbols that etched the crafts metal surface.

Crafter sat in the middle of the strider, huddled low in his crimson velvet long coat against the slashing winds that had continued to gain intensity as night closed in on them. He held a small bronze cube, its sides deeply etched with pictograms and angular sigils, similar to the ones that decorated Aleister. The cube hummed softly as he studied it, though he could feel the vibrations through his black glove more then he could hear them. His eyes strayed to the small open hatch on the side of the strider where he had gotten the box, and where another just like it still sat. Just one more. The journey had been long and supplies were low. He gave the box another glance and then looked back over his shoulder. The clouds had spent the late evening building a wall across the sky and now towered upwards no more then a few miles behind him.

He stood up sharply, turning to face off Aleister's stern. The wind leapt sharply off the water and lashed his short salt and pepper hair into his eyes. He brushed his hair back off his forehead with his free hand and watched the lightning a moment longer, squinting into the wind; then with a decisive motion reached down and spun the lid of the box a quarter turn. The result was immediate. The soft hum built to a deep, subsonic rumble and the geometric patterns crisscrossing the brass started to glow with a golden luminescence. He held the box for a moment longer, then with a sigh he tossed it off the back of the strider into the water. He watched behind him for a moment longer as the glowing box bobbed, strangely buoyant on the surface of the water. He turned and walked to Aleister's bow, his boot heels clicking across the deeply etched metal of the craft.

The sea ahead was a sharp contrast to the sea behind. The waves were low and even and the gentle breeze that rose up to meet him was warm. The sky was utterly clear and in the low, deep blue distance he could see the first few stars chasing sunset into the sky. He squinted into the distance ahead but could see nothing but gray water tinted red with the last dying rays of sunlight. His thin, pale lips tightened and he walked back to the middle of the vessel and resumed his seat on the flat deck.

He sat for a time with his eyes closed, trying to stretch his senses out in all directions; forward for his destination, and behind in search of danger, but after three days he had grown impatient. He opened his eyes and reached into his coat to draw out a crisply folded map. Careful of the wind and the damp he spread the map out on the deck. Much of the map was blank. The upper edge showed a patch of coastline and there were a few small islands littering remote corners of the parchment, but the bulk of the map was just a grid of navigational lines. A bit left of center and somewhat to the north a broad dot showed his current position on the map. It would shift across the parchment to show his progress, a process that had been painfully slow in the past days. The dot was drawing close to a think slash of ink marked in the ocean however and he allowed himself a small smile. He was finally getting close.

He carefully folded the map and slipped it back into his coat. He pushed himself to his feet and moved towards the front of his craft. As he did he glanced back at the storm. He had gained a little distance, and the clouds had stacked higher, but not moved forward like water trapped and building behind a dam. The smile grew. His play had worked, and though he knew the small power the box had contained would not hold off the storm nor its passenger for long it might be long enough.

Night had arrived in full force and the only hint that the sun had ever sat upon the sea was a low gray mist that clung to the edge of the horizon. He reached into his coat again, and withdrew another small box. This one was obsidian black and etched with more of the angular markings. He grasped it by two of the sides and with a little jerk began to stretch it. It moved with little pops and

3

clicks, pieces hinging one onto the next, little flashes of silvery light igniting the markings briefly until he had pulled it out into a long four sided cone. He raised the point to his eye and turned the broad end out towards the ocean ahead of him.

The images that cascaded across his eye were blurred and choppy, fragments of ocean from various distances, various magnifications. He relaxed his eye and kept his mind clearly focused on his destination. It took the seeker only a few moments to bring into a clean focus a sweeping span of metal that arched out of the dark abyss like the rib of a long-dead sea monster. It was all that remained of a once great bridge, which was all that remained of a once great city that had been swept away by the Waters. The pitted metal was almost completely dark except for a flickering patch of light at the zenith of its arch. He angled the seeker towards the light.

"Closer," he muttered softly. His voice cracked after more then a week of disuse and three days of hard salt air. He cleared his throat and repeated himself, "Closer."

On cue the image projected to his eye by the seeker rushed forward. He could see a frequently patched and ramshackle house lashed precariously to the flat span of the arch, ropes and guy-wires running from the walls, over the edge of the metal to the thick cables that plunged off the span and into the waves below. The light leaked from countless holes in the walls, and gaps between the boards.

With a quick clapping motion he collapsed the seeker back to its box size. There was a short flash of silver light and then it was still. He tucked it back into his coat and turned to face the storm one more time. The clouds had continued to stack up dauntingly, but still had not moved forward. That fact gave him a grim satisfaction. He leaned forward and laid a gloved hand flat on the deck of the strider.

"Come on Aleister, almost there, give me just a little more." The strider rocked alarmingly as a particularly large wave passed beneath the low flying craft, but with a dull groan of metal parts it picked up speed towards the bridge, a pale sapphire shimmer of light rippling through the script covering its hide.

The moon had risen in earnest by the time Aleister pulled up along side the dark steel of the bridge, and it glinted dully on the old and corroded metal. He edged the strider up the span away from where the low churn of waves clutched greedily and then stepped off the craft. He stood for a moment, rocking from heel to toe and relishing the feeling of something solid beneath his feet.

"Aleister, come," he said, reaching a hand back towards the strider. With a low groan the strider began to shake, then shift; parts of it pivoting, others sliding as it collapsed in on itself. Metal folded into metal in seemingly impossible patterns, marked by the occasional blue flash of a rune across its surface. When nothing more then another small box of burnished silver remained the strider drifted up into the air and floated to his hand.

"Thank you Aleister, you have done well." He glanced back at the storm, which was only now beginning to close ground. "Very well, and you will be rewarded." He tucked the cube into his coat and started up the length of the beam.

Though the storm would not reach him for some time, the winds came on quickly and whipped away the sound of his boots on the metal. It was just as well. He would prefer his presence went unannounced. He kept his eyes focused on the patch of light far atop the bridge, watching for any sign of movement or defenses. The only movement he could make out was the flickering of the light that leaked through the dilapidated walls of the little hovel. It was a long walk up the archway, but he traveled quickly, impatient to be done with this leg of his journey and before long he could make out the details of the little building.

The seeker had given him a sense of its shabbiness, but that taste was nothing compared to the real squalor of the place. It was windowless and the door hung askew, held in place by a length of twine around the knob. The wood that made up the structure seemed to have been stolen from a hundred different places and no two boards looked the same. Some were actually nailed poorly in place, but others were lashed up with twine like the door and rattled with the storm-winds passage. The whole structure gave a low moan as the wind slithered through the countless holes.

As he drew closer still Crafter could make out a thick odor, strong enough to overpower even the briny smell of the sea. He could not identify it, but it was heavy and clung to his nose unpleasantly. He slowed his pace and walked cautiously across the last few yards to the door, his every sense keyed high to any sign that his presence was detected or that some trap was waiting to be sprung, but the only sounds were the pitiful moan of the wind through the gapped lumbar and the occasional clink of glass from inside the building.

He grasped the door by its edge and yanked. The twine around the knob snapped easily and the rusted bolts holding it to the frame tore free. He let the whole thing twist to the side and fall over the edge of the beam. It spiraled off into the darkness below, dancing and spinning in the wind like a fluttering moth and was gone. The initial rush of light struck him and he blinked rapidly to clear his eyes as he stepped across the threshold.

The interior of the building was as poorly executed as its exterior. It was littered with tables and shelves, some wood, some metal, and others sagging plastic that looked hard pressed to bear the weight of the beakers, burners, and books that covered every flat space. Around the room a number of pots boiled out acrid smoke that, if strong out side the shack, was overwhelming in the poorly vented interior. With all the holes in the walls some of the vapors escaped, but most swirled upward and collected in the low rafters. The ceiling itself was stained a dirty rainbow of colors by these various smokes, as were most of the walls. The flickering light came partially from a few candles stationed in metal brackets around the room. The rest of the light came from the burners working on most of the tables, some with something boiling above them, others just burning away as if waiting for a chance to set some loose page or falling board alight. In the farthest corner from the door he could make out a tiny cot that was more a nest of filthy blankets then a real bed, but as he scanned back and forth with his red eyes narrowed he could find no sign of the hovel's occupant.

He took another step into the room and from against the far wall behind one of the largest tables, a great mahogany thing with vast lion's legs for feet came a clatter of breaking glass and a soft curse. He waited a moment longer and then called out,

"Come out, I know you're here and there is no reason to prolong this."

Slowly a head appeared from behind the table. It was crowned by wild brown hair that scattered in all directions as if attempting an escape. Narrow eyes of an indeterminate brown, like mud after a long rain peered out from between two tall glass vials. They met Crafter's cold red orbs for a moment, and then deciding he had been truly found out the hider stood all the way up. All the way was not far. The little man on the other side of the room was hardly bigger then chest high to the table. He wore a loose smock shirt that hung off his narrow shoulders and a

7

brown leather apron that wrapped almost twice around his narrow hips. Various instruments protruded from the aprons pockets; clamps and filters made of silver and brass, wrenches and several objects that were best left unidentified. A poorly chopped beard clung closely to the broad flat chin.

"Sorry!" the little man called out to his sudden guest, "didn't hear you come in. I was looking for ..." his eyes cast around the table in front of him, then the ground at his feet for something he could have been looking for, but finding nothing he looked back up to meet that bloody stare, "... for something!"

Crafter took another long step into the room, though he couldn't go far without running into a table blanketed by yellowed parchment. He glanced down and saw that the pages were maps, well annotated in tidy black writing. His eyes narrowed.

"Let's dispense with the pleasantries alchemist." His voice was level, but cut clearly through the sound of the wind and the bubbling chemicals. "I know who you work for, and I know what you are doing here."

"I work by contract," the little man replied, puffing up his chest as best he could. "And I have many very powerful employers. To which do you refer?"

"I refer to your only employer, the one that helped you haul all this junk up here, and the one that set you on your present course."

The alchemist furrowed his brow and thinned his lips at having his equipment referred to as junk and his voice was high and shrill as he responded.

"I do not work directly for anyone, and as for my things... I have many friends to help me move them."

"Unfortunately for you all of that statement is a lie. I am not interested in your working arrangements however. What I am interested in is the whereabouts of the Bearer.

You have found them, and you will tell me."

"I will tell you NOTHING!" the alchemist shrilled. Only too late did Crafter realize that the alchemist had been sidling towards a small glass globe full of a golden liquid. The little man snatched it up and hurled it across the room.

"DIE DEMON!" he roared as the globe burst across the crimson velvet of his guests' floor-length coat. Nothing happened. With a tight sneer Crafter reached up with a gloved hand to brush off stray shards of glass that clung to the velvet.

"I am no simple and nameless demon you fool." He fixed the alchemist with a level gaze. "I am one of the Named."

The alchemist's eyes widened for a moment, but he quickly regained his composure and tried to regain his sneer, though with little success.

"It is no matter," he said. "Demon or true Devil my master is mightier then you!"

"Yes," the devil nodded. "Your master is a great deal mightier then I."

The man's grin returned, vicious and ratlike.

"But," the devil continued. The grin faltered. "Your master is not here... and I am."

A crash of thunder cut through the wind. It was not close yet, but time was running out and Crafter knew it.

"Enough of this alchemist. Tell me what you know."

"I'll never tell you!" His voice climbed an octave in panic. "You will never know of the Bearer!"

Another roll of thunder shook the hovel.

"Time is out. You will not tell me, but I will have it from you. No more cat and mouse."

The devil waved his hand dismissively through the air. The shelves and tables that filled the alchemist's workshop responded at once, lurching sideways in a shower of glass and strange liquids. They exploded through the weak wall and cascaded down to the waiting sea. The alchemist let out a horrified shriek, and for a moment it seemed he would dive after his precious experiments. His eyes fixed on the dark, gaping hole where his life's work had been swallowed by the night. His head snapped back around fast enough for vertebra to crackle in his neck. His eyes found Crafter. No obstacle remained between them. The alchemist let out another shriek.

"I'll tell you!" he cried out. "I'll tell you what you want to know." He pressed his back to the slats of the wall and sunk to the floor, his eyes wide and pupils dilated until they swallowed any color.

"We've tried that," the devil told him softly. He reached out a gloved hand and plucked a fluttering piece of parchment from where it was drifting towards the floor. It was a map scrawled on yellow parchment with careful notations. It showed a rocky and jagged coastline.

"Please ..." The alchemist's voice was barely a whisper.

"No," the devil told him, "I think not. I tried nice, now we do it my way."

He held the map out towards the huddled man on the floor with one hand as the other hand caught the split of his coat and began to draw it open.

The alchemist began to scream.

2

ELLIS SAT HUDDLED and shivering on the bare floor of his small shack atop the old bridge arch surprised to still be alive. The devil was gone, and had taken with it all it had wanted. The feeling of a foreign presence inside his head lingered like a sunspot in the eyes but he was still breathing. Most of the light in the room had gone when the devil had cast his precious instruments into the ocean, and many of the remaining candles had guttered out in the sharp wind that billowed in through the blasted hole in his wall, leaving the room almost entirely in darkness. He closed his eyes against the intruding shadows, hugged his knees to his chest and rocked back and forth.

His mind turned into itself, seeking a place that harbored some comfort for the alchemist who suddenly felt very small. He remembered a white lab coat that in his head had always been the representation of his father. He remembered standing on a stool so he could see over the black varnished edge of a table as a number of colored liquids bubbled and boiled. His father's voice came back to him deep and resonant explaining the properties of each.

"This is a simple boiling point experiment Ellis," his father pointed to a beaker of clear liquid. "That over there is our water, our control group." He said this last part slowly – control group – and the young Ellis had known that meant it was important. The phrase rang over and over in his mind – control group, control group control group controlgroupcontrol – slowly morphing from his father's bass to the higher rasp of his own nasal voice. The table and the burners were gone and he was watching men in black habits shepherd frightened looking people into small corrals.

"Keep them separate," he heard himself say, gesturing to a cowering group of doe eyed teenagers who were staring frantically around, "They're young and strong and will make an excellent control group."

His father was with him again, lab coat a mess of wrinkles just like his face, but his voice was strong as it had always been. Ellis was sitting behind his own desk, an important man at the College.

"Ellis, this isn't science. You're dabbling in things that have no place in this world!"

Ellis' response was course and dismissive.

"It is in this world, and it's just waiting for us to control it! We just have to be brave enough to reach out and take what is ours! I have found resources-"

"I've heard of your resources Ellis," his father cut him off harshly, spittle frothing on his lips. "And I know evil when I see it."

Ellis stood up from his chair and leaned forward, one fist on the burnished brass surface of his desk and leveled a finger at his father. The desk had been a gift from his new benefactors at the High Church and leaning on it made him feel as if they were there supporting him as he challenged his father.

"You're just afraid dad, but you taught me that science must always move forward! Alchemy is the end result of chemistry, don't you see that? And these people, they have opened up whole new worlds to me." He paused and added quietly letting his extended hand sink down to his desk to rest on a small silver incense burner that rested there, still warm with embers, "And they have protected me."

His father threw his pale liver spotted hands toward the ceiling.

"Protection! Ellis we're scientists, not mad sorcerers, what would you need protection against unless you were up to no good!"

A low wail crept out from behind the dark metal door in the sidewall of the room. His father fell silent and slowly turned to face the door. Ellis felt a chill, the blood draining from his face as he watched his father, waiting for a response. Slowly that old face that looked like a broader version of his own turned back to face him.

"What is behind that door son?" His father's voice was quiet for the first time since he had come down to the lower floors of Coalbridge College to visit his son.

"Father it's noth–"

"What is behind that door!" The roar caught Ellis completely off guard and he fell back into his leather chair with a thump. His father drew breath to yell again, but it seemed to catch in his throat and a series of deep coughs shook his heavy frame. Ellis hurried around the desk and caught his father by the shoulders.

"Dad, are you ok?" he asked, leaning in close.

His father shrugged him off with surprising strength as he shoved himself to his feet and lurched towards the metal door.

"I'll find out what your up to down here, Ellis!" he half growled half coughed. He stumbled and caught himself against the wall. Ellis recovered himself and started after his father.

"They said you were up to no good Ellis, that you were doing things no sane man would do, but I told them that my son would never do such things as they whispered of, but now..."

He turned back and fixed Ellis with a cold stare as he

took another faltering step towards the door. Ellis caught him by the shoulders again and held him fast.

"Dad, I can't let you go in there, they'd kill you for seeing."

His father's eyes widened and he tried to again wrest himself from his son's grip. Ellis was much smaller than his father, having taken more after his mother, but his father's strength was failing and Ellis held him fast.

"Let me go boy!" his father snarled at him, "Let me go!'

He burst into another fit of coughing, this one longer then the last. The force of it took him to the ground. Ellis crouched next to him, watching terrified as those brown eyes that had watched him grow up rolled to whites. The coughing continued and red flecks splattered across his father's lips and onto his cheeks. Another fit brought his limp body up to a sitting position and the blood continued to come, splattering onto Ellis and dripping in long strings onto the white of his coat, staining it crimson.

A new scene drifted into Ellis' mind. A crimson coat hung from broad shoulders, framed in the slanting doorway and haunted by flickering ghosts of candlelight as a much older Ellis cowered behind the broad lions leg of a table and for the first time since his father's death felt a real trickle of fear start down his back. He had never gotten over the irony that for all his father's righteousness he had died of lung cancer contracted from breathing too many fumes in too many traditional labs while the experiments he scorned had made his son stronger and stronger, maybe even immune to death. Ellis had almost come to believe himself immortal until his door had burst off its hinges.

Not many had been able to find him once his masters had moved him to the bridge in the midst of the Great Waters, and those that had almost never made it more then half way up the bridge. The arch had many protections. Only two people had been able to approach the lab itself, and he had marked their faces and sent word to dispatch them as soon as they had realized that trying to get in was useless and gone away. The devil however had walked right up and torn the door off the wall and with a sweep of its hand ruined Ellis' entire life. He had never for a moment considered that his meteoric rise to power would attract the attention of one of the Named.

A storm had come up around the small cabin and cold rain blew in through the hole in the wall, soaking into the thin wood of the floor and spraying against his closed eyelids. He shivered, partially from the cold, but mostly with lingering terror. Somewhere in the darkness around him there was a soft cackle, like someone crushing long dead leaves in their fist.

His eyes snapped open and raked the darkness. The wind and the rain had put out the last few candles and the storm clouds had long since devoured the moon and stars. Nothing but blackness greeted him. He pressed himself hard against the wall, tucking his knees up to his chin and covering his mouth with his hands. The cackle rattled out at him again, from the far corner near the hole in the wall. He narrowed his eyes and tried to cut through the shadows, but could see nothing.

"You'll forgive my laughter," the voice was much like the laugh, dry and broken. "It's just that I take great amusement in seeing those who thought they were great because they dwelt in a very small world cut down to size when they see how big the world really is."

The inky black in the corner shifted and moved forward, a patch of shadow that created a hunched silhouette against the lighter darkness of the night sky that loomed outside his shanty. He fought for each breath around the clutching pressure in his chest as that dark shape shambled closer and closer. It took no pains at haste.

"I have powerful friends," he managed to choke out. The figured laughed again, and he realized that from the voice he could not tell if it was man or woman who menaced him.

"I know little man, I am one of them." The dark shape of arms spread out to either side of the figure and the silhouette hunched down in a bow. As it rose back up, a shot of lightning cut through the dark.

In the brief flash Ellis made out the gnarled shape of an old woman clad in Victorian black lace with a veil drawn down over her face that turned the worn lines of her age into shadowed valleys of infinite depth. The flash left him blind and when her voice sounded a split second later it was only inches from his ear.

"You know me alchemist, for we serve the same master."

He let out a half-swallowed cry of shock and tipped to the side, banging his shoulder against the wall as he fell. The leaf crack laugh sounded again, this time from across the room where the old woman had stood when the lightning flashed.

"Cr-crone?" he whispered into the wind.

"You are smarter then you first appear," she told him. "Yes, I am the Crone, the Rider of Storms, Wench of the Winds; I have many names."

"Why are you here?"

"I am not your first visitor tonight Ellis Carter," she told him. "After your first encounter you should not be surprised at more."

"I didn't tell him anything," he cried out, then thinking better of the lie amended more softly, "I tried not to tell him anything, but... but he did things... are you going to kill me?"

She laughed again. Each titter scrapped away a little more of his nerves.

"No little man, not even our unforgiving master could hold you responsible for what the devil took from you. No amount of preparing could have given you the ability to keep him from your thoughts. He is powerful beyond your reckoning. Now, let us make ourselves more friendly and we will see what you have learned, and what more you can do to serve our master."

There was another flash of lightning, but this time the bolt leap through the open hole in the wall. The heat of it scalded Ellis' face and the thick scent of ozone, copper, and burnt wood filled his nose. His vision cleared slowly, and when it did he found a small fire burning in the center of the room with a black iron pot suspended above it on a spit. It was full of a dark green broth that smelled of meat and pepper. The Crone sat next to the fire, a small ball of black in the amber glow. The shadow of her vale made it impossible to see her eyes as she turned her face to him. She gestured to the ground next to her with a withered hand.

"Come," she encouraged him, "sit and eat with me."

He pushed himself slowly to his feet. His legs were still weak and trembling and his first step almost slipped out from under him on the wet wood. He paused, looking at the hole in the wall and realizing that though it was still pouring rain none of it was being blown inside anymore. He looked back to the Crone who smiled at him with parchment lips. He took a deep breath and moved the few steps to sit next to her at the fire. It was pleasantly warm after sitting in the cold, and steam rose off him as his damp clothes started to dry.

The Crone picked up a small wooden bowl off the floor and ladled a spoonful of the thick broth into it. She held it out to Ellis. He eyed the green liquid suspiciously. Again she laughed at him.

"Come now little alchemist, do you think that if I was going to kill you I would have to poison you?" She gestured to him with the bowl again. "You have been through much, now eat."

He reached out resigned and took the proffered bowl. The wood was warm from its contents and he cupped his hands around it. He looked around for a spoon or fork, but saw none. He looked at the Crone, who smiled thinly at him again and motioned as if drinking. Catching her meaning he lifted the bowl to his lips and tipped a small portion of its contents into his mouth.

The stew was incredibly rich, with heavy spices seasoned into the chunks of beef that floated in the broth. He chewed slowly, savoring the tastes before swallowing and feeling the warmth slide down to settle in his belly. It had been a long time since he had eaten anything more then salted meat and the few fresh vegetables that were delivered to him by servants twice a month. He took another mouthful out of the bowl before turning his attention back to his second strange guest of the night.

She was smiling and watching him eat quietly. Her dark gaze was unsettling and the warmth that had sunk to his stomach turned to a cold stone. The bowl in his hand shook and he lowered it to his lap to avoid spilling any.

"You have long been a valuable asset to us. Often you have served in less then ideal conditions." Her round head swiveled slowly back and forth to survey the hole-laden walls that had housed him for almost a year.

"Our master regrets that we were unable to prevent this attack by one of our greatest foes; that I could not get here before your valuable work was scattered." She gestured towards the hole. As she did one of the lace cuffs fell back and he saw deep red slashes across her wrist that vanished into her sleeve.

"Ah yes," she said, catching his look. She tugged back down her cuff to cover the wounds.

"You are not the only one the devil has attacked this night. He left a nasty little surprise for me. Nothing truly dangerous, but enough to slow me down and give him time to do his work."

Ellis didn't know what to say. The idea of the Crone being attacked was strange to him, and the idea of something powerful enough to do it having been in the room with him was terrifying. He lifted the bowl and took another deep drink of the stew to cover his unease.

"That is not important now," she told him. "Neither he nor I would have come here tonight had you not touched upon something deep and central, the reason for your being sent here in the first place. You have found the Bearer?" It was not really a question but he replied none-the-less.

"Yes, in a small coastal town to the West. It was much as we suspected."

The Crone nodded, her veil rustling against the high neck of her gown.

"And the devil knows all of this?"

"I don't know what he knows," Ellis told her. "He rutted in my head like a hog digging truffles. I can't say what he found."

"Then we assume he learned everything and I must be after him quickly. I will send word." She rose to her full height; it was not a long trip.

"Don't you want to know which town?" he asked her. That laugh.

"No little man, you're truffles are not buried deep I fear. As soon as you spoke of it I knew." His eyes widened a little. She ignored his surprise as she rummaged in a little bag that hung around her wrist. She pulled a heavy medallion out of it. The buffed metal glowed a dull gold in the firelight. At first glance Ellis thought it was the mold of a wolf, but upon closer inspection it looked more reptilian in nature, though it was a rough cast and the details were not clear.

"Now our alchemist, the master has a new task for you." She held out the medallion towards him. He set down the stew and took it with two hands, catching the chain in one and the pendant in the other. It was heavier then he'd expected.

"What would he have of me? My lab is destroyed. Am I to return to the College?" He unknowingly held his breath as he waited for a response. He yearned desperately for the softer life of the College with its well-furnished laboratories and generous amenities, and of Coalbridge with restaurants, taverns, and booksellers. Mostly he longed to be back inland away from the damnable Waters. The Crone shook her head slowly.

"I'm afraid not. Our enemies are on the move and the College is too exposed now, we've had to abandon it. I fear your experiments have come to a close."

"Workings then?" he asked. "Workings to confuse and hinder our adversaries, fatal blows struck from great distances?" Again the old woman shook her head.

"There are mightier sorcerers then you by far in our employ seeing to those needs alchemist. There is a war upon us Ellis, and what the master requires now is soldiers to fill the ranks."

Now it was Ellis' turn to laugh, short and self-deprecating.

"I am hardly a warrior! I will gladly serve the master, but I am ill suited to battle." He held up his thin arms as example, gesturing with them to his whip thin body.

"We are well aware of your failings Ellis." Her voice was cold and he let his arms fall limply back to his sides. "But it is warriors the master needs none the less, and now that the Bearer has been found you have fulfilled your other purposes so a warrior you will be. You are a coward Ellis, but your fear has made you cruel, and often enough that will pass for bravery." With a bony finger she pointed to the icon of the creature in his hand. "Wear the amulet. Journey to the mainland. There is a boat at the base of your bridge that will see you safely there. Once you're there you will receive further instructions, and when the time comes you will know what to do."

She started towards the hole in the wall and the storm beyond it in a slow shuffling waddle. He pushed himself to his feet and started after her.

"But I am a brilliant alchemist!" he protested to her back. "Surely there is some facet of scientific research where I can still be of use! Please Crone, it is my life!"

She turned slowly to face him. As she tilted her head back to look up at him the firelight stole under her veil and lit up her face. In the depths of her eye sockets were not eyes, but empty pits full of roiling clouds and mist.

"Do not question the master. Your time as an alchemist is through." she told him flatly. When he opened his mouth to protest she raised her hand to silence him. "If you wanted to choose your own path in life Ellis Carter, than you should not have sold your soul."

She did not wait for a reply. She turned and with two more steps came to the shattered edge of wood that marked the steep drop of several hundred feet to the water. With surprising agility she leapt through the hole. There was a loud roar of wind and she hung for a moment, suspended in a whirlwind gale.

"Go to the mainland and wait Ellis Carter, do not fail us."

Then she was gone, lifted away into the cloudy sky leaving behind a peel of thunder in her wake. As soon as she disappeared the rain started to blow through the hole again. Ellis folded his arms around his narrow chest and hugged himself against the sudden chill. He moved back towards the fire and crouched down but it gave off only a fitful warmth as it sputtered in the misting breeze. He gathered up the small bowl and drank down more of its contents, but it had grown cold since his first few swallows and the meat was chewy and bland. With a sigh he set the bowl down and lifted the necklace.

He still couldn't identify the animal it represented. It had the basic carriage of a wolf, but the tail was broader and came to a sharp point, the head was more conical, almost like a vipers arrowhead jaw. He lowered the amulet and looked out into the blowing storm again. Another jagged bolt of lightning cut open the darkness and he closed his eyes against the lingering glow. Another moment and he slipped the heavy gold chain over his head. The weight of it hung heavy around his neck and the creature bumped against his abdomen just below his breastbone.

He looked around the little building one last time, but there was nothing left inside it to gather so he turned and walked through the doorless doorway. The rain was coming down in sheets and he was immediately soaked to the skin. He considered for a moment taking off his apron and leaving it behind, but the well-worked leather was his one protection from the weather. He wrapped his arms tightly around his chest again and started walking slowly down the archway. The metal was slick and the gusting winds hit him from all sides like leviathan fists threatening to at any moment tip him off the narrow steel span and into the long drop below. He had to move at a snails crawl, sometimes even crouching down on all fours to keep his balance.

He couldn't see more then a few feet in front of him and so he looked back, hoping to catch a glimpse of the firelight from his home to gauge how far he had come. He cried out in shock at what he saw. The fire that had been neatly contained when he had been inside had spread quickly once he had left and the whole building burned in a bright conflagration. There was no turning back. From his estimation he was maybe one third of the distance to the bottom of the arch, so he turned his face away from the ruins of the last year of his life, tucked his chin to his chest against the wind and continued his slow plod along the beam.

The rest of the walk passed in blur of melancholy, and miserable cold. It was with a start that he realized he was standing at the foot of the beam with churning waves lapping at his once nice tasseled shoes. He lifted his head and looked around to discover a small barge sitting in the water beside him. There was no light anywhere on it and it almost vanished against the storm washed sea. A raise cabin took up the center of the vessel, and a wide stack belched black smoke into the black sky. A tall, broad figure appeared on deck through a hatch in the central housing, and a booming voice carried the short distance to him.

"Ahoy there! Let's get you on board." A skillet of a hand stretched across the short gap between the ship and the bridge. Ellis reached out and let the bigger hand close around his own. He was lifted bodily from the beam and plopped unceremoniously onto the deck of the boat.

"Lads!" The big man's voice boomed into the night and all around the deck dark figures stirred up from sitting positions and half crouches. Ellis realized there were men and women all around him that he had not even seen.

"Time to get underway!" The man told the crew. "Reichlad, come show our guest to his quarters." One of the shadowy shapes moved away from the railing and approached the David and Goliath pair. The figure motioned for Ellis to follow towards the housing where the big man had first emerged. Ellis looked to the big man who stood straight, as if unaware of the rain.

"Go on with ya!" he told the smaller man. "Wouldn't wantcha catching pneumonia out here and dying before yer supposed to!" The crew joined him in a long laugh. Ellis scowled at him, not finding the joke at all funny, but the big man turned away and started bustling about checking ropes and talking low to the rest of the crew. Ellis watched him a moment longer and then turned to where Reichlad waited patiently half way between the rail and the door. Ellis motioned him onward and fell in step. He was lead into the cramped dark quarters below deck where he could hear the snores of still more crew members.

Reichlad stopped before a hammock slung low to the ground. The sailor, who had never been more than a narrow shadow, pointed to the hanging bed. There were blankets folded on the foot of it and a pillow at its head. Ellis turned to ask about food or the restroom but Reichlad had already disappeared. Ellis slipped out of his wet apron and shirt. Shivering he wrapped the blankets around him and crawled into the hammock.

The hammock above his was scarcely a foot from his face and occupied. The contented snores of the person above him told him it was a woman and the smell told him she had been at sea for a long time. Despite his fear that he would never be able to sleep in such claustrophobic conditions it was not long before the weariness of his night overtook him and he drifted off into a fitful slumber full of dreams of blood stained coats and blood colored eyes.

3

EPIPHANY HADN'T SLEPT in two days and the deep bags under her eyes bore testimony to her exhaustion. Her body tingled with fatigue. The wind that crawled up the sea cliffs and coiled around her felt like a thousand ants running races across her skin, and the sound of the people gathered in the vale behind her was muffled and dull. She knew she should be there, accepting their sympathies with grace, but she had run out of patience for her neighbor's sympathy months ago. Instead she stared out over the blue gray sea where a low laying storm front had begun to gather on the horizon. If the winds held, the storm would be on the town by nightfall.

A little shiver ran through her and she took a deep breath, trying in vain to force the air past the knot in her chest. She released the breath in a short burst, almost a sob. She didn't cry though – couldn't; she'd cried herself out. Behind her the sounds of a shovel moving earth cut through the murmuring voices like claps of thunder. She didn't turn around, but she could picture the attendant in his dirty overalls tipping heaping shovelfuls of dirt into the twin gashes in the earth that had, a short week ago been her parents. She wondered whether he would cover her mother or father first. Perhaps he would alternate shovelfuls between them in the name of equity.

She was drawn out of her revere by footfalls crunching through the dry autumn grass. She didn't turn. They stopped a few feet away, but she folded her arms around her stomach and kept her eyes in the distance. The silence drew out and she let her mind wander across the open waters. When she had been a child her parents had taken her sailing on the Great Waters many times. It had been one of their special family outings, and though she had never though much of it at the time, even dreaded it sometimes in her teenage years when she could find countless 'better things to do' she missed it now. Her father had loved sailing, though by the end of the day he had always been green and it had taken him several days to stand up completely straight again. Her best memories of him were tied to the sea.

Once, all three of them had taken their little skiff and traveled almost a whole day to one of the islands that still held fast above the all-consuming Waters. Epiphany had been young, and spending so much time with nothing but endless waves and blue skies around her had been terrifying. She had clung to her father's arm and begged him to turn back. Her mother had gently called her over and shown her the old bronze compass she'd gotten from Epiphany's grandmother and explained how they were navigating not by visible markers, but by the angle of the sun and the compass. Epiphany had been so intrigued that she spent the rest of the day plotting courses to remote lands they would never visit. By the time she remembered her fear of the open sea they were within sight of their destination, a little cove with a blanket of lights that shimmered in the ebbing light.

It had been strange to visit that other town. It resembled her own so much that she found herself looking for familiar shops and neighbors. The buildings, built up from a patchwork of scavenged parts, the stonework lanes deeply pitted by the constant salt in the air; all of it was familiar, and yet just different enough to leave her out of sorts. Epiphany knew that there were towns, and even cities farther from the coast that were older, better kept and still had buildings and roads from before the Waters. She had never seen any of those, had never even been off the coast. She'd only been to the other town across the Waters once, and she wished she'd remembered more, but she'd been very young and they'd arrived late. After a light dinner of steamed cod her parents had put her to bed and vanished for whatever business had brought them there.

The next morning a low fog had clung to the strange village and Epiphany felt like she was walking through a half formed dream of home as they moved down the short road to the dock where their boat bobbed, bumping quietly against the wooden peer. A few of the early risers in the streets had seemed to know them and bid them farewell as they pushed off and turned back to home. She remembered that despite his remarkable fortitude of the previous day, her father spent most of the trip back huddled miserably in the bow of the little boat with his head close to the railing and left her and her mother to steer them home.

It was the one long trip they had taken together. Her parents went away from time to time, but she'd always been too busy, or in school, or just disinterested. Their last trip had kept them out for almost four days. They hadn't said where they were going when they left. When they'd come back something had changed. They still wouldn't tell Epiphany where they'd gone, or what was troubling them, but there was fear haunting their expressions. They jumped at shadows and had tense, whispered discussions when they thought Epiphany couldn't hear. Whatever was wrong, in a few short weeks they'd started to slip away.

"Epiphany?" Gerold's voice was soft, almost lost in the wind. He waited for a response but she gave no sign that she'd heard him. A crunch of grass as he dared a step closer.

"Epiphany, are you alright?" His voice was tight and low, full of real concern. Gerold had been one of her dearest friends for a long time and it hurt her to ignore him, but at that moment she had nothing to give, no reassurance that all was well, or that with time it could be well again.

"It's cold," he said, trying to sound matter of fact. She waited for something more, for the platitudes she'd grown so accustomed to or to some recrimination for not mingling with the other mourners. Nothing. There was another crunch of grass, still closer and then the weight of his coat settling across her shoulders. He said nothing, but she heard him start back down the short hill to the graveyard. With trembling hands she drew the edges of his coat tighter around her.

She waited at the edge of the cliff with the sea growling below her and watched the slow march of the storm until she could no longer hear the murmur of voices from the bottom of the hill. In all the time it took for the funeral to clear, no one but Gerold braved her solitude. Perhaps he had warned them of her cold shoulders on his way past. Once silence fell behind her she waited a few more minutes for good measure and then turned slowly.

At the bottom of the hill the graveyard huddled in the mid-day gray, cast by the high clouds that preceded the storm front. The tombstones were tucked close together, and her parents' graves were mostly hidden by the closer, older graves. She could just make out the freshly turned edge of her mothers resting place around the corner of a wide, well-weathered block that marked the last slumber of a whole family. They had died before she was born, but she'd heard that a monstrous wave had taken their boat one day and that the graves were actually empty, just a memorial to prove they had existed.

She started down the hill at a measured pace, letting

gravity and her long legs do most of the work. She passed through the gap in the low, white picket fence and weaved her way between the grassy mounds until she stood at the foot of the earthen humps of her parents. A chill ran up her back and she drew Gerold's coat tighter around her.

"It's not right you know." The voice came from within the graveyard, but Epiphany had seen no one as she'd walked in. "Well of course you know, they were your folks."

She snapped around to find the gravedigger slouched on the ground a dozen feet away. He was leaning back against a headstone; a casual slouch that seemed out of place against the somber granite slab. His face was smudged with dirt, a long line of it across his forehead where he'd wiped his brow. The top of his overalls had been unhitched and puddled in his lap. The front of his shirt was tacked to his body with sweat, showing a narrow line of pronounced ribs. He lifted a large canteen to his lips with a wide hand and took a long drink. He raked a sinewy forearm across his forehead, further smearing the dirt and let his hands fall back to the ground beside him.

"Sorry if I startled you," he told her. "I can go if you'd like a moment. Everyone else scooted off, some hubbub about strangers arriving this morning. I figured since I was still here... just though I'd tell you it's a shame about what happened."

She considered sending him away.

"No, it's alright, you can stay." Epiphany decided that she liked his matter of fact tone; none of the sickening sacchariny lilts that most of the town heaped upon her like a mountain of meringue. Just a simple fact – simply stated.

"It is a shame," she agreed.

"Strange too," he said, holding out the canteen in offering. She took it gratefully. The salt on the air had dried her throat. She lifted the heavy metal bottle to her lips and drew deeply. His dirty lips had left grit around the mouth of the bottle but the metallic taste of the dirt was somehow refreshing.

"Yeah," she agreed again as she handed back the bottle. "They say it was something they caught while they were out sailing a while back."

He nodded, pursing his lips in a sage fashion.

"Yeah, I've heard them say that. I've never heard of a disease that makes you grow old and die in the space of two weeks, is what I've never heard of."

"I haven't either." Epiphany shrugged. It was something she had been over time and again. At first it was denial. It was impossible. Her parents were barely out of their forties, and yet with each day that passed they seemed to wither away, as if the years had come looking for them early. Once she could no longer deny the truth then she turned to fury that something so strange could come out of the blue and strike her and her family.

Her denial and her rage changed nothing. In the short space of two weeks her young vibrant parents had gone through graying hair, to loosing hair; through cataracts and arthritis and more. Her father sank into a brain fog early in the second week and before the end of it didn't even remember who Epiphany was. In some ways the fog seemed kinder then her mothers crystal clear and knowing eyes fading away into the dark. Unbelievable though it may have been it all came down to one question in the end. "What else could explain it?"

"There have always been forces out there, weird stuff. Since the Waters all sorts-"

"No." Epiphany was emphatic. The caretaker looked at her with his mouth still open. "You sound like my grandfather with that stuff. I'm not interested."

Epiphany's Grandpa had often told her stories of the

Waters and their coming, semi-mystical tales full of God, angels, and magic. He had no love for the High Church, but no lack of faith either. He, and Epiphany's parents had their own brand of spirituality that often seemed to boarder on folk magic to their pragmatic, 'I'll believe it when I see it' minded daughter.

Of course they weren't the only ones. It had been centuries since the Waters had swept over the earth and covered everything. Theories about what happened were as numerous as their were voices to speak them. Many, like her Grandpa's were full of wonder and superstition, but Epiphany had no interest in religion and the mysticism that came with it. In her years she'd seen a lot of strange things, but nothing she needed magic to explain.

It looked as if the gravedigger was about to continue this argument, to pose some counter-point but Epiphany raised her hand to stop him. He closed his mouth and pushed himself to his feet using the headstone behind him. He latched one overall strap back over his shoulder to hold them up and then gathered up his shovel.

"It's not right what happened, either way it is; magic or disease." With the handle of the shovel he pointed to the cozy cottage at the edge of the graveyard. "I'm going to go clean up. With this storm coming I won't be scattering grass till at least tomorrow, so you can have some time with them if you like."

"It's alright," she told him as he started away through the narrow lanes between the graves. "I need to get back anyway. Strangers in town you said?"

He paused and nodded, pointing towards the bundle of houses that was Seacliff as if marking out the newcomers at a distance.

"That's what they say." He started away again.

"Thanks," she called after him. "...Thanks for everything."

He turned and gave her a small tilt of lips and she tried to return it with her best impression of a half-hearted smile. He raised his shovel in a parting salute and then made his way to the cottage with its neat rose bushes. Epiphany watched his back until the door swung shut behind him. She turned back to face her parents.

Epiphany searched for something to say, but no words came, just that same dull ache in her chest as if something she had tried to swallow was stuck. She moved forward between the heaps of dirt and rested a hand on each of the headstones. The marble was cool beneath her fingers. She stood for a little while, just breathing and trying to remember all the best memories of her parents. She got a few flashes to come; smiles and piggyback rides, but it was too soon, too close to wasting flesh and aging faces. With a sigh she let her hands drop from the stones and started into town.

The buildings looked surreal; flat like a painting. The bleached out light that filtered through the clouds cast no shadows and without relief it was like walking through a mural of her life. It made Epiphany's head spin. She knew she was still tired. She could feel how slowly she was processing, and how heavy her feet felt in their leather boots. She could have gone home to rest, no one would have faulted her on that day of all days, but she felt like she needed to keep moving, to resist the urge to curl up under a blanket and try hard to disappear. She set her course through Seacliff for the tailor shop where she worked.

The people she passed in the narrow lanes turned their faces away even as they murmured apologies and sympathies. It had been that way the whole time her parents were sick. No one knew what to make of the illness or whether it was contagious and so her family had been treated like plague bearers. Everyone was really sorry it was happening to them, but hoped it only happened to them. Epiphany couldn't really blame them, they were just trying to protect themselves, and so she bit back the sharp replies that bubbled up from that tight place behind her heart and murmured equally insignificant thanks.

She'd got so used to everyone giving her a wide berth that she jumped when thin strong fingers wrapped around her arm. She jerked around to see Juniper standing in the street beside her, the spindly arm that wasn't restraining Epiphany pinwheeling above his bald head.

"It's too much of one day girl!" he declared as if they'd been in conversation for the last hour. When she didn't reply he barreled on. "Your parent's funeral and strangers all at once! Too much for an old man!"

She could smell the whiskey on his breath as he leaned in to emphasis his point. Rumors said that once Juniper had been a great explorer and mountaineer, coming down from the hills that shoved the little town against the coast with furs and meats the likes of which no one had ever seen. For as long as Epiphany could remember he'd been crazy. People said – not loudly – that he'd found something up in the mountains that had pushed him past the edge and he had come back from one of his regular trips far from regular. Epiphany suspected that all he had found was a moonshine still with some bad shine.

"Well if it's too much for you Juniper you should go lay down somewhere." Epiphany was in no mood for craziness and she wrestled her arm free.

"They're cloth men!" Juniper threw both his hands to the sky, open in a wide 'Y' of invitation. "Come to bring us salvation!"

"What are you talking about Juniper?" Juniper was always crazy, but he wasn't usually incoherent or given to evangelical tirades.

"I saw them earlier, when I came back into town after

your folks' funeral," he pointed up the road towards the tree-lined rise that lead away from the coast.

"You were at my parents funeral?" Epiphany was shocked. Juniper always seemed to have a grasp of what was going on around town, but never seemed to engage in any of it. He turned his liver-spotted face towards her, suddenly quiet and earnest.

"They were my friends young one. Part of the cause for which we've all made our sacrifices. I wouldn't have missed it." The moment of startling sobriety passed quickly and his face snapped back up the road. "And after all the goings on at the cemetery they were walking past right up there, all black robes and white collars."

The realization dawned on Epiphany. It struck her that she had been fending off arguments about superstition only moments before and now priests had come to town. Official clergy didn't often venture out from the larger cities farther inland where their iron fisted rule held tightly, and there was wealth and influence to be had. The poor coastal areas held little interest for the High Church and its functionaries.

Their presence, when priests did turn up never changed much around town. They would keep to themselves, slinking around on unknown business; talk to anyone that still claimed to be faithful to the Church and then disappear just as they had come. Epiphany laughed softly. The sound of it was hollow, as if it had come from the depths of a cave rather then her chest.

"Not cloth men Juniper, men of the cloth! And I don't think they'll be saving anyone, especially you." She turned away and resumed her trudge as the old man continued to address her.

"Cloth men Epiphany. There's no substance to them you see! You watch yourself daughter of my friends; such as they are no friend to you and me!"

She waved over her shoulder to him, part farewell, part dismissal. Anyone in the street to see the exchange shook their head sadly. It made her suddenly sorry for Juniper, not because he was in the state he was, but because she had been the recent recipient of just that kind of pity. She turned back. Juniper was listing down the road in the direction from which she had come.

"Juniper!" She called out to him, making sure she spoke loudly enough that everyone else could hear her. He turned on his heel, rocking back and forth as his balance turned slower then he did. "I'll watch out Juniper. I'll be careful."

He nodded deeply, crushing his thick beard down against his chest and leveled a long finger at her.

"And I'll watch out for you too!"

She chuckled at the thought. What she needed at that moment was the town drunk leering in her windows at night to make sure no priests were attacking her. It was only a few more blocks to the shop, so she put it from her mind.

The air inside the tailor's was thick and muggy with the ocean humidity and the heat of the lamps they had to use for light on cloudy days. A few of the buildings in town had electric lights run off the town generator, but the little shop didn't rate that kind of expense.

Epiphany let out a low cough as her lungs made the adjustment to the stale air. She squinted around the little one room building. There were no customers, only Jacob, the middle aged tailor that serviced the entire town.

He was a thin and stooped man with a small paunch from his hours of sitting slumped over his sewing table. Epiphany reflected that if she continued on her path to replace him when he retired she could someday look forward to a similarly plump and hunchbacked physique. He peered up at her over the rims of his magnifying glasses, letting the pair of tall waders he was mending drop to his lap.

"Epiphany, my dear! You know you didn't have to come in today." He spoke slowly, hesitantly and there were tense lines around his eyes. His lip trembled slightly as if he had taken a bight of rancid meat and was trying to choke it down.

"No, it's ok Jacob," she told him, trying her best to sound casual and reassure him with her tone that she wasn't going to have a breakdown. Jacob was good with clothes, bad with people, and worst with emotion. He was one of the town's lifelong bachelors, and no one had to ask why. "I know we have a lot of work this week and I want something to keep me busy."

Jacob shrugged, his shoulders moving more forward then up. He gestured with his needle at a pile of clothing stacking in a corner.

"If you want something easy and mindless there's a whole ton of mending to be done. Everyone's trying to tidy up their winter clothes before it really gets cold, or if you want more of a challenge," he redirected his needle to a stack of papers on his desk, "the Kelly girl dropped off the specifications for her wedding dress."

Epiphany scrutinized both options and decided that though she wanted to stay busy she was in no state to be creating an object of lasting beauty for some young girls special day. She nodded to the mending and with a broad sweep of his arm Jacob indicated that it was all hers. She took the two steps across the room to the pile, picked up a heap from the top of it and carried it to her workbench.

The top item was a dismally battered sweater. It was in need of a great deal more then mending and patching, but people held on to the strangest things. She selected a sharp fresh piece of chalk and started going over the sweater visually, marking the most obvious offenders for patches and making small dashes at the seams that needed mending.

"Ah!" Jacob's sudden exclamation startled her enough to drop her chalk. It fell past her leg and bounced off the floor, chipping one of its edges.

"Dammit Jacob," she snarled out, rounding on him. His eyes were doubly wide through his magnifiers and she immediately regretted the outburst. "I'm sorry, it's just been a long day and you startled me. You know how much I hate breaking my chalk."

"Of course," he said with a gracious nod, but his eyes marked off a tick of indignation in his mind that Epiphany knew she would hear about later. He let the silence draw out as he surveyed her, allowing her to drink in his displeasure. Normally she treated him with respect and did her best to tolerate his eccentricities; he was after all teaching her a trade, but today really had been a long day.

"Did you need something Jacob?"

His eyebrows almost met in the middle and his lips tightened.

"Yes." His voice was clipped now and Epiphany regretted coming to the shop when she was in such a foul mood. She knew Jacob was less then friendly most of the time and should have known he would be put off by her demeanor.

"I just remembered. Your grandfather came by. He told me that if I saw you I should ask you to stop by his home at your earliest convenience. I told him that I very much doubted you would come in on such a sad occasion, that you would surely have more important things on your mind then troubling yourself with little old me." By which he meant that he thought she would have more sense then to bother him with her sadness. Sometimes she wondered if Jacob was human, or just some mechanical throwback from the time before the Waters that was made to sew and snipe. "Clearly he knows you better then I, for here you are."

Epiphany seized on the opportunity to rectify her mistake.

"Oh... I guess that could be important. I should go check on that... if it's ok with you Jacob?" She fought the urge to cringe while she waited for his reply, but he too seemed relieved at the chance to part company until she was back to herself and could just sit quietly and learn to sew.

"By all means, today of all days family must come first." Again he gestured broadly, this time at the door. Epiphany quickly carried the clothes back to their pile and ducked for the door.

"For what it's worth Epiphany," he said as she stooped down to get out the low entrance. "I'm sorry you had to go through all this."

She looked back at him and he gave her another little forward shrug as if to say that it was as good as she could expect. She gave him a quick smile and then headed out into the day.

She hadn't been inside long, but while she had the sky had darkened and the high, light pre-storm clouds that had filled the sky had been replaced by low dark rain soaked things that threatened to burst at any moment. She pulled Gerold's coat tight around her again as the wind picked up. The storm was moving strangely fast. She tucked her head down and hurried towards the upland edge of town, hoping to make it to her grandfather's house before any of the rain started to fall.

As she passed by McAurther's farm, the only place in town that offered lodgings, she saw two men standing outside the barn. One was tall the other short and thick, each wearing dark robes. They looked up as she passed but made no gesture of greeting so she ignored them and hurried on her way. Visitors were big news in a town as small and isolated as Seacliff, but Epiphany was not so astonished by strangers-even priests – that she needed to stop and gawk.

Just past McAurther's was a short field that led up to the tree line beyond town, and nestled comfortably at the edge of the trees was her grandfather's house. It was larger then most of the homes in town, but not because they were wealthy. Her family had lived in the home for three generations and each had added on to it with the tenacity of a clan of beavers ever building up their damn. It would have been her parents' house when her grandfather died, but as it was it would pass to Epiphany. She didn't want it.

She found the old place off-putting. Her grandfather and great-grandfather had both had an affection for pre-Waters things. Some they had come to upland in the cities that had been affected less by the flood, but most of it had been salvaged from coastlines and more from the ocean floor itself using the giant brass-fitted diving suit they had found somewhere. Most of it was machine bits that would never work again, though some was books or art. Mixed in were curios that no one knew the meaning of anymore. The stuff exploded out of the maze-like rooms that had been added haphazard at the whim of each new owner. Even when she knew where she was Epiphany felt lost and claustrophobic inside.

The stone chimney, which had been taken stone my stone and moved down from a collapsed home up one of the nearby mountains, puffed thin gray smoke into the dull sky. The wind snatched it up and scattered it into the trees. Through the bizarre collection of windows that splattered the side of the eclectic building Epiphany could see a lantern bobbing hurriedly from room to room which meant her grandfather was trying to find something in the clutter.

She moved up and hammered the side of her fist against the large oak door, which family rumor had it was lifted from an old church when the house was first constructed. Her grandfather had insisted to her many times that she was family and didn't need to knock, but she always felt awkward just walking in to the old man's house.

She looked back at Seacliff as she waited quietly at the door and saw one of the priests standing by the corner of the McAurthur barn. He was a fair way off and vanished quickly from view, but it seemed as if he'd been watching her. She watched the wide, red building intently until the door in front of her swung open.

Her grandfather looked so much like her father that it hurt. He had the same long chin and broad cheekbones that made his face look like a spade, and though his hair had turned white he wore it in the same low on the neck ponytail her father had favored. He'd had more time to get used to old age then her father had though, and his wrinkles were well tempered with laugh lines, and his dark brown eyes sparkled with razor sharp awareness. By then end her fathers had been empty, though by the end her father had probably been much older then her grandfather was now.

Her lips tightened and trembled as the old man reached forward and folded her to his chest. She and her grandfather had never been overly close, but it felt good to have him hold her now. She nestled her cheek into his shoulder as he ran a hand loosely over her short-cropped hair.

"Come in out of the cold Epiphany," he cooed at her, drawing her slowly into the house. "You're like a woman made of ice. Come sit by the fire."

He released her slowly from the embrace and smiled. The skin around his eyes was swollen and dark and he looked more pale then usual as he lead her out of the small entryway and into a side room. The room was one of the least cluttered in the house and was used to receive guests. There were a few scavenged paintings on the walls, and some archaic machine sat on the mantle. It had a heavy motor housing with a long black tube sticking out of it and Grandpa said it was used to make wind, but if it did then Epiphany had never seen it work. For furnishings there was a couch, and two mismatched but plush chairs and a coffee table.

The fire was stoked up high against the late afternoon chill and it bathed the room in a warm cherry glow. Her grandfather stepped to the side of the door and motioned for her to choose a seat. She smiled at him. It was the closest to a real smile she'd felt in a long time. Though the house usually made her uncomfortable, today it felt safe and familiar. She moved over to the thickly padded armchair nearest the fire and sank down into it with a sigh. Her grandfather followed her and dropped onto the edge of the couch. He studied her for a moment, head tilted back and eyes half-lidded in thought.

"You have always reminded me more of your mother, but the older you get the more of Francis I see in you." His face broadened with a smile. "Which is unfortunate for you, because your mother was a good deal more attractive then anyone in my family ever was!"

He let out a short bark of laughter and Epiphany let herself smile a little at the joke.

"I always told Francis it was a miracle that he managed to woo someone so lovely. You were always his greatest joy though Epiphany. I hope you know that."

"Thanks grandpa," she replied. She wasn't sure what to say. Her grandfather had watched his only son grow old and die before his eyes, and as much as Epiphany hurt she knew that her grandpa hurt to; she just had no words of comfort for him. Instead she changed the subject.

"Jacob told me you needed me?"

He nodded.

"Indeed. There are," he seemed hesitant, faltering between the words as if treading his way carefully through a sleeping nest of snakes, "things you should know about this family, and something I must give you."

She didn't say anything, but her warm mood was beginning to fade. Her grandfather was notorious for broken ramblings and religious babble; stories of angels and demons and magic and wars that no one had any time for. Her father had seemed to buy right into the whole thing and her mother at least tolerated it, but it had always annoyed Epiphany. It seemed like clinging to moonbeams when you needed a rope. This sounded very much like the introduction for one of his tirades.

"Epiphany, the world is not what you think it is," he began. "I know I have told you many things in the past, and I know that you have never really believed me, but you must believe me now. With what happened to your parents I can't help but feel that you and I might be in grave danger."

"Grandpa, Mom and Dad got sick, that's all. Please no fantasies today." She turned towards the fire, offering him the back of her head.

"Epiphany I-" he paused, sighed, then continued, "Maybe this would be easier if I had you get the gift I have for you first, though I don't know if it's a gift so much as an obligation."

She turned back around to face him. She could feel heat in her cheeks, though she wasn't sure if it was the fire or her ire.

"Alright then, where is this obligation that will make it all make sense?"

"It's not here. Your father and I hid it for safekeeping.

Anyone that tried to take it would come here first. Buried under the alter at the old church there is a secret compartment. Bring me the black box that's in that compartment and I'll explain everything."

"It's getting late Grandpa, do you mind if I come back with it in the morning." She pushed herself to her feet and her legs trembled as an unwilling emphasis to her fatigue.

"I'm sorry Epiphany," he said, bowing his head in apology, "but this cannot wait."

"Fine," she grumbled. "I'll be back in a few minutes."

"Thank you," he told her, rising and giving her another hug as she headed for the door. She returned it warmly, despite her irritation. He may have been crazy and annoying, but he was family and he'd always been good to her and to her parents.

"I'm sorry this has to happen now of all times," he told her as he let her go.

"It's ok Grandpa. It'll be good to be with family tonight." She pulled open the front door and started out. "Anyway, it's going to be quiet a storm tonight and your place has a fire!" She gave him a smile as she pulled the door shut behind her.

The day had crawled away and left an early dark tucked beneath the thick clouds. A light mist had begun to fall and it clung to her hair and jacket like tiny diamonds. She took a moment to button Gerold's jacket closed and thrust her hands deep into the roomy pockets. She would have to remember to thank him a great deal for it when she returned it tomorrow. She started away at an almost jog towards the old church. She veered around the outside of town rather then taking the streets. The church sat out to one side on a little rise, and though the grass clung wetly to her pant legs it would be a shorter trip then going all the way through Seacliff. The houses threw puddles of light out into the early evening but she stayed wide of the glow, preferring to keep her own company rather then being spotted fluttering around in the dark as someone bolted up a shutter against the coming blow.

The town was small and the church, a small slatted wood affair came quickly into view. It was a dark silhouette against the dark skyline of the cliffs behind it. There were no lights on, which came as no surprise. Almost no one went to the services on Sundays, and no one at all went there at any other time. It wasn't High Church sanctioned, and there was no real clergy. A Sunday consisted mostly of the towns folk who still went telling each other stories that they found 'faith inspiring' from their week. Epiphany had gone once, and had been privy to the wonders of cows getting suddenly well from intractable illness, a rainstorm waited just long enough for a fisherman to reach home dry, and one old woman who swore that she saw and angel smelling her tulips. Epiphany had never gone back.

When she reached the church she slipped around the side to use the anteroom door rather then levering open one of the big main doors. The inside of the building was completely dark and she stood still inside the doorway to let her eyes adjust. It didn't help much. Everything was still lost in shadows, so she stretched out her hands and felt her way around the low desk that held the parish notes and to the door that lead into the main hall.

The main hall was long and thin and had high windows that let a little bit of the light in from outside. She could make out the clusters of chairs that filled the room and the wide altar where the speakers stood as they regaled the listeners with the wonder of their prosaic miracles. She moved slowly towards the altar, sliding her feet along the dirt floor to avoid tripping over any unseen obstacle in the dark. She reflected that it would have been smart to either stop by her house for her lantern, or ask her grandfather for one before she'd come She hoped she'd be able to find this trap door in the dark and wouldn't have to go all the way to her house and back for light.

She crouched down next to the altar and pulled aside the cloth that was draped over it. The back of the altar was a series of shelves that held books, candles, and alcohol for whatever version of a sacrament the people felt like doing that day. She reached down and felt beneath the bottom shelf for any sort of latch or door. The space between the bottom shelves was tiny and she'd have to move the altar to get into it, which explained why no one had ever found this secret chamber of her grandfather's. No one ever did anything to the church, certainly not rearrange the furniture.

She stood up and braced her shoulder against the edge of the wooden fixture and slid it across the dirt. She moved back and crouched down to next to the spot it had been and started feeling around. She brushed away a few layers of the dirt before she felt wood beneath her fingers. She was surprised that her grandfather hadn't been making the whole thing up.

Carefully she started to work her way out from where she'd first felt the wood, brushing away the layers of earth till she found the edges of what seemed to be a large box. She worked slowly in the dark, and again she cursed herself for not thinking to get a light before she came. She felt along the edges for any sort of release or catch until she found a small raised button on one corner. She pressed it, and with a click the lid of the compartment sprung free.

She couldn't see anything in the compartment but trusting her Grandpa wouldn't set a trap for her she reached into the shadowy hole. Her hand immediately found cool, smooth lacquered wood. She picked up the box, a rough cube about a foot to a side, and examined it as best she could in the dark. She could see no latch or button on the box that would allow it to open. For that matter she couldn't see any hinges or the split of a lid. She shrugged again and set the box down next to her and closed the compartment. She brushed the dirt back onto it as best she could and slid the altar back into place, taking a moment to kick away the skid marks where it had been displaced. Her grandfather might want to use the compartment again, and Epiphany saw no reason to give away his secret. She gathered up the box and slipped back outside.

TSAYYADIEL WOKE into the quiet darkness. He did not open his eyes right away, nor did he move. Instead he laid still, letting his mind travel the long unused corridors of his body, touching stiff muscle and coaxing brittle sinew back to life. When all was ready he let his eyes slide open. In the darkness of his little room they glowed with a soft blue light. The flat stone of the walls drank in the light and gave back only shadows. Slowly, carefully he pushed himself up to a sitting position and let his bare feet swing down to rest on the cool floor. He let them get used to the touch of ground again and then pushed off his bed and drew himself to his full height. He was long and lean and his head almost brushed the low ceiling of his chamber.

He rolled his shoulders, stretching his back and breathing deep in satisfaction as his vertebrae cracked and released. He bent forward, letting his fingertips brush the ground and relishing the dull ache in the back of his thighs as his hamstrings slowly elongated after long disuse. The stretching routine continued for several more minutes and only when he felt that he had regained his strength and suppleness did Tsayyadiel finally turn and open the rough hewn door of his room.

In the dimly lit hallway stood a small round man wearing a long rough spun brown robe. The man's stature was such that the robe puddled on the floor around his feet and the sleeves were turned back in wide bells to expose his hands. It had been the sound of the man's approach that had first awoken Tsayyadiel. In his fat little arms the man cradled a pile of cloth and a bundle wrapped in heavy canvas. Without a word Tsayyadiel took the parcels from the man. He turned and laid the canvas package on his cot and unfolded the heavy cloth to reveal a thick white robe with a deep cowl. In one smooth motion he pulled the robe over his head, letting it fall over his lean naked body and tossing the hood back to lay around his shoulders. He picked up the canvas wrapped item and tucked it under his arm. Satisfied that all was in order he motioned for the little man to lead him.

They walked in silence down a curved hallway lined with more rough wooden doors. Many were open to reveal more small rooms. Within, more of the brown robed men were engaged in quiet reading or transcribing, some were praying, and a few were on their knees, naked and scourging themselves, their blood dripping in soft plops onto the stone floor and filling the hall near them with a heavy copper scent.

At the end of the hallway was a wide double door. The little man fished around inside his voluminous robes and produced a wide flat key which he inserted into the cherub's mouth that served as the door's keyhole. With a deep and resonant click the lock sprung and he pulled the door open, dipping into a deep bow to one side and allowing Tsayyadiel to pass. Once Tsayyadiel was inside the door swung shut and the lock clicked back into place. The click echoed off bare stonewalls. The room was small and unadorned, the only feature a thin spiral staircase that swept away and up into the darkness above him. There were no torches or windows so the only illumination came from the pale glow of Tsayyadiel's eyes, but it didn't matter, he could see in the dark.

He took the stairs two at a time, and it wasn't long before he stepped out of a narrow archway into a round tower room at the top of the stairs. Four torches in sconces high around the walls threw flickering light through the mostly empty room. The only furnishing was a wide wooden table in the center of the room with a pitcher, a heavy iron goblet and a platter of bread. He crossed to the table with long strides and laid aside his canvas burden.

He took up the pitcher and poured a rich dark wine into the goblet and then tore off a thick chunk of the bread. Holding the bread in his right hand he picked up the goblet in his left and bowed his head. His eyes slid shut as he intoned softly,

"As this is his blood." With measured motion he gradually upended the goblet, spilling the wine onto the floor, "and this is his flesh." Tsayyadiel threw the chunk of bread into the puddle of wine and with a sharp motion ground it beneath his bare heel.

"The heresy will be undone, the treason punished." With that he set the goblet back on the table and opened his eyes.

Across the table stood a thin man with gray eyes and hair to match. A long beard tumbled down his chest and stomach and fell low enough to vanish behind the broad table between them. He was clad in the same white robe Tsayyadiel wore and he scrutinized the other man with quiet probing. Tsayyadiel spoke first.

"Hello Enoch, it's been a very long time." The other man nodded.

"Very long indeed. Much has changed Tsayyadiel."

"I have been awakened, so I can only presume that much has not."

"We have found the Bearer." Enoch paused to let the information soak in. "Our triumph is closer then ever in hand. The Crone has already been dispatched to begin the collection, but we felt that perhaps such an important task should be monitored by someone who understood the old ways."

"Very well. What are his wishes?"

Enoch reached into the folds of his robes and pulled out a leather envelope and laid it on the table between them.

"The last known location of the Bearer is indicated on the map I'm giving you. Go there and find him. Take back what was stolen."

Tsayyadiel picked up the envelope and opened it. Inside was a map of a jagged coastline with a town indicated by a quickly dashed 'x'. He tucked it back and laid it next to the canvas bundle.

"What of the others?"

"I assume you mean the Three?"

The name made Tsayyadiel's eyes narrow and his lips turn down in an angry sneer.

"All that remains of their venomous clan's treachery." He nearly spat the words at Enoch. The old man's lips twisted into a thin grin.

"All that remains?"

Tsayyadiel's eyes were murder, but Enoch just laughed.

"The Three have continued to plague us during your repose, but nothing significant. Mostly they harry our servants and trouble our trade routes," the old man told him.

"I should have been allowed to deal with them long ago." Tsayyadiel's hand strayed out to brush the canvas.

"You know as well as we the futility of such an action, but," he quickly interjected detecting Tsayyadiel's thinly veiled rage, "that time may swiftly come. If they realize, as they are sure to that the Bearer has been found then they will do as we are and seek him out."

"Then I must hurry." Tsayyadiel snatched up the two packages and tucked them into the pocket in his robes and started back towards the stairs.

"You must be cautious," Enoch called after him, "things are not as they once were."

"We are unchanging Enoch," he said without turning or slowing. "That is all that matters."

"You cannot come back you know, not until the task is done."

Tsayyadiel still did not slow his pace.

"I have never come back until the task was done, even when I could."

Enoch may have had more to say, but Tsayyadiel did not wait to find out. His journey back through the stronghold was brisk and spent lost in thought. So many things were finally coming full circle. The Bearer had been found and the Three had reemerged. Debts long left unpaid were going to be answered. A dark grin twisted his thin lips at the thought and his fingers tightened around the canvas satchel the monk had brought him.

Within he could feel the hard lines of his dagger. He unwrapped it from its swaddling as he strode through the dim corridors. He tossed the canvas to the floor once it was off, trusting in one of the lessers to see to it. The knife, long, slender, and single edged glowed with a polished silver luster in the torches that lined the hall. He flexed his fingers around the wire wrapped grip. It felt good to have its hard lines back in his hand, made him feel whole again.

He was still holding the knife, turning it back and forth between his hands when two hooded monks drew aside two vast, black metal doors. He paid them no mind, striding through and tucking the blade into his belt as he went. The doors boomed shut behind him and Tsayyadiel found himself standing on a narrow walkway around the outer edge of the stronghold. Above him the wall stretched away farther than even he could see, dotted here and there with narrow windows that shot narrow beams of light into the darkness beyond.

51

And beyond there was only darkness.

In the inky blackness Tsayyadiel almost felt he could make out hints of motion, coiling forms in the dark that hid just at the edge of perception, but that was probably just his mind trying to make sense of the nothingness. The darkness was just that: nothing. The Void was the blank palette where the stronghold of the Word had stood since the beginning of things and it was the dividing line between the world of humanity and the worlds beyond. Once there had been a bridge between those worlds, but the Word had closed the Gate and now the Void was unending.

Tsayyadiel slipped forward, sliding his feet until his toes hung over the edge of the smooth walk. Despite the emptiness there was a slight breeze. It drifted down the face of the keep behind him and tugged at his robe as if trying to draw him over the edge. He looked down, but there was no more to see below than there was beyond. The smooth line of the wall swept downward and disappeared into the shadowed distance.

He knew that somewhere down there was a wholly different sort of wall, one he would have to past through to reach his goal. He did not relish the thought. He was not fond of humanity the way some of his kin were and each trip to their realm convinced him all the more of their inferiority. None they less, they were the heart of the Machine and whoever controlled the Machine controlled everything. The rebellion had to end and the Bearer was the key.

He laid a hand on the pommel of his knife, meditating for a moment on its reassuring presence. Then he let his eyes glide shut and with a gradual shifting of weight pitched himself forward from the lip of the wall. He could feel himself falling, but paid it no mind, focusing on only one thing. In his inner eye was the frozen image of a map, with a quickly scrawled X.

5

IT HAD STARTED RAINING in earnest while Epiphany had been in the church and fat drops spattered onto her head and shoulders with chilling impacts. She hunched down, tucking the box into her chest and took off at a run. Despite running, the trip back to her grandfather's house seemed to take longer with the cold rain pounding down around her and half blinding her. Her familiar town took on a strange foreign quality of blurred lines and dark slumped shapes. Curiosity about the box churned in her gut and made everything seem more ominous. She squinted into the downpour and tried to make out the house as she shuffled quickly along.

It emerged like a ghost out of the rain, one moment nothing, and the next a wide shadow blocking out a patch of dark sky. She tucked herself close to the wall in hopes of dodging a bit of the shower, though she was soaked to the skin as it was. She rounded the corner to the front door and found it partially ajar. It was strange, but she was just grateful to get out of the cold and wet.

She opened her mouth to call out to her grandfather when she heard the low drift of voices from farther inside the house. She strained her ears to hear what they were saying or see if she could identify which of the villagers had come to visit her grandpa on such an unpleasant night. Few people ever came to visit and it was always on strange business.

"– around a bit. You check and see if the old man's still

alive." It was a voice she did not recognize, and the last words chilled her more deeply then the rain. There were sounds of rummaging from one of the rooms deep in the house. As quietly as she could quickly move Epiphany started towards the noise. She slipped into side rooms rather than going down the main hallway. She moved through a narrow office heavily cluttered with papers and books and then through the little breakfast nook that looked out over town. She glanced through the large window, but the rain had built a wall between her and the rest of the world.

The sound of the rummaging was close by and she peaked around the corner of the nook door and into the study beyond. She ducked back quickly when she saw the figure in the center of the room, then more cautiously leaned her head around.

The man crouched over her grandfather hadn't noticed her. She held her breath and watched from the shadow of the doorway as stubby fingers pawed her grandfather's throat for a pulse. A half hooded lantern sat on the floor a few feet away from him and threw phantasms of light over the round toad-like face. She could see the thin white collar wrapped around the squat man's neck and realized that she was looking at the shorter of the two priests from McAurthur's barn. From farther back in the house she could still hear the sounds of rummaging and guessed that it was the taller priest.

The toad craned his head around and called over his shoulder in a musical voice ill suited to his trollish features,

"He's still alive!"

"Good," The voice that drifted back was the first one Epiphany had heard when she'd come inside. "Then we can question him when he wakes up and I can stop digging though mountains of junk. Leave him there; I'll tie him up.

You go wait by the door for the girl to come back."

"How do you know she's coming?" Toad called back to his companion.

"When we came in the old codger thought we were her. That means he's expecting her. Now go wait. If we grab her we can torture her to loosen up his tongue."

"Straight to torture eh?" the Toad asked. From his thick-lipped grin Epiphany could tell he wasn't bothered by the idea.

"I don't want to be here any longer than I have to be. I don't like these coastal towns, and I don't like coastal people. Plus you know what's coming." The voice was getting closer.

"They're on our side," the little man said, glancing up as his partner entered the room. Despite their differences in height the two priests might have been related. The tall man shared the same fleshy features as his squat companion, but they looked as if they had been stretched to fit a frame that was a size too large for them.

"So they say," the tall one said. "I don't like being around them anyway."

"Torture it is then!"

Epiphany had to fight down a gasp of horror. She had to bite back another gasp as the squat priest stood up and she saw the shallow pool of blood on the floor around her grandfather's still form. The priest move away from him and into one of the hallways that lead from the study back to the front door. She thought about trying to sneak past them and go to the town for help, but watching the pool of blood slowly expand around her grandpa she knew she didn't have much time. For the first time ever she was glad that the house was like a maze. She slipped back out of the breakfast nook and ducked into the series of rooms that paralleled the hallway.

Epiphany couldn't stop shaking and her heartbeat was

an oceanic roar in her ears. She found herself half holding her breath for fear that she would be heard as she slipped from room to room. Her eyes danced across every surface, each bit of junk taking on the sinister shape of a new attacker. She had only seen the two priests at the farm, and only heard the two voices, but could she be sure they were alone. Panting as if she'd run a race, she finally emerged into the living room where she'd talked to Grandpa earlier that evening.

She lingered in the shadowed door and glanced towards the entryway but didn't see the priest. She looked around for something she could use as a weapon. Whatever she found she'd need her hands to wield it so she set the black box down on the floor next to her. It hit her like a landslide. It was the box they were looking for; the terrible obligation her grandfather had mentioned and the danger they were in. That was why the tall priest had been ransacking the house.

She picked the box up again. She couldn't leave it out in case – she hated to think it – in case they got her as well. She didn't want to make it easy for them to find. There was a closet sized room next to the living room, and it was overflowing with knickknacks and heaped linens. She tucked the box into a shadowed recess under an old quilt and then peered back into the living room and through it into the entryway.

She didn't see anything, but she waited. Every moment that slipped past made her think of her grandfather laying there and bleeding, but she knew if she moved too soon and got captured then she'd be no help to him at all. Finally she saw a bit of movement in the hall just beyond the living room, the flash of an arm rising to scratch a nose and then dropping back down. The toad priest was standing in the entryway with his back against the wall of the living room, right next to the door.

Epiphany again looked around for something she could use as a weapon. Her eyes settled on the heavy iron poker next to the fireplace.

She moved across the room on tiptoe, her eyes never leaving the dark square of doorway in case the priest should glance back in her direction. She reached the fireplace and lifted the heavy poker in two hands. Tensely, she slunk towards the doorway. He was straight through the wall from her now. She could imagine him there as if she could see through the paint and plaster, squat body leaned back but ready to spring should she come through the door. In her minds eye she could see her grandpa's blood on his hands. It made her hate him. She took a deep breath and tried to focus. She needed to do this quickly and quietly so she didn't alert the other priest.

She cocked the iron bar up by her shoulder and stepped through the doorway. The toad was standing with his hands by his sides and his eyes fixed on the main door. He had just enough time to register the motion next to him and start to turn before the fire poker took him full swing across the chest. He was sandwiched between the wall and the poker and Epiphany heard several dull pops inside his body. His eyes bulged out and then rolled back as the man slumped to the floor. Epiphany stood over him for a moment, the breath heaving and in and out of her lungs as blood trickled from the corner of his mouth and his eyes continued to roll in their sockets.

She looked down the hall into the house, but she neither saw nor heard the other priest. Hopefully he hadn't heard the thump of the attack over the drum of rain on the roof. For the first time she was grateful for the downpour. Epiphany slipped back into the living room, and poker still in hand retraced her steps through the well-shadowed side rooms to the breakfast nook.

She could see through the door to the study where her

grandfather lay on his side, his arms bound behind him, his eyes still closed. There was a dark stain on the left side of his shirt and his face looked even paler in the lantern light then it had earlier. The tall priest was checking the knots that held grandpa's legs together. The dim light of the shuttered lantern shown across his bald pate as he gave a satisfied nod and stood up. Epiphany pressed herself back into the shadows by a set of cupboards and willed him not to see her as he glanced around. His eyes passed over her but never paused. He strolled with a long sloppy gait towards the front of the house. Epiphany pressed forward to the edge of the study and watched as he leaned a little out into the hallway. His face was hidden behind the doorjamb and Epiphany took the opportunity to slide into the room and across the wall towards him.

Again her foe had the briefest moment to register the movement next to him as he drew his head back into the room before the heavy iron bar crashed down in an overhead swing across the top of his hairless head. There was a thick crunch and the body crumpled like a rag doll to the floor. Epiphany stood frozen for a moment as a rapidly expanding pool of crimson formed around the priests still head. She realized with lightning bolt certainty that she had probably just killed a man. She looked over her shoulder to where her grandfather was stretched out on the floor and she shed her guilt like a snake its skin. She dropped the poker unceremoniously next to the priest's body and crossed quickly to her grandfather.

He groaned as she rolled him onto his stomach and started to work loose the ropes holding his wrists. From this position she could see the long angry gash torn down the left side of his lower back. The wound was deep and at the top edge of it she could see the dull white of exposed bone. Blood continued to leak from the cut. Once she'd untied his wrists she rolled him back over. She knew she should do something about the wound, but she didn't know what.

His eyes fluttered weakly open.

"Epiphany?" His voice was less then a whisper.

"Hush Grandpa, I'm going to get you to help."

He shook his head and tried to push her limply away.

"There's no time," he told her. "You have to go. Did you get the box?"

"I got the box Grandpa, but I took care of them, of the men who attacked you. We're safe now and I'm going to get you help." She started working furiously at the ropes around his ankles.

"Never safe Epiphany. We're never safe, but that doesn't matter. The box girl, you have to protect the box. It is our family obligation. Take the box to Friar Brendiwald in Newridge."

"Hush grandpa," she told him again. She finished freeing his legs and moved up to his shoulders. She tried to lift him, but he was like a sack of loose flour and she couldn't get a good grip.

"I'm dead Epiphany." The words came without fear, just a dreadful certainty. "They killed me, but you have avenged me. Now do as I've told you. You cannot go to the town council; they will bow in fear to the people after you. Take the box to Friar Brendiwald. Now you have to flee, there are more where these came from and you haven't much time."

He limply pushed at her again. The effort seemed to take the last out of him and his eyes slipped shut. Epiphany held her breath, trembling as she watched the slow rise and fall of his chest grow still with a last rattling exhale. Her body shook with a violent sob as she pushed herself to her feet. She didn't know what to do, only her grandfather's last request thundered over and over in her mind. She needed to get the box and take it to Friar

Brendiwald in Newridge.

Epiphany had no idea where Newridge was, or how to get there. She had never traveled inland, only out to sea. She puzzled over this as she moved quickly back through the house to the little closet where she'd left the box. She pulled out the quilt and the box under it. She wrapped the box in the quilt, making it into a makeshift satchel and tucked it over her shoulder.

In the entryway there was a pool of blood, but the priests body was gone. A long smear of sticky red lead towards the half open front door. She took two long steps across the room and yanked the door open. Her grandfather's last breath and the vivid slash down his back were still crystal clear in her mind and she had every intention of finding the Toad and finishing what she'd started. Outside the rain was coming down harder then ever and in the darkness she could find no trace of the man. For a moment she considered continuing her search, but her grandpa's warning about more pursuers chimed in her head. Toad could have crawled off for reinforcements and so Epiphany turned and hurried down the road towards town with the box bumping against her back through Gerold's jacket.

The idea came to her in a flash. Gerold had traveled inland. His family was pearl farmers and sold many of their wares in the bigger cities. She would go to Gerold and ask him to come with her. What would she tell him though, that her grandfather had been murdered by priests and she had in turn killed one of them, and that she was now on the run to an inland city?

She stopped in the middle of the road, the rain curtaining her off from everything around her. The realization of what had transpired in the last fifteen minutes hit her like a boulder. Her vision swam and the thud of the drops on the hard packed dirt around her sounded like the roaring of lions. Her stomach lurched and she doubled forward at the waist, her hands flying to her knees for balance.

She'd eaten little throughout the day and so it was mostly bitter bile that poured out of her. Her eyes were blind with tears and her throat burned. She felt as if she'd been kicked hard in the gut and she retched again across her muddy shoes. She stood there, hunched over with her short brown hair veiling her from the world and panted for breath. For a moment she considered throwing the blanket wrapped box into the darkened field and pretending that nothing had happened, but her grandfather's corpse was still warm behind her and his commands were fresh in her mind. If she had to go she might as well enlist what aid she could. Her grandpa had warned her of the council, but Gerold's family had nothing to do with the bureaucracy of the town and they had been friends since childhood. She would tell him what had happened and hopefully he would help her. At that moment she dearly wanted a friend.

THE WOMAN HUDDLED in the corner, her head tucked to her chest as if she was trying to curl into herself. Her round shoulders shook with violent sobs. Gasping breaths rasped in her throat between each long bout of tears. The man crouched quietly next to her reached out a hand, but when he touched her shoulder she let out a soft jagged cry and recoiled away. Her head struck the wall, but she didn't seem to notice. He let his hand fall back to his denim clad knee.

"Shhhh ... quiet now," he whispered to her, his voice mid-range and only slightly modulated. "I know what you've seen today has been terrible, but it was all for the best."

She gave no sign that she heard him but he continued on, speaking slowly, his words creating a melodic cadence.

"I know the people you loved are gone; I know you feel like you're world is over; I know you fear you're in danger." When he mentioned danger there was a hitch in her sobbing, a moment of held breath.

"You're not in danger," he continued, seizing the moment. "You are innocent. I'm sure after what you've seen in the last hour you must believe that we are indiscriminate and terrible, but I assure you the innocent have nothing to fear from us. Those people – the others – I know they were close to you and you thought well of them."

A frightened glance flicked out toward him and he

quickly held up his hands.

"Of course you did, you are a good person and you loved them. We never want to think ill of the people we love, especially family. I know." Something dark drifted through his robin's egg blue eyes; there for a moment, then gone. "You thought well of them, but deep down you know what they were, and what they were becoming... and I know that with time you will see that what happened here was for the best."

He reached slowly towards her again and this time when his hand touched her shoulder she didn't pull away. He squeezed her shoulder gently. Her breath slowed and her wracking sobs died down to a low sniffling. A wave of relaxation flowed outward from the point of contact, easing tense muscles and settling her whole posture. The room seemed quieter.

"You'll see. Someday you'll understand. You're husband, his brothers, and even your sons," at the mention of her sons a tremor ran through her wide body and he tightened his hand on her shoulder, "They were tampering with dangerous things beyond their control; evil things and you should be happy that they can no longer endanger you with their greed."

Slowly, hesitantly she uncurled her head from the nest of her arms, mud brown eyes rimmed in red looked up to meet soft pools of blue. His full lips turned up in a gentle smile that parted his curly red-brown beard. She managed a small smile in return.

"You see, when you really look at it all you have lost is a group of people who never thought of your well being," he continued, reaching out with his free hand and brushing the lingering tears from her eyelashes with the broad flat pad of a well calloused thumb. "You see don't you."

She seemed to search through her thoughts, uncertain

of whether she agreed with him or not. He caught her gently by the chin and brought her gaze back to his. Their eyes locked for a long moment and he nodded. She nodded in return. His smile broadened and the whole room was brighter for it. He gathered her gently into his arms, her face settling against the soft flannel of his shirt. He made soft cooing sounds as he rocked back and forth on his toes and stroked her tangled brown hair.

"Who are you?" she whispered against him.

"I'm an angel of course," he replied. "I am Heart."

"I've never heard of an angel just called Heart," she whispered.

"I had another name once, but that was long ago and it is lost." He continued to pet her hair. "For today though I am Heart, and my concern is the weight on your heart."

Her smile widened and she nestled her face deeper into his chest.

Abruptly the woman let out a throaty scream and thrashed away from her comforter. She threw herself against the wall, her sobs renewing immediately in both force and volume. Heart's eyes widened in shock as the peace in the room crumbled away like a sand castle in an earthquake. The woman's stricken gaze was locked across the room. Her eyes were frantic and she screamed again before slamming her face mindlessly back into the wall as if trying to hide inside it.

Heart pivoted on bare feet to face the only door. It was filled with a tall figure dressed in a long black duster. Long dark hair was pulled sharply back from his face and gathered into a ponytail and his eyes were sapphire pinpricks under heavy brows. His right hand held the door open and his left held a pistol. His pants were covered in blood.

"For the love of lost heaven Reaper, I had her calmed down, what are you doing?" he barked quietly across the room at the new comer.

"Sorry Heart," came the flat and obviously insincere response. "We have to go."

Heart glanced back across his shoulder at the increasingly frantic woman. Her face was pressed to the wall so hard that blood was trickling in tandem from a broken nose and split lip and she was clawing at the plaster as if she could dig her way out of the room.

"She's an innocent in all this Reaper. You know I can't leave her like this and you just undid all the good I had worked. What's the rush?"

"Can't you feel it?" the man in the doorway asked. "He's on the move, and if he's on the move..."

Reaper didn't finish, just waited as Heart tilted his head to the side as if listening. It didn't take long. His head snapped back up and his eyes were fierce and alert.

"If Tsayyadiel's back then the Bearer is on the move," Heart said. "Alright, I'll finish quickly, though you know I hate to rush these things."

Reaper shrugged.

"Fist is almost done outside," he said, tilting his head out the door where the dull sound of flesh being struck repeated blows could just be heard. "Hurry and we'll all get on the move."

He turned in a swirl of duster and pulled the door closed behind him.

Heart turned back to the woman in the corner.

"It's ok," he said to her, his voice falling back into the same almost monotone cadence. "He's gone now, and he won't come back. It's ok."

The woman didn't react to his voice at all, and when he reached out yet again to touch her the reaction was so violent that he was afraid she was going to hurt herself in some permanent way. He heaved a deep sigh and stood up. He straitened his jeans and plaid shirt and looked down at her with pursed lips.

"Alright." His voice was still soft, but the gentleness was gone, replaced by a stern forcefulness. "You will be calm."

His voice filled the room, and the pulse of it washed across the woman like a tranquilizer. She immediately fell silent, but continued to tremble against the wall. He inhaled deeply and as he exhaled a warm calm flowed out from him like a cresting wave.

"Today was a terrible day, but it was necessary to quell the evil in this house. You have been found innocent of the wrongdoing and so you are spared. You will find peace in the knowledge that your life is better and safer without those others around. Your fear and trembling is past."

He took a step towards her and laid his left hand on top of her head. This time she didn't pull away. He raised his right hand above his head.

"You are loved my child. When the time comes you will find the Gates of Heaven thrown wide for your arrival, but that time is not now. Until then let my love and the love of all that is fill your heart and take away all your pain."

The woman pushed herself away from the wall and wrapped her arms tightly around Heart's legs. When she looked up at him she was crying again, but the rapt look on her face was all adoration and gratitude. Around his head she could see a pale aura of golden light and two dove gray wings swept back from his shoulders.

"Thank you," she whispered, her voice still raspy from her crying and screaming. He left his hand on her head for a moment longer before pulling himself from her and walking away, the light around him fading and the wings folding into his back and disappearing into themselves. She whispered 'thank you' again but he didn't turn around, just moved to the door, opened it, and went outside.

Reaper stood in the middle of the scrub filled yard, his face turned to the gray, cloud riddled sky. The detritus of a short and ugly battle was littered around him. Blood stained the stunted grass and the earth had been churned up by scuffling feet. At Reaper's feet lay a shattered haft of wood decorated with bones and feathers, a hex stick the woman's husband had tried to use against them. He kicked at it idly with a bare toe. He didn't turn when Heart came out but asked,

"Is she alright?"

"Not that you really care," Heart said curtly. Reaper glanced back, his gaze dark and unreadable to any but those that knew him best. "I'm sorry, I know you care. I know you only fill the role that was given to you, there have just been so many lately. It wears on me. Yes, she's all right. Where is Fist?"

Reaper tilted his head and Heart followed the motion to a low hill. Around the corner of it strode a tall, sinewy woman with curly red-brown hair. Her square and muscular shoulders jutted out from a tight black tank top and she was wiping blood off her hands with a torn scrap of cloth that she tossed casually on the ground in front of her and tread bare footed across. Her blue-gray eyes flicked from Reaper to Heart and back again.

"What's going on?" she asked in a light voice that seemed ill fit to her strong frame.

"Tsayyadiel is on the move," Heart told her.

"The Bearer?" Her question was as much a gasp as words. Reaper nodded, finally looking away from the clouds to face the other two.

"We have to go." He said flatly.

"Newridge?" Heart asked him, but Reaper shook his head.

"Brendiwald will have to find out on his own. We go to Seacliff. Tsayyadiel will go straight for the Bearer and we can't let him get there first."

"Do we travel fast then?" Heart asked. This time it was Fist that shook her head.

"To risky. If he doesn't know where the Bearer is then we would lead him there."

Reaper nodded in agreement.

"We'll travel as fast as we can, but we'll have to go overland."

"There were horses in the barn out back," Fist suggested, motioning back the direction she had come.

"No." Reaper's voice was again firm and flat. "The innocent lives, and she still lives here. We won't steal from her."

"I'm impressed," said Heart with a thin smile. Reaper's brows furrowed down over his narrow eyes in a deep glower.

"Don't push your luck Brother."

"If no horses," Fist cut in, "then we have a long road ahead. We should get to walking."

"Not walking," Reaper told her. "Too slow. We run."

The other two fell in behind Reaper as he started down the road with long loping strides, his duster trailing behind him like black wings. A low roll of thunder chased them into the shadows of the tree line.

"At least we're in the woods!" Heart called out. "Looks like rain!"

7

TO SAY THAT GEROLD and his family were well off would be like saying that the ocean was deep. Wealth didn't mean as much as it once had, especially near the coastlines, but it still meant enough to secure the Ipsens a sprawling manor on one of the sea cliffs overlooking a private bay where they kept their small fleet of ships docked. Even with the rain still coming down in heavy sheets Epiphany could make out the dark bulk of it framed against the seaward sky. It looked like a giant crouched down on the crest of the hill and Epiphany could almost imagine a great arm reaching down into the ocean to pluck up its treasures.

She squinted through the rain, but couldn't make out any lights within the house. She had lost track of time in the chaos of the evening, but she would have guessed it was past midnight. Part of her quailed at the idea of waking the whole house, but she had nowhere else to turn so she put her head down and trudged up the steep hill.

Once she reached the house Epiphany wasted no time in hammering on the door. Inside she could hear the sound echo in the broad entry hall, while outside the first crashes of thunder exploded through the sky. She waited for a brief moment and then hammered the side of her fist against the door again. Gerold had to be home, he was not the type that would be out on a such a night. Epiphany leaned over and peered through the frosted glass pane next to the door. She could make out the bobbing globe of a lantern coming down the hallway. Gerold's family had their own generator of course, and the house was wired for electric lights, but no one would waste valuable fuel to keep lights burning in the middle of the night. The lantern swam closer and the door swung open to reveal Gerold standing bleary eyed in a long silk robe. A hooded lantern was held up by his cherubic face. His blond hair was pointing sharply up on the left side and Epiphany knew she must have rousted him from bed.

"Epiphany?" He squinted out at her, huddled on his doorstep like a stray dog. Like a stray dog he seemed unsure if she needed help, or was going to bite him. Epiphany glanced over her shoulder, though the effort was wasted. Even if someone were standing ten feet behind her she wouldn't have been able to see them. She put a hand in the middle of Gerold's chest and pushed him into the house, pulling the door closed behind her.

"Epiphany what's going on?" He lifted the latch and unhooded his lantern. The entry was bathed in light. It sparkled off the pearl inlay in the floor and off the golden candelabras around the walls. Gerold blinked in the sudden light before refocusing on her.

"Oh my god Epiphany! What happened to you?!" His eyes were wide, tiny pupils in a sea of brown in the sudden burst of light. She glanced down at herself and for the first time realized that she was covered in blood. Gerold started to push past her towards the door, though where he thought he was going in a silk robe with no shoes in the middle of a rainstorm Epiphany couldn't say. She reached out and caught him by the shoulder.

"It's my grandfather," she told him quickly. "My grandfather's been murdered." His eyes widened further until Epiphany had to fight down the urge to reach out and catch them in case they fell out of his head.

"The priests that came into town today, they were

looking for something that he had and they killed him."

"They... but they... but... what?" Gerold was quickly running himself out of breath trying to find his question. Epiphany steered him by the arm away from the door.

"Hood the lantern Gerold," she instructed him. He quickly complied. "I don't know if they're still after me. I killed one of them, and hurt the other pretty badly, but he got away."

"You killed someone!" Gerold slithered out of her grip and took a long step away from her. Epiphany again questioned her wisdom in coming to Gerold.

"It was self defense Gerold," she insisted. She took a step towards him but he took a step back to match. "They killed my grandfather."

"We have to go to the constable, the Magics, or to the town council"

"No." The word and Epiphany's flat tone struck Gerold like a slap to the face. "Gerold listen to me please. We've been friends for a long time and I need you to just listen to me for a minute."

Gerold didn't respond, but he didn't run away either which Epiphany took for a good sign. Gerold was not a strong man, and certainly not someone comfortable with killing and blood, but he was a good friend.

"There's something big going on here Gerold. I don't know what it is, but it has something to do with this box."

She brought the blanket off her shoulder, carefully unwrapped the box and set it on the floor. The black wood gleamed in the low light. Gerold leaned in to look at it and then looked expectantly back at Epiphany, unsure what he was seeing.

"I don't know what it is," she admitted, "but it was what the priests were looking for, and my grandpa said my family's been protecting it for a long time. Look, I don't know how long I have before they start looking for me so

I'm going to make this quick. Grandpa told me with his dying breath that I need to take this thing to a Friar in Newridge. I'm going to do it. I've never been inland, but you have. I'd love it if you'd help me, at least just to get to Newridge. A map, supplies... come with me."

The last was ventured forth with great hesitation. Gerold started to respond, but Epiphany held up her hand to stop him.

"Wait. I'll tell you up front that it's probably going to be dangerous. This isn't one of our kids games anymore, and I thought hard about not coming here, but... but I feel way in over my head and I didn't know who else I could trust."

Gerold stood for a moment gazing at her, and then set down the lantern, spread his arms and stepped forward to embrace her. She threw her arms around his soft waist and buried her face in his chest. She could feel the cold dampness from her clothes soaking into his silk robe, but he didn't seem to care and neither did she. The events of the night again overwhelmed her, and this time it came in the form of tears. She bawled against him and he held her tightly, rocking slowly back and forth.

"This whole running inland thing seems like a mistake Epiphany," he said softly, still rocking her. "I know your grandfather told you to go to Newridge, but we're hardly great adventurers, and if there are people after you, people obviously willing to kill then we need to think hard about what our next step is."

"You won't help me?" Epiphany drew back to gaze up at him. The light from the lantern threw dark shadows off his round cheeks and made his eyes into unreadable pools of black.

"Of course I'll help you," he whispered softly. "What are friends for? And if we decide to make a run for Newridge then I'll even go with you. I'm just saying that we shouldn't run off into the night without thinking things through."

She pulled herself together quickly. She drew out of his embrace and knelt down next to the box, dabbing at her eyes with the sleeve of his coat. She started to wrap the box back up.

"We need to move quickly. Grandpa said there'd be more and I don't know how long we have."

He watched her wrap the box up and then nodded towards the back of the house.

"We'll start with some dry clothes for you, and some real clothes for me," he told her, starting down the hall. Epiphany followed.

"Mom and my brothers are all inland right now, so we have the house to ourselves, which is good. I don't think mom would take any of this well." He laughed quietly as he stopped at a large hall closet and pulled out a set of pants and a heavy wool shirt for Epiphany. He passed them to her and pointed to the door across from them.

"You can change in mom's room, I'll run put on some clothes and meet you back in the hall." She caught him by the arm again before he could move away.

"Thank you Gerold, for even hearing me out." He gave her arm a reassuring squeeze and turned down the hall to his room. Epiphany stepped into his mother's palatial bedroom and pulled the door shut behind her. The room was dark and cavernous with the lantern gone, but Epiphany changed quickly in the dark, grateful for the dry warmth of the clothes. Gerold's mother was larger then Epiphany and the clothes hung off her shoulders, but she was well beyond complaining. She balled her wet clothes up under her arm and stepped back out into the hall.

It took Gerold longer to return and when he did his hair was wet and patted down and he was wearing a pair of leather pants and a pressed shirt.

"Much better," he told her with a nod, "Now we can get down to business."

He motioned for her to follow him and lead her farther down the hall to the small family kitchen in the rear of the house. Once there he pulled some bread out of the pantry and poured her a glass of water. Epiphany attacked the food, tearing large chunks off the bread and gulping them down.

"So what now?" Gerold asked her, "I already suggested the council, but you seemed against that."

Epiphany shook her head and spoke around a mouthful of the sweet honey-bread.

"My grandpa said not to go to the council or the constable. He didn't have time to elaborate, but I guess they must be connected to the priests somehow."

"That seems unlikely," Gerold said and Epiphany had to cram a hunk of bread into her mouth to avoid a sharp comment about his condescending tone.

"Why would some vast conspiratorial group take the time to infiltrate the leadership of our tiny little town?"

"It seems as likely as my family being the sworn protectors of a mysterious box in this tiny little town." He nodded in concession and tore off his own piece of bread.

"There has to be someone we can go to for help Epiphany, I just don't know how well we'd fair trying to sneak off through the woods, especially if there's someone after us."

He tore off another piece of bread with one hand and gestured sweepingly at his small potbelly and heavy arm.

"I mean, I appreciate you coming to me, and I would do anything for you, but you'd probably have better luck protecting me!"

"I didn't come to you for protection Gerold. There's always safety in numbers I guess, but I came to you mostly because you've traveled before and I haven't, at least not inland. The bottom line is there is no one else I can go to, and by extension no one else you can go to either. It's just us."

Before he could reply she continued.

"I'm heading for Newridge, and I'm doing it soon. You can come or not, but I'm going it either with you, or alone."

"I already told you I'd go," he replied petulantly. "This is just a lot all at once."

"I know Gerold. I'm sorry."

"It's a shame my brother's aren't here!" he exclaimed suddenly. "This sort of grand escapade is just right for them!"

Epiphany had almost forgotten about his family.

"Won't they be worried when the get back and find you gone?"

He shrugged.

"I'll leave them a note explaining everything." He must have seen the worried look on her face because he quickly amended, "Everything they need to know. I've never been the favorite son anyway. Mom prefers my strapping brothers." When it looked like Epiphany was going to protest he interjected more seriously,

"I just run the books anyway, and any of them can do that. But come on, if we're going to do this then we'd best start packing."

He tore a last piece off the bread and stood up. Epiphany followed suit and followed him back into the hall.

"Are we going to try to leave tonight?" he asked.

"I think we have to," she replied. "The storm will give us cover and erase our tracks."

"Makes sense."

They moved quickly through the house, grabbing supplies as they went. Gerold threw a few changes of clothes into a rucksack for her and moved on. He grabbed a few sets of clothes for himself and pulled a long oilskin overcoat around his shoulders. Though Gerold wasn't the most physical of men he was an experienced traveler and as he moved with smooth efficiency through the routine of packing Epiphany had to admit that he cut a dashing figure in his leather breeches and overcoat.

Gerold lead her into a side room and gathered up a few tarps, a compass, more lantern fuel, wicks, and strikers, along with a short, broad bladed knife and a heavy hatchet. From there it was back into the pantry where he grabbed several stacks of non-perishables and two large canteens. All these he packed carefully into the two bags he'd pulled down from a high shelf.

"Gerold, I don't want you to feel like your manhood is challenged or anything, but I can carry just as much as you!" Epiphany gestured to her half empty backpack and Gerold's brimming one. He shook his head.

"If that box is getting people killed I'm not really interested in having you carry it around in a blanket on your back for everyone to see. I left space for you to put it in the bag and cover it."

In the sudden bustle of business Epiphany had almost forgotten about the box, and had willfully been trying to put her grandfather's death out of her mind. She tightened her lips and took a deep breath. She again unrolled the box from its blanket and slipped it into the space left in her bag, shifting some of the clothes around so they laid across the top. She shouldered the bag and her eyes met Gerold's across the narrow kitchen counter where they'd been laying out the food.

"Are you sure about this Gerold? I'll understand."

"Are you kidding? If I don't go now I'd have to put all this back!" he laughed softly, though Epiphany could see the lines of tension outlining his eyes. "I think we're ready, and I don't think the storm is going to let up any time soon."

Epiphany could tell he was right. The rain sounded like a hoard of deer rampaging on the roof, and the sky was now regularly brightened by flashes of lightning.

He shouldered his bag and inclined his head towards the front door. Epiphany smiled weakly and started that direction. Her head buzzed, and each crash of thunder seemed to echo inside her skull. She was still exhausted and now that the initial rush of preparation was past the fatigue made the act of leaving seem herculean. She had no choice, so she kept moving, planting one foot in front of the other.

At the door Gerold blew out the lantern he'd been carrying and hung it on a peg. He lifted a heavy coat off another peg and handed it to Epiphany. She slipped it on and flipped up the hood as Gerold turned up the hood on his own long hemmed coat. The two pushed open the door and stepped out into the storm. Epiphany was grateful for the heavy coat Gerold had given her. The oil canvas kept out most of the wet, and the broad rimmed hood kept her face clear so she could see without the water dripping into her eyes. Even with all the protection she could feel the damp working its way in at the seams and splashing up her legs.

Lightning set fire to the night and for a moment she saw the whole town spread out in front of them. It was a dark and huddled mass cowering before the might of the storm. She closed her eyes and tried to burn that image into her mind. She knew she might never see it again. Gerold was a shadow next to her, waiting in silence for her to be ready. After a moment more she turned and motioned along the road. He took the cue and started down the incline that lead away from his house and she fell into step at his heel.

They moved quickly out of town and Epiphany couldn't help but wonder as they passed into the tree lined dark beyond the reach of the village if the surviving priest had perhaps dragged himself to reinforcements and was waiting somewhere just out of sight to spring a fatal trap. If he was then the storm proved to be the ally they had hoped for, offering them concealing shadows every step of the way. Even so Epiphany jumped in alarm at every sound she couldn't immediately place, and she was glad for Gerold's presence.

The two slogged on as long as they could bear, but Epiphany had started the day exhausted and the specter of fatigue chased her every step. Even Gerold showed signs of wear. Though he had been resting when Epiphany rousted him, he hadn't had long and the weight of the water seemed to pound him into the ground. Without any moon in the sky there was no way of knowing what time it was, but the night was still dark when they slipped off the road and moved into the forest to find a safe place to sleep. The rain had slackened from a torrent to a constant and oppressive drizzle and Epiphany had began to feel as if she would never be dry again.

Once they were far enough from the road to be safe from passing eyes Gerold went about the business of putting up a tarp, a process made more difficult by Epiphany's insistence that they light no lanterns. The hasty cover provided some solace from the storm, but the tarp dripped and the wind blew the rain in around the edges.

The two huddled close together under one of the heavy blankets that Gerold had packed and tried to share warmth in the cold night. Epiphany couldn't shake off the image of the dead priest or her grandfather's body vanishing into the depths of his house. She feared that she would never sleep again, but the exhaustion of the day quickly overwhelmed her and drew her down into a deep slumber.

THE NEXT TWO DAYS were a wash of half-light and constant drizzle. It was five days travel to Newridge, but that first morning over a hurried breakfast of cold bread and poorly ground coffee full of grit, the pair decided that they should travel overland, staying near the road as a guide, but never on it where they could be seen by other travelers. The choice would add several days to the trip as they fought through the often thick growth of the forest. Once they reached the mountains they would have another decision to make. The only pass through the high peaks was the road, and while it was possible to navigate the slopes themselves neither of the pair was certain it was a challenge they wanted to meet. For the moment staying off the road seemed the safer option, at least until they knew if they were being followed.

The question of their pursuit was a regular topic of conversation between Gerold and Epiphany. Were they being pursued, and if so than by whom? Epiphany knew next to nothing about the High Church with its robed clergy and deep ritual. Her family kept no ties to the Church and when her parents and grandfather did speak of it wasn't complimentary. They talked about conspiracies, control, and violence, but always in obscure terms that Epiphany couldn't help but relegate to the realm of legend; at least until the High Church had showed up and murdered her last remaining family member.

Gerold's family on the other hand still had deep ties

with the High Church. One of his uncles was even a priest. Epiphany had met him once, a round bodied and jovial man that didn't seem the type to be wrapped up in conspiracy and murder, but just because one priest wouldn't didn't mean another couldn't.

That was perhaps the most hotly contested issue. Gerold insisted that the two men that attacked her must have been disguised as priests, and though she had no real proof otherwise something in Epiphany's gut told her that there were no disguises involved. After a few fiery exchanges they made a tacit agreement not to discuss the issue until they could reach Newridge and learn more about what was actually happening.

That arrival couldn't come soon enough, and not only because it would finally shed some light on recent events. It was strange to Epiphany to be so long in the woods. She had grown up near the forest, but had never spent more then a night in the hills and she was accustomed to the open sky of the Waters above her head. The tight green canopy combined with the solitude made her feel claustrophobic.

Near the end of the second day Gerold lead her farther from the road without explanation. They had been going up hill most of the day, clamoring over low ridges and climbing embankments, but as they walked farther off the path the ground became even steeper and low shelves of rock thrust out of the ground like the armored spines of a great beast not only long since dead, but forgotten. Epiphany tried to press Gerold as to where they were going, but he insisted he had a surprise for her.

Working together they slithered up onto the widest of the shelves. The grayed sandstone curved around a steep face of the mountain. It was slippery in the misting rain and more then once Epiphany had to pause and catch her balance. Gerold moved with surprising confidence even in the poor conditions, and not for the first time Epiphany wondered at how natural the normally awkward man seemed in the wilds.

The previous day he had quickly built a lean-to of branches and leaves to augment their tarp and caught several rabbits to add some fresh meat to their dinner. He had shown no squeamishness as he gutted and cleaned them, talking the whole time about how his father used to take him and his brothers hunting and camping, and Epiphany wondered how different Gerold would be if his father were still with him.

Now he leapt the short distance between two ledges and reached back to offer his hand for balance. She took it and made the short leap as well, catching his shoulder for stability and then following Gerold around an outcropping. What she saw took her breath away.

The ledge they stood on thrust out from the side of the mountain and stood high enough to clear the tops of the trees on the slope below it. The mist obscured much of the world, but she could still see the landscape rolling down and away from her. With the pale light turning the hills into grayed shadows the vista almost looked like the swell of waves rolling across the Waters. She squinted into the farthest distance, wondering if she could still see the coast. It might have been her imagination, but she thought for a moment she could see the glimmer of daylight on water.

She stood frozen, taking in the grandeur of the scene. The sea cliffs had a power all their own, but she had never seen anything like that sweeping vista of the mountain-side. She turned to find Gerold watching her with a small smile nestled between his cheeks.

"You kept saying the forest made you feel trapped," he told her softly. "I saw this from down the hill through the trees and thought it might give you a chance to clear your head a bit."

She threw her arms around his neck and hugged him close before turning back to the vista.

"Thank you so much. It's beautiful."

"We can't stay long. I don't know if we can be seen from the road. I could just make it out from deeper in the woods so I don't think so, but you can never be too careful."

Epiphany nodded and stood for a few moments longer taking in the open space before turning and following Gerold back along the rock the way they had come. Around the outcropping and across the short hop and they were back in the cover of the tree line. They slid and dropped back down the steep rise that had taken them to the vista, making much quicker work of the decent than they had of the climb.

Without warning Gerold spun on his heel and grabbing Epiphany by the shoulders, lunged behind one of the low boulders that littered the landscape. Before she could ask him what was going on he pressed his fleshy hand over her mouth and with wide eyes urged her to silence. With his free hand he pressed a finger to his lips and then waved at her to stay put. He let go of her mouth, and crouching low to the ground, peeked around the edge of the rock. He snapped back like a spring and pressed his back to the stone.

"There's someone in the woods," he whispered to her. She started to speak, but he pressed his finger hard to his lips, urging her to hold her tongue. He motioned for her to move closer to him and slowly the two of them inched upwards until they could just see over the rock.

At first Epiphany couldn't see anything but the tightly clustered trunks of the trees. A flicker of motion caught her eye, and she squinted through the mottled shadows. Her breath caught in her throat as what only moments before had been the shadow of a tree moved away from the broad trunk. It was a man clad in loose brown and gray leathers and draped with a cloak covered in leaves and grasses. He moved with a lithe suppleness that made Gerold's seeming ease in the woods look offish, and though he moved quickly he never seemed to make a sound. As she watched Epiphany saw a second man emerge from the gray mists behind the first. The lead figure paused and motioned in the direction where the two youth cowered. He cupped his hand to his ear.

Epiphany snapped her head back down below the shielding rock, her heart hammering in her chest with such force that she thought she would shake the stone behind her. She tried to control her breathing which pushed at her chest in ragged bursts, tried to slow it so the approaching men would not hear her gasping breathes, but it was no use. Her heart pounded her ribcage and shook the breath out of her. She looked to Gerold, but he was no comfort, his face was ghost white and his eyes so wide they looked as if they were loosely balanced on his cheekbones.

The anticipation was unbearable. Epiphany wanted to look around the rock, to see how close the men were, but she was too afraid that she would peak around only to come face to face with one of the motley clad men.

The woods around her seemed horribly quiet, so quiet that her own short breath sounded like a symphony in her ears, and every snapped twig felt like a explosion all the way to her bones. With each little sound her mind conjured images of the two men creeping ever closer, wicked knives clutched in their hands and lurid grins on their faces as they prepared to pounce. It was too much, and Epiphany could feel her legs tensing almost against her will beneath her, preparing her to bolt like a grounded deer. There was a sudden loud crash of breaking wood farther down the road. Without thinking Epiphany jerked her head up over the concealing stone to see the two men – now joined by a third – no more then five feet from where she and Gerold hid. Luckily all three of them were looking in the direction of the sound so none of them saw Epiphany. The lead man motioned for the other two to follow and the three dashed off into the woods with lithe leaps, still making hardly a sound as they moved. She watched them go, afraid they would look back and see her watching, but at the same time transfixed by adrenalin and unable to look away. In the distance there was another crash of breaking wood and tearing underbrush and then silence.

Gerold, his face still a death mask, sat up slowly and looked towards the sound, but by then the men had gone and only trees greeted him.

"There must have been someone else in the woods," he whispered, his voice a harsh rasp. "Thank God it drew them off."

Epiphany could only nod mutely. Her voice was still in hiding even if she was not. It took Gerold only a moment more to regain some sense of composure. He pushed himself up to his feet, staying low in a crouch as he did so. He reached out to Epiphany to help her up, but she continued to stare off into the forest where the men had disappeared.

"Epiphany, we have to go," he told her. "I'm pretty sure they're after us, and it won't take them long to figure out that's not us their chasing. They'll be back."

Epiphany shook her head to clear the lingering traces of panic from her brain, but they wouldn't go, clinging instead like cobwebs to the corners of her thoughts. She accepted that and took Gerold's hand. She let him draw her up onto her haunches.

"We should cross the road," she told him. "They're already looking for us on this side and it might not be much of a ruse, but it's better then walking along behind them and hoping they don't turn around."

Gerold nodded, even laughed a little and then started down the hill towards the road. When they reached the edge of the road they stopped, nestling themselves behind trees and gazing up and down the wide expanse of packed dirt for a long time to make sure there were no well concealed adversaries hiding in the dappled green. When they could wait no longer they clasped hands in unspoken support and dashed across the gap. Then they waited again, crouching low in the tree line, breathing far harder then the sort sprint merited. There were no running footsteps and no shouted alarms. Satisfied that they had made the dash unobserved the pair moved father into the trees, leaving the road behind them.

When they were a suitable distance up and again ensconced in a dish of the jagged rocks that seemed native to the hillsides they stopped. Gerold pulled out one of their canteens as Epiphany let her head fall back again the cool stone and closed her eyes. Her heartbeat was finally starting to return to normal and she felt like she'd been holding her breath since Gerold had first pulled her down behind the rock.

Epiphany didn't know how much time had passed, or whether she had been asleep or just awash in a daze of the past weeks events, but Gerold's soft voice clanged against her ears, causing her to jerk her head up and her heart to pick up its double-time tempo.

"I'm sorry, I didn't mean to startle you," he said nervously, watching her the way a person watches a coiled snake. She took a slow deep breath and her heart settled again.

"It's ok, I was just drifting I guess. All this just has me on edge."

He nodded.

"I can understand that. These aren't normal days for us. We're supposed to live quiet lives and not amount to much, you know. We aren't supposed to be the type that go running around in the woods dodging dangerous pursuers."

"I killed a man Gerold. I've lost track of the days, but not so long ago I killed a man."

Silence; then a change of subject.

"I think we should travel at night," he said, forcing a thin determination into his voice. "During the days we can find good hiding places and take turns sleeping. We'll move when it's dark. It'll be slower going, but I have to imagine they'll have a harder time finding us if we travel at night."

Epiphany nodded. He waited to see if she had anything to add but she just watched him with a flat gaze so he continued.

"We should move farther up for now, find a better place to hide out and then we can get some rest until nightfall."

This time she didn't even nod, just pushed herself to her feet and waited for him to join her. When he stood up she turned and started up the hill. He took a quick step after her and caught her shoulder. She turned slowly to face him.

"You did what you had to do."

She smiled thinly. It wasn't much, but it was a crack in the mask she had started to form and he took what comfort from it he could as he fell in next to her. They trudged up the slope of the mountain. It was steeper on this side than it had been on the other and so the going was slow and arduous. Through the trees Epiphany could see the mountain sweep up and away toward snow-capped peaks and hoped they wouldn't have to climb that high to reach their destination.

"No, we may not go through the passes but we also won't have to go anywhere near the peaks," Gerold told her when she asked about it. "At least I hope we won't. I can't imagine them being able to drive us that high, and honestly I don't know if I could make it up there anyway. It takes training and equipment to summit the mountains. The only people I know who've even ever done it were my brother Elton and old Juniper."

"Juniper?" Epiphany knew the old man had been a great woodsman once, but she had always known him as the town drunk and it was hard to imagine him conquering anything so daunting as the mountain. From where she stood the top seemed more like a dream than a real place. Gerold laughed.

"I know, it's hard to imagine. The only thing I can think of when I think of Juniper and the mountains would be him rolling down the side of it giggling all the way."

That made Epiphany laugh, and the laughter helped shake away some of the tension that had been haunting her.

"Elton is old enough to remember before Juniper came back... you know... wrong. He says that Juniper was one of the most able woodsmen he ever knew. There was no one quieter or smarter in the wilds."

"What happened to him?" Epiphany asked.

"I don't know." Epiphany already knew that. Everyone in town talked about what was wrong with Juniper but no one really knew. It gave them something to talk about other than their own plight however. "He once told me there was a witch living in the mountains and he was crazy because of her. I always assumed that the witch was some fishwife selling cornbrew out of the back of a shack. I've heard that stuff can rot your brain, especially if it's low quality and heavens knows Juniper likes his drink."

"That's true." Epiphany was reaching a point where

she had to keep her answers short to conserve her breath. The incline was becoming increasingly severe and she was repeatedly having to use her hands to scramble over terrain. Epiphany had always been active and in reasonably good shape, and she was surprised to find out how quickly the slopes were exhausting her.

She was profoundly grateful when they found the cave. From outside it was just two low rocks leaning against each other with a sliver of shadow nestled between them. Gerold ducked his head into the gap and emerged smiling.

"It opens up on the other side," he told her. "It doesn't look like it goes too far back, but I think far enough that we can both fit with the packs. As long as we don't light any fires and stay quiet I think people would be pretty hard pressed to find us here."

Epiphany moved gratefully into the shade of the cave. The space was cool and dark. Without a light she couldn't make out the dimensions, just hazy impressions of dark stone all around her, but Gerold was right, it was big enough for both of them. He slipped in after her.

"I'll take the first watch," he told her. "You get some rest."

She thought of objecting, but decided he would just fight her about it anyway so she pulled out her blankets and bedded down. The floor of the cave wasn't soft, but it wasn't hard for her to find sleep. Her dreams were filled with crimson and the dull crack of metal on bone, and in all of them she could see her Grandpa's eyes fading away.

9

ELLIS WAS NOT GOOD at plots and subterfuge so it took him a long time to notice the two men watching him from the corner of the room, even if their efforts at shadowing were amateur at best. His observers' only real effort at secrecy was to quickly glance down and pretend to converse any time he looked their direction. At first Ellis tried to be furtive in his own right, but quickly decided that since they were already looking at him he might as well just stare.

The two men were cut from the same block, both square bodied and square faced. The same person also butchered their dirty blond hair into short spiky crowns. They might have been brothers, or even father and son as they were the sort of well-weathered coastal folks whose age could never be accurately guessed. Ellis watched them shovel sullenly at bowels of stew, their meaty hands making their spoons look like children's toys.

The Crone had told him that some one would come for him, but these two didn't seem like the sort he'd been expecting. He sat watching them for a time longer, sipping down the watery mess that the restaurant was trying to pass off as ale. When the mug was empty he pulled a few coins from the bag the ferry captain had given him when he'd disembarked and left them on the table as he pushed himself up and headed for the door. His new friends huddled down over their stews and tried to be invisible, a comedic picture for such large men.

Ellis eased out the door into the brisk evening, glancing over his shoulder before the door closed, but the men hadn't moved. He milled in the dirt street for a moment, wondering if he should wait to see if they followed, but found he lacked the patience. He started off into the last fading gray of twilight toward the town's only inn. Like most of the towns that had sprung up along the Newcoast this one was hardly more then a jumble of houses and a few basic businesses, and so the walk was a short one. Ellis watched behind him constantly, but the only people he saw emerge from the restaurant were a young couple that spilled out into the street in a wash of amber light and laughter. They were both obviously drunk and groping frantically at each other.

Seeing the two of them stirred something in Ellis. It had been a long time since he'd been with a woman. He was hardly a ladies man. He knew he was small and unattractive, and he had thrown himself too much into study to develop any real social skills, but at the college his employers had seen to it that all his needs were met.

His musings on trysts of the past carried him up the inns exterior stairs to his room and he didn't emerge from them as he fished out his wooden key and opened the door. He'd left no candles burning and the little room was dark. He stepped just inside and felt along the shelf next to him for the candle and matches he'd left there on his way out. Ellis had never been tidy, and in only a few days time he'd turned the room into a warren with the clothes he'd purchased and what paper and maps he'd been able to find in the rural village. The supplies had been utterly inadequate. It seemed that fisher-folk had very little use for quality paper, good pens, and even less for mathematical tools. At the least they'd had readily available maps of the area and good scales at the general market. The rest he'd had to haggle off a passing merchant on his way up the coast.

As he struck the match and put it to the candle, he again found himself longing for the convenience of the college days when all he had to do was give a secretary a list of items and it would appear for him the following day, and when light took only the flip of a switch. The candle caught and threw illumination across his clutter. He waited a moment for his eyes to adjust before attempting to navigate his little maze. At least he had been given adequate funds to keep himself comfortable, and though the hard straw bed was hardly opulent it was no worse then what he'd had on the bridge. At least here he didn't have to contend with the constant wind.

He reached back to close the door, but before he could a rough hand caught his shoulder and shoved him into the room. His foot scattered a stack of notes and tangled in the clothes he'd worn the day before. Reeling he turned the best he could to find the older looking of the two men from the restaurant. With two saucer-sized hands he shoved Ellis in the chest, and the little man toppled back onto the hard cot against the back wall of the room. The younger man shouldered through the door behind the older and pulled it closed. The two locked their cornflower blue eyes on Ellis.

"That's him," the younger one said. The older man didn't look back at his companion; never took his eyes off Ellis. He nodded slowly.

The younger surged forward, but the older held up a hand across his chest. The young man held fast, but his whole body was taut and trembling for violence. With the two standing side by side above him Ellis could see them more clearly. They were definitely father and son. Though both their faces carried a wealth of deep furrows, there was a deep tired in the older man's eyes that whispered stories of long years in the world, and his calm control of his son spoke volumes about their relationship.

"I'm sure ya don't remember me." The old father's voice rumbled up out of his chest with a sound like storm waves breaking on a cliff.

"A' first I didn't believe it could be you. Ya' look a mess, an' withou' your guards an' assistants running all around ya'." He shook his wide head. "Ya shouldn't have come back."

Ellis sneered at the two men looming over him, anger warring with fear in his guts.

"You've mistaken me sir!" He spoke quietly but clearly, "I've never been here before." He started to stand up, to explain that this was his first time traveling this far down the coast, but the father wrapped a hand across his face and shoved him back to the bed.

"I told ya, ya woun't remember. I imagine ya came collecting at a grea' many towns 'round here."

Collecting. Ellis had a vision of black habited men shepherding terrified people up a swaying gangplank onto waiting ships as he stood to the side on a narrow strip of beach and surveyed the work like a king. A ripple of fear passed through his little body.

"Ah!" The father's lips turned up in a cold smile, an awkward expression for his big face. "I see ya remembering the stop, or one like it a' least."

Ellis started to reply, but before he could form words the man hit him with a great block of fist; not hard, but enough to silence him and leave him rattled with his jaw aching. Ellis was still holding the candle and it wavered dangerously, threatening to topple onto the straw pallet beneath him.

"My daughter lef' on one of those ships." The man's presence seemed to fill Ellis' world, and a soft growl from near the door reminded him that the son was still in the room as well.

"Course," the father continued, "she was returned to us, as were alo' of foks. Wish she hadn't come home."

"She was still breathing," the son cut in, his voice raspy with tears, "but she wasn't alive. There... there wasn't nothing lef' in her." He cut off in a strangled sob.

"And now ya' come back to us," the father took over. "And now we're gonna kill ya'."

"Kill ya' slow!" the son snarled out through his grief.

"Aye, gut ya out jus' like my little girl."

A slow tendril of rage uncurled inside Ellis, the anger winning out over the fear that nestled in his belly. Who were they to judge his work and its products? They knew nothing of power and determination, and whatever fate the girl had suffered was surely no worse then life condemned to the drudgery of the little fish town. The thoughts gave strength to his rage and it reached out farther, worming up through his chest and constricting his throat. He sat up straighter on the bed as the father pulled out a broad pitted knife from his belt.

"You are nothing," spat Ellis, holding the candle up between them. "Nothing but ants railing at the sun for being inconveniently warm."

The father's lips drew into a tight bloodless line.

"And ya' are abou' to be nothing but guts on the floor."

As he leaned down to grab Ellis the little man breathed words from a dead language under his breath and exhaled his wrath across the raised candle. Belying the soft breath the little flame exploded forward like it had hit a pocket of gas, enveloping the old man's head and shoulders in a cloud of rippling flames. The father let out a startled cry of agony and reeled backward, the heavy knife falling from his hand as he reached up to bat at the flames that crawled across his skin.

The son didn't react the way Ellis had expected or hoped. Instead of rushing to his stricken father's aid and giving the alchemist time to prepare another attack or make his escape, the burly youth let out an inarticulate cry of rage, shouldered his burning father aside and charged. Ellis tried to bring the candle to bare for another lethal puff but a strong hand swatted it aside as the other clamped around the smaller man's throat and started to squeeze. Ellis clawed at the fingers crushing his windpipe, but the man was too strong; too much grip from years of hauling ropes and nets. Ellis tried to claw at his assailant's eyes, but his arms were to short to reach. He thrashed wildly as black stars started to creep into his vision. The horrible realization dropped into his belly that he was going to pass from the world with the worn and snarling, tear streaked face of this vindictive brother as his last sight.

Abruptly the young man's deep snarl turned into a gurgling choke and his fingers went slack though they didn't fall from Ellis' neck. Ellis gulped desperately at the air, sucking it in so fast that it caught in his throat. He rolled to the side and vomited off the edge of the bed, remnants of fish stew and watery ale splattering onto the mess of papers scattered there.

A flicker of light drew his head up. Where the burning father had fallen in his death throws the heaped clothes and piled papers had caught fire and the blaze was starting to spread across the floor and up the wall. Ellis turned towards the door. The young man that only moments before had been determinedly throttling the life out of him lay slumped on the floor. Behind him stood a tall broad man in a white robe with a simple silver knife held loosely in his left hand. He stepped over the corpse of the fisher-boy and extended his empty hand towards the bed.

"Come Ellis Carter, I am Tsayyadiel," he said. "The fire spreads quickly and we should be going."

Ellis hesitated only a moment before he reached out

and took his saviors hand. Tsayyadiel's skin was cool and smooth. He pulled Ellis to his feet and headed toward the door. For the second time in a week Ellis' world was burning. At least this time most of the paper was blank.

Outside the night air was cool and the town still quiet. Ellis wasn't sure why he was surprised. The fire had only just begun to spread in the room and it would be minutes yet before anyone even noticed the blaze. Nonetheless it was strange to move out of the dancing hell of fire and corpses and find the world still going on as if nothing had changed.

Tsayyadiel lead him quickly back down the stairs and away from the inn. His clothing caught a few glances. It wasn't often you saw a stark white robe in a fishing village; you didn't often see the color white really, but if the attention bothered him Tsayyadiel gave no sign. Ellis had to jog to keep up with the tall man's long stride.

"You were sent to meet me?" he panted out as he rushed along.

"No," Tsayyadiel replied flatly. "You were sent to meet me. I am sent no where on the needs of a human."

"On the needs of a... so you're..."

A cold glance silenced the question before it was asked. A week ago Ellis wouldn't have been so cowed. A week ago he had believed that he had power and that he could do battle in the arena of the mighty. A red-coated fiend had taught him otherwise and now he wisely held his tongue.

"Where are we going?" he asked instead. Tsayyadiel simply gestured toward the edge of town.

"Do you have horses waiting?"

Tsayyadiel rounded on him and Ellis was off footed enough that he crashed into Tsayyadiel's chest before he could stop. The big man was unswayed by the impact, but Ellis almost fell to the ground.

97

"I am tired of your ceaseless prattle. I have need of you but it is not so great that I cannot do without you. Be silent and when I need you I will tell you. Until that time there is nothing you need to know except keep up."

He spun, white robe swirling out around him and resumed his ground-devouring stride. Ellis stood stuck in place for a moment. He'd seen the look in Tsayyadiel's eyes. That look had been his death. Not for the first time since the devil had come to his door Ellis wondered what he'd gotten himself into.

Behind him the first cries of alarm were being raised. He glanced back to see a thin tongue of flame crawling slowly out the window of his former room. It teased at the edge of the wood shingled roof until that too began to burn. The town was slowly coming to life, with people pouring out into the street to see what the commotion was. Thus far none had noticed Ellis, but he saw no reason to wait until they did. He ran to catch up with Tsayyadiel and then fell in with his brisk pace.

They moved out of the village and into the dark beyond. Tsayyadiel didn't remain on the road for long. The village was situated in one of the low-lying coastal areas and the area around it was given over to farming the rich loam that flowed down out of the mountains and settled in the deltas just inland from the Great Waters. It was across this farmland that they traveled, Tsayyadiel heedlessly trampling heads of cabbage as he went.

Across the fields Ellis could see a small farmhouse. There was smoke rising from the chimney and soft light glowing through the shuttered windows. It seemed too tranquil to be their destination, but looks could be deceiving.

"Do..." He was going to ask 'do we have allies there,' but a cold glance from Tsayyadiel reminded him of the prohibition on talking and he kept the question to himself.

When they reached the homestead Tsayyadiel did not pause, but pushed the front door open and strode through. Ellis followed him. The light inside was not bright, but after the empty night it was enough to blind Ellis for a moment.

Even before his vision returned he could smell death. It was sickly-sweet rot and the copper tang of blood and his stomach rolled over at the thickness of it. He blinked his eyes clear and looked around the house.

It was a one-room affair that was common on these little farms, with a narrow balcony that ran the circumference of the roofline for sleeping. Everything else, cooking, eating, bathing would all take place in the main room. With no walls there was nothing to hide the massacre that had occurred there. Ellis wasn't sure how many bodies there were, but at a glance he could see at least four.

They had been left where they'd fallen. Near the front door was a short man in patched overalls slumped over a broken shotgun in a pool of dried blood, likely the man of the house. In the kitchen there were two women, probably mother and daughter judging by their ages. Both had their throats cut. The younger woman had fallen forward into a sink full of dishes and the water had darkened with her vitae and flies buzzed over the sticky morass. There was a young man who had been sitting at the rough wood table when he'd been taken. The narrow hole in his chest had leaked a red bulls-eye onto his shirt and the look of shock would be forever frozen on his face. There was a dark stain across the boards of the balcony and Ellis guessed there was at least one more body there.

"What happened?" Ellis gasped. He knew he'd been told not to ask questions, but the overwhelming horror of the scene was too much to swallow in silence. It wasn't the killing. Ellis had seen plenty of death in his life, it was the absolute disregard. There was no brutality to the scene, no passion, no concern. It seemed like the casual snuffing of life without a second thought. Turning off a person they way you'd blow out a candle when you were done with it.

"When I fell I came down close to here. I knew we'd need a place to talk after I secured you and this seemed as good a place as any."

Tsayyadiel tipped the dead boy off his chair with a bare foot. He gestured Ellis into it and took a seat in the only other chair at the table.

"You needed a place for us to talk so you killed them all?" Ellis knew he was treading on dangerous ground, but in all his experiments there had always been a part of him that cared, a part of him that felt for the people he had to use. He tried to treat them well and make it as easy on them as possible, and none ever died if he could help it. The idea of exterminating an entire family so you'd have a place to chat was too much.

Tsayyadiel didn't respond, just gestured at the chair again. His dark blue eyes were emotionless, but Ellis was smart enough to read the threat in them. He knew Tsayyadiel could just as easily leave him with the rest of the corpses and move on alone. Ellis slipped into the chair. He gripped the carved seat in an effort to stop his hands from trembling. He couldn't stop the flinch when Tsayyadiel reached into a hidden pocket in his robe. That elicited the first expression Ellis had seen, a thin smile. He hoped he would never see it again.

Tsayyadiel pulled out a leather envelope and withdrew a piece of parchment. He spread it across the table between them, holding it flat with his long, thin hands. On it was a rough drawn map of the coast with a quickly jotted X near a set of coves.

"Where is this?" Tsayyadiel asked.

"North of here," Ellis told him. He considered for a few

moments. "Probably a days journey by swift horse."

"And what is here?"

"I don't know," Ellis said with a shrug. "I know that the Bearer is there. I found them through my workings, but what else is there I couldn't say. My best guess would be another forsaken coast town full of fishers and farmers and nothing of note. But it's the Bearer you're looking for isn't it?"

Tsayyadiel shook his head.

"Not looking for, no. Hunting. If this is where the Bearer is to be found than this is where we will go. What is the swiftest route if we take these swift horses of yours."

"It's a little out of the way, but if we take about a quarter day moving inland we can pick up the Great Coastal Road and follow that north. It will better traveling and we'll avoid having to pass through every hamlet between here and there."

As he spoke Ellis traced out the route on the map with his finger.

"Very well, it will be as you say."

Tsayyadiel rose, returned the map to its envelope, and tucked it back into his robe. Ellis rose as well.

"Aren't we even going to rest?" he dared the question. He didn't fancy sleeping in the house of the dead, but it was the end of the day and he was weary.

"There is no time for rest Ellis Carter, the hunt has begun and time is of the essence. We are not the only ones on this trail." With that Tsayyadiel was out the door and Ellis had no choice but to follow him. As he left the house he glanced back at the family they were leaving behind, murdered so they could have a five-minute conversation. He ran quickly to catch up to Tsayyadiel who was moving swiftly over the fields again toward the distant shape of a barn. He didn't want to fall behind, it was clear what happened when Tsayyadiel was inconvenienced.

10

EPIPHANY WOKE with a start. She would have cried out, but Gerold's thick hand clamped down over her mouth before she could. He was crouched low above her, a finger pressed to his lips and his eyes hunting back and forth through the mouth of the cave. She could see by the deep shadows that clung around the rock and pooled across Gerold's face that it was past dusk and true dark was well on its way.

Once Gerold could tell that she was awake he lifted his hand off her mouth, but his finger didn't leave his lips, nor his eyes the cave mouth.

"Gerold?" Epiphany whispered as softly as she could. She wasn't even sure if the word was audible or if she just knew she'd said it, but Gerold shook his head and motioned with his free hand for her to move farther back into the cave. She didn't argue, slithering over the rough floor until her back was against the wall farthest from the mouth. Gerold followed slowly, inching backward without shifting his unwavering gaze.

"Gerold?" she hissed again when he reached her. Finally he let his finger drop and turned to face her.

"There's someone out there," was all he said. It was enough. Her heart leapt up into her mouth and she could feel it pounding against the base of her brain. She couldn't get air in past it and the mouth of the cave suddenly seemed like a glaring spotlight shining right on her.

"Is it the men from before?"

He nodded; then shook his head; then shrugged.

"I don't know. I haven't gotten a good look. They're making more noise than those other men did, but they're quiet enough that I can't really spot them. They're definitely looking for something though because they keep switching back and forth."

"Are we safe here?"

"I don't know. The cave mouth is small and it's not obvious. It's dark now, but we found it so obviously it can be found."

"What do we do?" Epiphany was concentrating on staying quiet and not letting her panic drive her voice into a shrill scream.

"The cave goes deeper," Gerold told her. "I found it by accident earlier. There's a narrow crack in the sidewall. It's barely wide enough for me to squeeze through. If we take our gear and move in maybe whoever it is won't see that crack and assume this is all there is of the cave."

"What if they don't? What if they find the crack?" Epiphany didn't like the idea of being trapped underground with nowhere to go.

"If they do than we have a better chance of fighting them off while they squeeze through the crack than if they come through the entrance."

Fight. Epiphany tightened her jaw. Just days ago she had fought two men – killed one – there was no reason she shouldn't be ready to fight now. She took a deep breath and forced her heart back into place.

"Alright, let's go."

They slipped back to their bedrolls in the middle of the little cavern and quickly gathered everything together. When Gerold showed Epiphany the crack she was shocked he'd found it. It seemed more like a shadow on the wall than an actual opening, but when she reached her hand in she could feel it get wider, and at the very end of her reach she could feel it open up completely.

"You go first," she told Gerold. She hefted one of the hatchets they'd brought and turned to face the entrance. He lingered for a second, but decided against arguing with the woman with the hatchet. He pushed his bag through the gap first and followed after. He'd spoken true and he barely fit between the rough walls of stone. It took him several minutes to worm through and the whole time Epiphany expected the three men to burst through the cave entrance and fall on her. She was ready to fight; tired of being afraid, but she wasn't sure she'd win if it actually came to blows.

When Gerold softly called that he was through it was with great relief that Epiphany crammed her bag through the gap and followed him. Epiphany was a lot smaller than Gerold, but even for her the passage was uncomfortably tight. She could feel the hard stone pressing in on either side of her, pulling at her hair and clothing. She had to side step and turn her head at the narrowest point. As the cold rock brushed her cheek a feeling of panic welled up inside her. She would be trapped. There was a whole mountain above her, pressing down and crushing her in place. She forced the idea back down and kept moving, exhaling and holding it to make her chest slimmer. Two more sliding side-steps and she popped free of the gap, gasping and grateful.

Gerold leaned close enough that she could feel his breath on her cheek.

"I think we should keep going," he whispered.

"But then we won't be able to block the entrance," she responded in her own quiet hiss.

"I know, but I can feel a breeze coming from deeper into the cave. I think there might be another entrance, maybe not too far from here. We might be able to get out that way and lose whoever it is entirely."

Epiphany took a moment. She could feel the breeze too, now that he'd pointed it out to her. It wasn't strong, but it stirred her hair and touched her cheek with warm fingertips. It was strange that the wind was warm with the chill of late Autumn in full control of the world, but it smelled fresh so it had to be coming from outside.

Still, Epiphany wasn't sure she wanted to go chasing that warm wind. There was a certain confidence to remaining beside the narrow split in the rock, a certainty that she could fend off anyone that came through, but how long would they wait; how long could they. At some point they would have to go back and if their pursuers found the cave, and found the gap than they could wait on the other side to ambush Epiphany and Gerold. The trap worked both ways. The idea of waiting indefinitely just to end up forcing her way back through the defile helped her decide.

"Let's go," she told Gerold. She could feel the bob of his head against hers as he nodded.

"I'll lead," he told her. "We'll go slowly for a bit and once we've put in a bit of distance we can use a lantern."

She took hold of his arm with one hand and reached out into the black with the other until she found stone. It was cool under her fingertips and rough. As Gerold started slowly, ploddingly forward she trailed her fingers over the rock to keep her bearings and balance. She slid her feet, using the toes of her boots to find rocks and cracks that could trip her. In the pitch black of the cave, time dilated endlessly and Epiphany couldn't say if they had walked for seconds or hours before Gerold stopped.

"We're far enough in now, we should be able to use a lantern as long as we keep it hooded. Epiphany had no more sense of how far they'd come than how long they'd traveled so she had to trust to Gerold's judgment. She could hear him riffle through his pack and then there was a sudden star burst of brightness as he struck a match.

Even that tiny bit of light was painful after so long in the dark and Epiphany squinted as he leaned down and put the match to the lantern's wick. It caught quickly and he turned it down as low as he could without loosing the flame. He shuttered all but one pane and lifted the lantern above them.

Epiphany's eyes adjusted quickly to the muted light and she had a chance to take in their surroundings. They were in a curving passageway, lined in smooth stone. At first she thought the passage must be man-made for how even the stone was, but when she looked closer she could see whirls in the rock created by countless ages of water flowing down the passage. She glanced back, but the curve of the tunnel prevented her from seeing where they'd been.

"How far in are we?" she asked.

Gerold shrugged, handing Epiphany the lantern. He dropped to his haunches and started tucking items back into his pack.

"Hard to say. Far enough that they shouldn't be able to see the light."

That was comfort enough for the moment. She could still feel the warm wind from farther into the cave. It seemed a little stronger.

"How much farther do you think it is to the other entrance?" She turned the narrow beam of the lantern back in the direction they were going, but there was nothing to see.

Gerold shrugged again as he stood and shouldered his pack.

"Only one way to find out." He took back the lantern and led them onward.

The lantern offered scant illumination, but the going was far faster than it had been with no light at all. Every turn of the passage looked the same however, and

Epiphany still had no sense of time or distance. She fell into a numb rhythm, treading along behind Gerold, using his back as a point of focus. She was paying little enough attention that she ran full into him when he stopped abruptly.

"Gerold-" she began but he held up his hand sharply for silence.

"Listen," he whispered.

Epiphany did as she was told. Somewhere in the cave water was dripping. It was impossible to tell where, the plop-plop-plop echoing ceaselessly off the bare walls. At first all she heard was the water, but after a few moments she was able to pick out what had caught Gerold's attention. It didn't sound all that different from the water, a soft rhythmic sound layered in with the dripping, but there was a sharper more metallic quality to the sound.

"It sounds like-" she listened for a moment longer, certain that she couldn't be right. "It sounds like a clock."

Gerold bobbed his head in agreement.

"That's what I thought too, but I figured I was crazy, or just hearing things."

"No, I hear it too."

"What should we do?" he asked her. The narrow beam of lantern light played over the corridor, but there was nothing to see, no clue as to the origin of the sound.

Epiphany glanced back the way they had come. She didn't relish the idea of trying to forge their way back through the dark to the gap in the wall and even if they did they would just be right back where they'd started, stuck with the question of how long to wait before they braved the risky crossing.

"We should go on." She did her best to sound more confident than she felt.

"Alright." Gerold continued on before either of them could think about the decision.

Epiphany wasn't mindlessly following any more. Every fiber of her being trembled with tension as they moved down the tunnel. She craned her neck as if reaching out with her head would make her hearing more acute.

The sound of the ticking became clearer as they traveled, and soon Epiphany was certain that she could make out the sounds of more than one clock tick-ticking away in the black distance. The sound grew louder and louder as they continued until it filled the passageway with endless echoes that bounded and rebounded in contrasting time. The off-rhythm ticking was maddening.

"There are-"

"– so many," Gerold finished for her. "And ..."

He twisted the knob on the side of the lantern. As the wick fluttered and died Epiphany expected to be plunged into darkness, but instead found that there was little change in the level of light in the tunnel. From somewhere ahead of them came the warm flickering glow of fire. They couldn't see the source yet, but the water-smoothed walls reflected the light well and the luminescence filled the area.

Epiphany took hold of Gerold's sleeve in a white knuckled grip and the two moved forward at a hesitant crawl. Epiphany felt like she had to force each footstep against her better judgment.

They rounded the next bend in the corridor and Epiphany couldn't force her feet any farther. She had conjured images of what she thought waited for her when they finally found the source of the sound, but none of them matched the reality. Around that next bend was not another cavern, but a room of dark wood paneling that drank in the warm light of crystal chandeliers. The room was both long and wide, easily the size of the whole first floor of her grandfather's house.

There was a wide round table in the center made of the

same dark wood as the walls with feet carved like some great cat's and a green velvet couch pulled up next to it. There were other pieces of furniture around the room as well, but the details were lost; lost because every inch of every surface beyond those two centerpieces was covered by clocks. They hung from the walls, they sat on tables and chairs, and they lined most of the floor space. Several were hung from the ceiling. There were clocks of every description, from tall grandfather clocks, to tiny wristwatches that were wrapped around the branching arms of one of the chandeliers. The only unifying feature of it all was the ticking.

"Gerold what is this?" asked Epiphany in an awed whisper.

"I don't know," he told her. He pointed across the long chamber. "But I know where we need to be headed."

She followed the line of his finger to a door on the far end of the room. It was made of the same dark wood as the walls and Epiphany missed it on first glance. Scanning the room it seemed the only way out other than the tunnel.

Rather than replying she gave Gerold a gentle nudge with the hand still holding his sleeve. He started forward, carefully weaving his way between clocks on the floor. Some were individual and free standing, and others were stacks of smaller clocks that made leaning towers and wide based pyramids.

"Good evening." Both Epiphany and Gerold had been so intent on not knocking over the piled timepieces that neither had seen the man approach.

Gerold yelped and jumped, his foot snagging a brass clock and tipping it with a clang. Had it not been for Epiphany's hold on his arm he would have fallen over.

"I'm sorry, I didn't mean to frighten you!" the man declared. He was tall and rail thin, wearing uniformly dark clothes. He had a stovepipe top hat as tall and thin as he was and he swept it off his head and downward into a deep bow. "It is not often I have visitors and I certainly don't want to scare you away!"

"Who... who are you?" Epiphany asked after an awkward silence that was far from silent.

"I am Mr. Samael," he said, sweeping into another deep bow. "And who do I have the honor of addressing?"

Gerold started to respond, but before he could Epiphany stepped in front of him.

"We're Mister and Misses Yelver," she told the strange man, choosing the names of two other people from Seacliff. The Yelver's were elderly grocers and unlikely to ever find themselves lost in the mountains, so it seemed a safe ploy. Epiphany was far from trusting at this point and she wasn't willing to give the stranger her or Gerold's real name.

"It is a great pleasure to meet you!" he cried excitedly, throwing his hands toward the ceiling.

"Likewise I'm sure." Epiphany gave Gerold another light push to get him moving again. He started clumsily forward, knocking over a small pile of pocket watches.

"We really can't stay though," she told Samael as she followed along in Gerold's wake. "We're just passing through. Sorry to have disturbed you."

Samael moved with a terrible grace, his long legs stepping over and around heaped clocks and piled watches as his tall hat bobbed between those hanging from above. He imposed himself between the pair and the exit, that wide smile never leaving his face.

"But I hardly ever have guests!" he exclaimed. "You must stay for a time."

He reached inside the long hemmed coat he wore and pulled out a brass pocket watch. He popped open the cover, checked it and then snapped it shut with a flick of his wrist.

"You see, you have plenty of time!"

He tucked the watch away, at the same time shooing them toward the couch with his free hand. Gerold tried to move around him, but each time Samael would take a long step and intercept him.

"I'm sorry," Epiphany said again, "but we really don't have the time."

"Oh you have all the time in the world!" There was something in the way he said it that turned Epiphany's blood to ice water. Samael had successfully herded them to the couch and Gerold sat down with a heavy thump when the tall man leaned uncomfortably close. Epiphany managed to keep her feet, but only just.

"Now let's see!" Samael said, spinning away from the pair and capering through his ticking army. Epiphany helped tug Gerold to his feet and they started for the door again while Samael was distracted.

"Mr. Yelver was it?" Samael seemed to be talking to himself, bent almost double over a table full of ornate ivory cased clocks. "No, I don't think so, I don't think so at all. Mr. ... Ipsen seems more the case."

They both froze. Ipsen was Gerold's real last name.

The hesitation lasted only a moment. Epiphany shoved Gerold hard, propelling him forward in a rush that toppled clocks left and right. The room echoed with the clang-bong of them falling. Samael began to laugh.

"I thought so," he said, his voice cutting through the clamor of ceaseless ticking.

Gerold cried out in sudden agony and pitched forward. Epiphany was behind him and could only partially slow his fall. He slammed into the edge of a table and the whole thing went over, spilling its contents across the floor in a clamoring wave. Gerold was clutching at his chest and gasping for breath. A thin trickle of blood rolled down his forehead where he'd struck it on the table.

Epiphany turned to find Samael holding one of the ivory-faced clocks and slowly winding the minute hand forward, that same wide rictus splitting his face. He stopped winding and behind her Gerold drew in a shuddering breath.

"Who are you?" Epiphany growled. "What are you doing?"

"Time. Time is such a funny thing don't you think? You little humans believe time is fixed, and that you all go through it at the same pace, but it doesn't have to be so."

He waved a hand expansively around the room taking in all the clocks.

"You see all these clocks tick in sweet synchronicity and perfect time together, until someone who knows better comes along and gives one a little... twist."

His finger flicked the minute hands a few clicks forward as he said it and Gerold let out another deep groan. Epiphany glanced back. To her horror Gerold had grown older in the last few moments. It wasn't a lot and the changes were subtle, but Epiphany had known Gerold long enough to see them. His cheeks were thinner, his eyes more lined, and a few threads of silver had crept into his hair.

Her horror redoubled as a creeping realization spread through her. She could see her parents growing older by the day; all over again watched them waste away to nothing without cause or explanation. She still didn't understand it, but now she knew the truth.

"My parents," she whispered.

"What?" Samael seemed legitimately confused. He looked around the room as if expecting to see more people wandering in at any moment.

"You killed my parents." Her voice was stronger, quavering with constrained fury.

"Who?" His brows folded together for a long moment

and then that wide grin returned in full force.

"Oh my!" he chortled. "I know what you are now! It seemed like you were protecting your friend there on the floor so I assumed he was the important one, that's why I started with him, but it was you all along."

"What do you mean you know who I am?" Epiphany growled, her hands balled into trembling fists.

"Not who you are, what you are," he corrected. He started to move toward her, his eyes sweeping back and forth across the timepieces he passed. "I couldn't touch you before because I didn't have your scent. I had your parents from the alchemist, but not you. Now you have come to me and you will not leave."

Samael stopped and bent down. He set down the ivory clock and lifted a small wooden desk clock. It was made of a rich rose-colored wood and burnished brass numbers were set flush into its face. The hands were of a darker wood and carved into elegant loops and whirls. When he touched it Epiphany felt an electrical tingle roll through her starting with her feet and rushing up to the crown of her head.

"Now," he said, weighing the heft of the clock in his hand. "You're going to answer some questions for me."

Epiphany didn't know what to do. She'd seen what Samael had done to Gerold, and even more seen what he had surely done to her parents. She knew if he twisted that clock's hands it would start to rip away the years of her life. She also knew he wanted the box, and even more knew that she didn't want him to have it. He was already reaching toward the dial with those terrible thin fingers so she did the only thing she could.

Epiphany leapt the short distance between them, her hands twisted into claws. He was much faster than she was, but the sudden pounce had caught him off guard and though he was able to twist his hand and with it the clock beyond her reach she was able to grab two handfuls of his coat. She used that precarious bit of leverage to throw herself against him, hoping to unbalance him. It was no use. Samael was impossibly strong and solid as the rock walls of the cave. He twisted in her grip and swatted her away with a casual flip of his hand.

He'd put almost no effort into repelling her, but the blow felt like a crashing wave. The breath was gone from Epiphany before she even hit the wall and dropped to the floor. She pushed herself up to her knees and elbows as his laughter mixed with the ticking of his clocks. In her hands, still balled into fists Epiphany had two scraps of dark fabric that had torn free from his coat when he'd thrown her. As she pushed herself up to sitting, a flash of metal tucked into the folds of cloth caught her attention. She shook it out and Samael's pocket watch dropped to the floor.

She snatched it up and held it before her by the chain. It swayed slowly back and forth.

"And what do you think you can do with that?" Samael asked her waving dismissively at the watch. Epiphany thought she'd heard a slight quaver to his voice though, at least she hoped she had. She tightened her jaw as the two stood locked eye to eye. Samael's eyes were such a bright green that they almost seemed to glow.

"Fine," he snarled. He reached for the hands of the wooden clock. At the same moment Epiphany spun. She snapped her arm out as hard as she could, swinging Samael's watch in a sweeping arc into the wall. It hit with a concussion like a gunshot and Epiphany was knocked from her feet again.

The sound of clocks was utterly drowned out by the ear-shattering wale of agony that erupted from Samael. Epiphany rolled over where she lay until she could see the man. He was standing with his arms thrust straight out to either side of him. His whole body was shaking; no not shaking, vibrating. His limbs twitched so rapidly that he seemed to be in several places at any one moment. He was changing as well. His hair would grow and then recede again, his face would grow older and younger in quick succession, and sometimes it seemed like part of his face would get older and another younger at the same time. Through it all he continued to scream.

It stopped as suddenly as it had started. Samael was there, vibrating and changing, and then he was gone. Where he had been was only empty air. His horrific shriek was replaced by the steady drum of clocks. Epiphany pushed herself off the ground and hurried to where Gerold was sprawled. He was righting himself as she ran up and he met her eyes with his own, eyes that were now lined with years he hadn't lived.

"Are you alright?" she asked him.

"I'm alright, you?"

She nodded.

"What just happened?" he asked her, looking around the room as if the clocks might leap to attack at any moment.

"I honestly don't know. It seemed... it seemed like magic." She hated the sound of it. Sensible people didn't believe in magic. There seemed no other explanation for what they'd just seen however.

"Did you hear what he said to us?" Gerold asked her as he got back to his feet.

"What?"

"Humans, he called us humans. That would mean he was something else Epiphany. And I've heard the name Samael before."

"What? Where?" She needed to hear the answer, but was terribly afraid of what it might be, in part because she already suspected.

"Samael is the name of an angel Epiphany. Samael was an angel of death who stole the lives of man."

Epiphany looked around the room again, at all the clocks piled everywhere. Were there enough clocks in that room to account for every living person? It was hard to imagine, but she couldn't discount it.

"What would an angel be doing here?" she asked.

"I don't know, but I think we should go while we can," Gerold responded. "I don't know if you can really kill and angel, or even if what you did was kill him. I... I think we should go."

Epiphany had no argument so they grabbed their bags and started for the door. Before they got far however, Epiphany stopped.

"Gerold, the clock he used on you; if we could find it we could-"

Gerold waved his hand sharply.

"Whatever he did it's done. Maybe we could reverse it and maybe we couldn't, but either way I don't think we should trifle with any of this. I'm still here, and I feel fine. We need to move on quickly."

This time she was inclined to argue, but Gerold didn't wait, continuing to push through the room until he reached the door. He glanced back once to make sure Epiphany was still following him and then opened the door and stepped through.

11

CRAFTER SQUINTED down the hill at the little town. It was nestled against the edge of a cliff next to the Waters, the buildings cluttered together like nervous youth trying to coax each other to jump. In the narrow lanes Crafter could see people doing a combination of hurrying and milling that meant something was wrong. There was a large house, set a bit away from the rest of the village and seemed to be the focus of the hubbub. Men and women in gray uniforms swarmed around it like agitated bees. Crafter strained his ears to catch any of what was being said. His hearing was supernaturally keen, but with wind and rain whipping through town he couldn't make out anything significant.

He had a grim suspicion what the chaos meant. It meant that he was too late and that something had happened to the Bearer. He knew he had a head start over some of his enemies, but there were many and it was possible that one of them might have beat him to the town. At worst that meant they had captured the Bearer, at best it meant the Bearer had fled and his pursuit would have to continue.

His pale lips tightened in a long scowl and he narrowed his eyes at the mountains that rose up like a jagged ridge of teeth farther inland. If the Bearer had fled, that was where they would have gone. The storm that had chased him, and now held the town in its thrall would make escape by sea impossible. Crafter hoped that was the case, that the Bearer was still on the move. At the same time there was a lot of ground to cover inland and he knew the longer it took him to find the Bearer the more likely it was that someone else would.

He needed answers. He would have to go into town, probably to the house at the heart of the ruckus and it wasn't a thought he relished. Crafter was powerful, but stealth had never been one of his strengths. He considered waiting until the commotion died down, or at least until darkness fell, but if there was a trail to catch it was getting colder with every moment. With a quiet grumble he started down the hill toward the house with his crimson coat snapping around his ankles. At least the house was on the outskirts of the town.

He moved around the fringes of the village. He had no interest in the spectacle it would make were he to walk into the middle of the square where most of the town's people were gathered to gossip and guess. Once he got to the house itself however, he would have to deal with people. The uniformed men and women didn't seem to be in any rush to leave the place and there was no chance he could get in without their notice.

He took brief note of the town as he passed. It was like so many that he had seen, solid but weathered buildings grayed by years of sea salt and wind; dirt streets well packed and rutted by simple folk living simple lives. He wasn't sure what he had been expecting. Perhaps he'd expected the Bearer to live in a monastery, or maybe in some fortress-like palace. All of that was foolish conjecture of course. The Bearer's greatest asset for so many years had been secrecy and a town like this, a town that blurred with every other town like it and where every person blurred with every other person was the perfect place to hide.

Crafter made it around the edge of the place

unnoticed, but now he was staring across a shallow incline of low grass between himself and his goal. He glanced around. There wasn't anyone paying particular attention, but when a man in a crimson velvet coat started across the distance they would notice. There was nothing to be done about it however, so he steeled himself and set out with long strides.

It took them longer to notice him than he'd though. He was maybe ten strides from the house when one of the grays glanced up from a worn notebook and saw him coming. It was a young man, sixteen years if he was lucky and his thick lips were surrounded by the lie of a beard. This close Crafter could see that what he had assumed were uniforms were simply mismatched gray clothes; clearly as close to a uniform as the constabulary had bothered to come. In a town this size everyone probably knew who they all were anyway.

The young man's mouth dropped open, flapped up and down once... twice... and then he reached back and caught the arm of the woman with him. She turned, an exasperated look solidly lodged in eyes well lined enough to mark her as a senior member of the group. When she caught sight of the approaching devil her look changed from one of exasperation to one of shock, and then to fear. She stepped protectively in front of the young man and squared her lean, hard frame to Crafter.

He stopped a few steps away from the pair and swept into a low bow, his arm tucked neatly across his waist. When he straightened the woman seemed less fearful, but no less confused.

"I'm sorry to trouble you, and I mean no trouble, but I have business of the most pressing urgency," he told her.

She pursed parchment dry lips and looked him up and down, taking in his odd clothes and lingering on his blood red irises. She clicked her tongue and jerked her head toward the house.

"Havish, be a good lad and get Magis Lubb." The young man lingered for a moment, transfixed by the sight of the strange figure, but another head snap and tongue click from the woman set him on his way. He turned faster than he was ready for and half-ran, half-stumbled through the open front door.

Crafter could smell the blood coming form inside the house. A deeper, older part of him stirred at the scent but he forced it down with an iron will.

"What can you tell me about what happened here?" he asked the woman. She hadn't taken her eyes off him for an instant. She hadn't even blinked as far as he could tell.

"Who are you?" she returned sharply. Her voice was rough and slightly accented.

"A concerned citizen. You're from inland," he told her, to shift conversation away from himself. "From Bighton, yes? From the Northside?"

Her eyes narrowed to mossy-green slits, deepening her crow's feet.

"Yes, how did you know that?"

He smiled his warmest, most charming smile. She was unimpressed.

"I spent time in Bighton. The accent is subtle after all these years away, but it's still there. As for Northside, I remember there being several factories there and being around the smoke would explain the rasp."

"Are you some kind of detective?"

"I am!" He decided to run with the idea. Crafter was always amazed by human's ability to rationalize virtually anything in their efforts to deny the supernatural and superhuman. It was something he had used time and again in dealing with common people.

"You got here awfully quick." It wasn't a question.

Crafter was saved from explaining by the return of the

woman's young companion, which was no more graceful than his exit. He was followed by a heavyset man with a mustache that devoured most of his upper lip and crept down to infringe on the lower as well. He was wearing the first thing that actually looked like a uniform. His gray coat was lined up the front by a double row of frogged buttons and epaulets which had once been gold crested his shoulders. Clearly this was Magis Lubb.

He eyed Crafter in much the way the woman had.

"Can I help you?" Lubb barked. His words were clipped and efficient, his tone firm but not harsh. Crafter suspected there was more politician than policeman in the Magis.

"I am Mester, a detective from inland. I'm here to assist with the murder investigation in any way I can."

Lubb snorted, his mustache dancing.

"Hardly an investigation to be had," he told Crafter. "The granddaughter, wracked by grief over the death of her parents lost her mind and killed her grandfather and a visiting priest. She tried to kill another, but he was able to crawl away. He told us the whole story when we found him in the morning; half dead at the edge of the woods. I know you city sorts love to come out here and play up for we idle bumpkins, but we can handle this I'm sure."

Crafter's hackles rose at the mention of the priests. He had suspected he was in the right place, but now he knew. There were several things he needed to do now. He needed to see the grandfather's body, if they priests had killed him there was a reason, and more importantly he needed to talk to the surviving priest.

"That's probably true," he told Lubb, again flashing his most charming smile. "Still I came all this way. I'd love to view the scene, and perhaps even talk to the witness."

Lubb shrugged, his epaulettes flashing in the diffuse sunlight. He stepped to the side and gestured into the house.

"We're done here anyway. If you find anything new let us know."

The Magis didn't wait for a reply. He strode past Crafter, who offered another deep bow. The other two fell in behind their superior and they moved down the hill as a group. A few other people in gray were trickling out of the house, but Crafter didn't wait for them to finish their exodus before pushing his way through the front door. People continued to give him strange looks, but he was already focused on the scene in the house.

Someone had been hurt in the foyer, and hurt badly, but not killed. He could smell the lifeblood, but no scent of death. There was a bloodstain on the carpet a few feet from where he stood. Crafter guessed that the surviving priest had been attacked here. He glanced around taking in the clutter and dismissing it in the same moment. There was everything from garbage to wondrous treasures, but none of it was important.

Crafter pressed deeper into the house. He could smell the lingering air of death farther in, a faint miasma of pain and regret. He followed it back into a small room, no less cluttered than the one he'd left. There were two dark pools here, a larger one in the center of the room and a smaller one near the wall. The other priest and the grandfather.

He crouched down next to the smaller stain and trailed his fingers over it. There was nothing, the blood had been spilled too long ago to still hold any animation. He suspected it was the same with the other blood but he checked it anyway. It was just as cold and dead as the first patch and he cursed under his breath. If either of these had yielded up answers he might have been able to avoid a trip into town. Now there was no other way. The Bearer had been here. Something had happened and Crafter needed to know what.

Once he knew there was no other way the devil wasted no time moving into town. He traveled quickly enough that by the time he was nearing the town center he'd caught up with Lubb and his escorts. Everywhere there were eyes following him, but he could already hear the murmured rumors about an inland detective spreading. He smiled a little at the reliability of human gossip.

"I've seen what there is to see at the scene," he told the big Magis as he dropped into stride beside him. "I'd like to talk to the survivor of the attack."

Lubb gave another disinterested shrug.

"He's in the infirmary," he said, leveling a meaty finger at a small building that had been white but had long ago lost claim to that color.

"Again thank you." Crafter snapped off another quick bow, which Lubb returned with still another shrug. The devil had decided that was Lubb's version of a salute. He also decided the Magis would make an excellent politician with his policy of deny nothing, commit to nothing.

Crafter broke off from the party of law-officers and crossed the small square to the infirmary. The door was cracked, propped open by an old shoe. He stepped gingerly over it and closed the door with care so as to not dislodge the impromptu doorjamb.

"It's to let in a bit of a breeze. When storms are on it's a good way to get some circulation in here."

The voice seemed to drift out of nowhere and it was only after several moments of searching that Crafter picked out the bald crown of a head and milky eyes that just crested a long counter across the middle of the room.

"Wise," he said as he stepped up to the counter. Behind it sat a woman who looked old enough to have stopped counting. She was not completely bald, but the only hair she had clung low around the nape of her neck and made a gauzy veil that trailed down the back of her shirt. She regarded him slowly, inch by inch as if she could barely take him in, and with the heavy cataracts on her eyes that might have been the case.

"I'm-"

"An inland detective," she cut him off. "I know. Word gets around fast when you can stroll across town in two minutes. I gather you're here to see my patient."

"I'm here to see one of them," he told her.

"There's only one," she replied, giving him a grin that was full of gaps. "Not enough people in this town to have many sick. Mostly I just fix bones when someone get's too drunk near the cliffs, and tell them fingers don't grow back when they lose one to the nets. Only one person here now though and he isn't from around here. Makes him a good fit with you."

She pushed herself unsteadily to her feet and picked up a cane that was hanging over the arm of her chair.

"It's alright, I can find my way," he told her, afraid that she might pitch over at any moment.

"What else am I going to do!" She laughed, and for all her apparent frailty her laugh was loud and bright. She didn't move quickly, but her legs were sure as she came around the counter and lead him to a side door. She pushed it open with a spider-veined hand and motioned him through.

The room beyond was big enough to hold four beds and from the thin layer of dust on the bedposts three of them had been empty for quite some time. In the forth was a squat man with broad toad-like features. His complexion was pale and his breathing came in labored rattles, but he didn't seem to be in acute distress. His eyes were closed and he gave no sign that he'd noticed their arrival.

"Thank you," Crafter said to the old woman, "I can see to things from here."

"Don't want me listening in while you give him the

once over?" She laughed again, bold and full of life, as she went back out the door.

The laugh had woken the patient and as his eyes blinked slowly open they found Crafter. The priest opened his mouth to scream but the devil was on him in a flash. He pressed a black-gloved hand over the priest's mouth, the supple leather devouring the sound. He locked eyes with the struggling man, settling against him and pinning him to the bed.

"You may as well be quiet and still," he told the priest. "You couldn't resist me on your best day, and this is not your best day."

He pressed down on the man's ribs where he could see wrapped bandages and was rewarded with a dull grind of bone and a pained groan.

"You see what I mean. Now, I'm going to take my hand off your mouth and if you scream and bring that nice old woman out there into this, things are going to get very unpleasant for you very fast."

The priest glared at him, jaw set firm in defiance, but Crafter could feel him trembling and didn't have to look far to see the fear hiding in the man's eyes. Slowly he lifted his hand away. The priest took three deep, pained breaths, but made no move to call out to anyone. Crafter nodded. That was good; he understood the nature of his situation.

"We're going to have a talk about a dead grandfather and a missing girl."

~ ~ ~

"He's sleeping again," Crafter told the hospitaler when he came back out of the sick room. "He was able to answer most of my questions, but I think it took it out of him. Best to let him rest a bit."

The old woman bobbed her bald head in acknowledgment.

"Glad you got what you needed," she told him. "Have a

safe journey, the world isn't safe for devils these days."

Crafter froze in the doorway. Slowly he turned back to face the woman behind the counter. Cloudy or no her eyes locked tight with his own.

"I'm not sure what you mean by that," he told her, but the words sounded hollow and forceless even as he spoke them. She laughed.

"You don't need to fear me devil, I don't want your name and I don't want to stop you. I know what I have in the next room and I have no love for it. I'm old enough to have seen what the High Church is capable of, and I'm crotchety enough to be angry about it. Now be on about your business. Where there's one of them there's more soon enough and I think you should be gone when they get here."

Crafter nodded slowly, shaken by being known for what he was.

"Thank you," he told her and passed out of the infirmary, careful not to disturb the shoe. Her laughter chased him back out into the dull afternoon. He took a moment to get his bearings, both in the town and after the strange exchange. It didn't take him long to find the building he wanted. Death hung all over the compact structure, and death was always easy to find.

The morgue was catty-corner across the square from the infirmary. Someone had planted flowers in front of it, bright sprays of pink and yellow buds that hunched low to the ground after the steady rains. The color only served to make the dark wood seem bleaker. Crafter pushed open the door, which swung in with a dull creak. Inside the smell of death was much stronger; fresh, pungent, and poorly masked with oils and incense.

Two candles cast only a dim glow through the entry, but Crafter had no trouble seeing. There was no one in the front room, but like the infirmary there was only one door leading deeper into the building. He pushed on, moving into a back room that was lit scarcely better than the front. There were four slabs in the cramped space and the synchronicity between the number of beds in the infirmary and the number of slabs here wasn't lost on the devil.

Only one of the slabs was occupied. The body was draped in a white sheet, and from the shape beneath Crafter could tell it was a man of small frame. The smell of the blood told him it was the old man that had been murdered by the priest. The surviving priest had told him about the dead grandfather. He had been the Bearer for a long time, but that had passed. Apparently the priests had been caught off guard waiting for a granddaughter who had then presumably fled.

Crafter needed to know more.

He crossed to the slab and gently turned back the sheet. He was always impressed with human's ability to create the appearance of peace in their dead. The old man looked like he had just drifted off for an afternoon nap rather than being brutally stabbed to death. There was even a faint hint of a smile. Crafter wondered if humans knew how little importance the body really had would they still work so hard to make it look nice once the soul had departed.

Of course as things stood now the idea of a soul moving on was not what it once was.

"I'm sorry," he said quietly to the old man on the table. It was true. The old man had done nothing to deserve what was about to happen, but Crafter needed to know what he knew and there was only one way to do that. Crafter parted the front of his coat and reached inside. When he withdrew his hand he was holding a small golden cube. It was etched with lines and swirls in eldritch patterns, but the cube was for the moment inert.

He drew the sheet down farther and laid the cube on

the grandfather's bare chest. He rested his hand on top of it and began to chant softly. At first nothing happened, and he feared he was too late. He persisted, chanting with greater urgency. As he did a light began to shine deep in his eyes, casting a ruddy red glow across the room. The dead man's cheeks seemed almost flush with life in the crimson light.

Finally a thin trace of golden light trickled down the carvings on one edge of the cube. Crafter fought off the urge to sigh with relief and focused on his chant. Once it began it happened quickly. More and more of the markings on the cube took light, flowing into one another like water rushing toward an unknown sea until the whole of it was wrapped in shimmering amber energy. Still Crafter continued to chant until the light began to pulse with the slow methodical regularity of a heart beat. Finally he fell silent, letting the cube rest on the man's body a moment longer before lifting it free.

"Again, I'm sorry," he said to the cube quietly. "I know this must be strange and even frightening to you, but you are in no danger and I will treat you well. We need to talk at length and I will explain further, but now is not the time or place."

With that he tucked the cube back into his coat. He was so intent on what he was doing that he almost missed the soft click of the door behind him; almost.

Crafter dove headlong over the slab where the body was laying. Even with his swift evasion the crack of the whip was only inches behind his heels. He hit the floor in a roll and came up with his back to the wall. The woman from Bighton, the one he'd met at the murder scene was standing just inside the door, her wrist flicking back and forth and keeping the whip hanging by her side alive with a sinuous roil. Crafter could smell the bile salts and unguents worked into the leather.

"You knew at the house," he said.

"Of course I knew. You reek of the Abyss and any fool could smell it," she spat back.

"I haven't been there in a long time," he told her. "There is no need for you to die today."

Her smile was cold and grim.

"Not if you do."

She snapped the whip forward. It unfurled with lightning speed, but Crafter was a devil, one of the Named and he was not so easily taken. He ducked beneath the leather and surged forward. The tang of the salts bit at his eyes. The woman tried to draw the whip back, but he was on her already, one of his gloved hands closing around her wrist. He squeezed hard and was rewarded by the crunch of bone breaking.

She didn't cry out. Instead she rolled with his lunge, drawing him farther in toward her. Too late he noticed the flash of light on honed steel in her other hand. The slender dagger had been hidden behind her when she'd attacked with the whip. With all the work done on the whip Crafter had assumed it was her primary weapon. He had been wrong.

The dagger slashed out, digging through the thick velvet of his coat cutting into where his arm... should have been. The dagger met nothing as it passed through the material and out the other side. She was nonplussed, but didn't allow it to slow her next attack. He was ready for this one however and his hand snapped down to intercept her strike. His fingers coiled, vice-like around her wrist and that one broke under his grip as well. She still didn't cry out. With inhuman power he knelt down and dragged her to her knees with him.

"Whoever sent you didn't give you the information you needed to survive this," he hissed at her. "Who was it who betrayed you to me?"

She spit in his face, a thick glob of sputum that clung to his pale cheek.

"It doesn't matter. I'll know either way. You sealed your fate when you cut me."

Her eyes flicked to where she'd torn a hole in the sleeve of his coat. An inky darkness was seeping out of the gash, like blood drifting into water. As she watched it took on a life of its own, pulsing and coiling; flowing ever closer to her. She struggled against him but he was too strong for her by far. As the first tendrils of darkness brushed across her cheek she finally began to scream.

Chapter 12-

12

"HE KILLED THEM ALL." Fist's voice was grim and flat. Her voice was all gravel and no finesse at the best times, but with a growl of fury in her chest it was like an avalanche.

"Of course he did, Sister." By contrast, Heart's voice was soft, lyrical, and full of sadness. He was kneeling on the floor beside the body of a young boy. The lad had been murdered in his chair and then casually cast to the ground. He had landed with one arm grotesquely twisted behind him and his staring eyes fixed on the ceiling. With gentle hands Heart lifted the boy and carried him to the wall where he had laid out the boy's father, mother, and sister. He crouched down and placed him gently with the others.

"We need to move faster." Reaper glanced around the farmhouse again. The first rays of dawn were fighting through the heavy drapes on the windows and casing a red charnel house light over the whole grisly scene. It was as if the rains that had dogged the sky for days had paused long enough to offer this hellish tableau. The ruddy glow made the pools of blood look black. Tsayyadiel had been thorough, but Reaper expected nothing less.

"Faster is not the answer, Brother Reaper," Heart countered, rising from his haunches. "We can go as fast as we want and you know as well as I that he can stay ahead of us. We have to be smarter, not faster."

"What do you suggest, Brother Heart?" Reaper asked. Fist was already moving toward the door. Reaper could see from the tense trembling in her shoulders that she was lost to her rage. She was a creature born of violence, and never one to balk at brutality, but always with a purpose. Fist didn't lash out at whatever was closest, she would bide her time and let her wrath build until she could vent it in a righteous rage on a deserving victim. The family in the farmhouse were clearly innocents and their wanton destruction did not sit will with her.

Reaper considered calling out to her, asking her to stay, but if she was a creature of violence she was not one of plans. At that moment they needed clear heads and a direction, not rage and destruction so he let her go.

"We should turn inland. Whether he reaches the Bearer or the Bearer is able to run that's the direction they'll go. There is nowhere over the Waters, but inland both sides have their strongholds. I don't know which they'll head for, but if we can cut across their path we'll have them, maybe both of them."

Heart had the right of it, though Reaper hated to admit it. He was loath to break off the chase but there were greater things at stake than his vendetta. He took one last look around the house. So many had suffered for this war already.

"Let's go round up Sister Fist before she starts beating up the livestock and we'll turn inland."

Heart joined his brother as they left the slaughterhouse, his hands folded penitently over his chest. As he went through the door he turned back and whispered a soft prayer for the dead family and then pulled it closed. Fist was standing in the middle of the yard, arms akimbo as she watched the sun slowly climb free of the horizon. The light turned her mane of curly hair into a flaming halo the color of fresh blood. The image seemed fitting to Reaper. She turned to face the other two as they approached.

"Brothers? What has been decided?'

"We're turning inland Sister," Heart told her. "We are hoping-"

She held up a knotted and scarred hand to stop him.

"I have no need of the details Brother. Simply lead and I will follow. I have never had any urge to take the reins of leadership in this family."

Heart laughed, a warm sound even in the wake of the horror in the house.

"And that is one of the things I love about you Sister dear," he told her.

Without waiting for them to finish their banter Reaper broke into a loping run and the other two dashed to catch up and then fell in beside him.

"Do you think he knows we are after him?" Heart asked as they moved swiftly across the fields toward the tree line.

"He would be a fool if he did not, not after what he did. He is no fool. He knows." Reaper's jaw set into a hard line.

"Where are we going? We decided inland, but you run as if you have a particular destination in mind?" Heart asked wanting to distract his brother from the line of thinking his previous question had started.

"We make for Newridge," Reaper responded. "It's the closest decent sized city to this coast. It makes sense that anyone who ran inland would go there."

"Sound," Fist grunted in response.

"Brendiwald will be happy to see us," Heart suggested with a thin grin.

"I'm sure he will," Reaper replied.

They ran in silence for a time, skirting the edge of the woods as the minutes of stolen sunshine slipped away, thick clouds starting to crowd out the sky again.

"They should have put the Bearer in our care long ago," Heart grumbled as they crossed into the shadows of the trees. "It would have saved all this trouble."

"You know why they didn't," Reaper replied.

As they moved farther into forest the rain resumed. At first the trees provided cover and the rain was just a soft patter on the leaves above them, but as the storm built in intensity the heavy drops wormed through the canopy. Soon the trio was running through a misty haze of water and green-black dappled shadows. The three pressed on undaunted and unslowing even as the drizzle built to a downpour, and the storm devoured the last of the wan daylight.

The first forks of lightning struck close and turned the forest into a sea of black pillars against a white washed world. A peal of thunder shook the ground and caused the trees to tremble. It shook the canopy and a wall of dislodged water dropped around the running angels. They had to slow as they were swallowed by the avalanche of water. After the next bright strike Reaper stopped.

"What is it Brother?" Heart had to shout to be heard over the pounding rain.

"Something is wrong," Reaper replied, wiping a hand across his face to clear the water from his eyes. "I don't know what, but something is wrong."

All three of them turned their attention outward, their eyes darting around the dark forest. The world was full of sound and movement, the trembling of the rain washed trees, the rain itself, the roar of the thunder, but none of it seemed out of the ordinary.

"Down!" Reaper roared suddenly. Neither of the other two questioned, just dove to the ground. As they did a bolt of lightning tore through the canopy above them and slammed into the ground where all three of them had been clustered only moments before.

Reaper was the first too his feet, the guns that rode his thighs already in his hands. Heart was on the way up as well, and Fist tucked into a low fighting crouch, her fingers digging into the soft earth for balance. Reaper swept across the clearing to stand with his siblings, his eyes and guns tracking together through the shadows. The smell of ozone mixed with wet loam and a faint smell of burning.

Even with Reaper's determined searching it was Heart that saw the intruder first.

"There!" he cried, leveling a finger through the trees. A dark shape hunched next to a thick boled tree. Reaper followed his brother's gesture, both guns flaring bright muzzle flashes and barking loud shots. The shots found nothing but empty air however, the dark shape blurring and ducking back behind the tree.

The scent of ozone grew heavier. Reaper lowered his guns to his sides. Behind him he could hear Fist's snarl even over the storm.

The next bolt of lightning came straight through the trees, twisting between the trunks like a living serpent. It struck Reaper full in the chest. There was a bright flash and a clap of sound so sharp that it blew the rain aside, leaving the clearing in a momentary stillness. In that stillness Reaper stood where he had been, four soot-black wings stretching back from his shoulders and the heat of the strike glowing white against his unscathed chest.

"You have been measured and found wanting Wind Witch," he shouted into the shadows. The rain resumed, turning his dark feathers into an ocean of shimmering black.

He felt Fist's hand settle onto his shoulder and he nodded a silent acknowledgment that she was ready. Otherwise he was completely motionless, his senses scanning the wood for his foe. She did not stay hidden long. That dark hunched shape slunk out of the trees in front of him, moving with a listing gate to stand a few feet away from the waiting angel.

"It was brazen of you to attack us Crone," he told the shriveled old woman. "You could not defeat me, much less all three of us."

Her cackle was like heavy rain on dried bones.

"Defeat you? You warrior angels are all so direct in your thoughts! I have no need to defeat you, at least not now. Your eventual and utter defeat is already assured, I simply have to stall you until it is done."

"You shall never have the Bearer!" Fist growled from behind her brother.

The Crone laughed again.

"Perhaps not, but neither shall you, and for the moment that is all that counts."

"You can't stop us," Reaper told her, shaking the water from his wings with a flick. "You are too weak to even slow us much."

He was growing weary of the old woman-thing's cackles.

"What you say is true, I lack the direct power to oppose you mighty angel, but again you warriors are so charmingly direct. You are subject to this world just as everyone else is, and though I may not be able to attack you directly I can, given time enough – say the breadth of our lovely little chat here – I can set into motion things in this world that are stronger than both of us."

"Reaper!" There was a subtle edge of fear in Heart's voice. Reaper could hear it too though, the sound that had set his brother's nerves on edge. There was a roar hidden behind the sound of the rain, a deep throaty growl that he could feel rumbling all the way into his chest. Reaper squinted in the direction of the sound. At first he could see nothing through the trees, but an obliging flash of lightening cast everything into all too clear a relief.

The swirling mountain of wind and cloud was black on black and almost lost against the sky, but Reaper could see it, picked out by the bits of debris that were already caught in its fearsome orbit.

"I am a creature of the winds warrior angel," the Crone shouted to him over the rapidly escalating howl of the cyclone. "You I suspect are not so lucky!"

With a curse Reaper snapped his guns up, but before he could fire the Crone leapt up and was snatched away by the gale.

"She's right, we have to get out of here! We won't live through that tornado!" Heart shouted, leaning in close to Reaper's ear.

"We have to move fast," Fist added. "We have to fly."

Reaper shook his head.

"We'd never make it with these winds."

"We have to go somewhere," Fist insisted. "We can't stay in the open."

Already the first edge of the tornado was cutting into the woods and the sound of splintering wood mixed with the pounding rain and the shrieking wind.

"The farm house," suggested Heart.

"It's the best we've got." Reaper pointed back the way that had come and the three dashed away in a sprint.

The wind was tugging forcefully at them by the time they broke from the trees and speech was impossible over the carnal growl of the spinning storm cloud. Reaper glanced back for a moment as they ran. The cloud reached from ground to sky and was surly a mile wide at its base. He could see what looked like half the forest caught up in the funnel and other wreckage that looked like parts of ships and even houses. He wondered where the Crone had started the tornado, and what had been in its path.

The farmhouse was in sight, and before they even reached it the angels were singing and chanting protections and wards into its walls. Sigils flashed and burned their way into the wood.

They pushed into the abode only a few hundred yards ahead of the killing storm. Heart came in last and he slammed the door shut, laid both hands on the wood and started to chant fiercely. The other two moved into the center of the room and continued their own workings, trying to shore up the walls enough to weather the monster tornado.

The funnel hit the house like a clapper against a bell, and like a bell the house rang with the impact. That first powerful gust of wind shook down everything that could fall and the house was filled with the crash of breaking things. Spider-web cracks exploded across the walls, but they held. The door bucked against Heart's hands, but he chanted louder and the jumping wood settled into its frame.

With the initial strike of the storm past and the house still intact the siblings gathered in the center of the room.

"How long do you think it will last?" Fist asked.

"Long enough," Reaper growled. "She played us for fools."

"How were we to know she had the power to call up such a storm?" Heart countered. "I'm still amazed she did it."

"She didn't," Reaper rejoined. "She put into place the elements that allowed the storm to make itself, then she just had to keep us standing still long enough for the cause to lead to its effect. We were fools."

"Perhaps," said Fist. "But we are alive, and when the storm passes we will be on the run again."

"No." The word seemed so final that both the other angels were caught off guard. They looked to Reaper waiting for an explanation.

"No not on the run. We travel fast."

"But-" Heart began. Reaper didn't let him finish.

"No. We are beyond the point of subtlety. We are past

the point of secret. If Tsayyadiel doesn't know where the Bearer is, which I doubt, than he will soon enough. We will lose enough time waiting for the damn Witch's storm to pass. When the winds cease we travel as once we did, and if anyone wishes to follow our trail..."

He didn't finish the thought, but his hands crept down to lay across the butts of his twin pistols.

The grim finality of that settled onto the angels. They turned back to back and sank to their knees on the floor. They resumed their chanting, working to keep the walls strong, the windows closed, and the wind outside. It would be a long wait, but they had waited far longer for this war to come to a head. Now that it had a handful of hours would not deter them.

13

EPIPHANY WASN'T ready for the daylight that streamed through the open door and she threw her hands up to shield her eyes. She could see the dark shape of Gerold, silhouetted against the light and doing the same. They had been in the caverns far longer than she thought if the sun was already rising. She was glad that the door led back outside however. Epiphany hadn't been relishing the thought to trudging through more caves. The light was dull and gray as it filtered through the still ubiquitous rain clouds, but it was like a flash of lightning after the caverns.

Epiphany was still blinking and scrubbing at her stinging eyes when Gerold let out a strangled cry. She forced her eyes open even against the glare. A shiver of panic rolled through her body when she saw that Gerold had been grabbed from behind by a man in dark woodsman's leathers. The assailant had a gloved hand over her friend's mouth and a wiry arm wrapped around his waist. Then she recognized the narrow face peering out over Gerold's shoulder.

"Juniper?"

She was shocked to see the old man here, so far up in the mountains, and right where they were coming out of the cave. The coincidence seemed beyond reason. The thing that surprised Epiphany the most however was the clear and rational look in Juniper's eyes as he fixed her with his stare.

"Shhhhhhhh!" he hissed at her. He flipped his head to

the side to indicate a rock fall a dozen yards away. Juniper let his hand fall off Gerold's mouth, but continued to hold him fast and drug him to the tumble of stones. Epiphany followed along wondering whether encountering an angel, or a Juniper in full possession of his faculties was stranger. Once they were in the rocks Juniper released Gerold who spun on the smaller man.

"What the hell Juniper you scared the hell out of me!"

His anger quickly faded when Juniper met his gaze with those knowing eyes.

"Juniper?"

The wiry old mountain-man couldn't suppress a chuckle.

"Yes it's me, crazy old Juniper."

"But... but you're not crazy," Epiphany stammered.

"No, not at all," Juniper agreed.

"What the hell?" Gerold repeated.

"We don't have long, but I'll explain as best I can," he told them. "We've known Samial was up here for a long time and at one point I came looking for him. I found the entrance to the cave, I even found all the clocks, but he wasn't there. I knew that when he came back he'd know I'd been there, so I acted like the experience had driven me crazy so he wouldn't think he needed to kill me. It seemed like a long shot, but angels often underestimate humans, and they're usually lazy when they deal with us so I figured it was worth a try. I'm still here so I guess it worked."

"Wait," Epiphany interjected. "You talk like you've dealt with a lot of angels."

"Not a lot," Juniper corrected. "But enough to have a sense of them."

"What the-" Juniper held up a hand to forestall Gerold's shocked repetition.

"I don't have time to explain everything so just let me get through this. When I heard what happened to your

Grandfather I knew you were in trouble. It didn't take me long to find out Gerold was gone and to figure out that you two had headed for the woods. I came after you and good thing I did because I wasn't the only one looking."

"The other men in the woods," Epiphany supplied.

Juniper nodded.

"I was able to keep them off your trail for the most part, though they're very good at what they do and not so easily distracted. They almost caught me a few times as well."

"That crash in the woods that drew them away; that was you?" Gerold said it as part question part suggestion and Juniper confirmed with another nod.

"I lost track of you last night, but then I found the cave. I'd been there before so I knew where it came out. I was going to come around this way and come in after you, Samiel be damned, but about the time I got here out popped you two."

"I appreciate all the help Juniper, but what's going on? I don't understand any of this," Epiphany asked. She'd gotten so caught up in just trying to survive that she'd almost forgotten how desperately she wanted to know why her Grandpa had died, and why there were priests chasing her.

"I don't have time to tell you everything unfortunately. They're still close and you need to get moving before they get closer. If they get too close you'll never shake them. The short version is that there is a war going on, The War really. It's the war for everything, the world, heaven, hell, all of it."

"Those things though, angels and devils, and heaven and hell ... those are all just stories."

Despite everything, Epiphany didn't want to let go of her comfortable sense of doubt.

"Just because something is a story doesn't mean it

isn't also true Epiphany. What is history really, other than a story without decent prose and some dates smattered in?'

"What does any of this have to do with me?"

"Your family has been involved in the war for a long time Epiphany. You have been the keepers of something truly important."

"The box!" she exclaimed. "What's in the box?"

Juniper shrugged.

"I honestly don't know, I just know that your family, with the help of people like me, and sometimes angels, devils, and all sorts of other things have been hiding that box for a long time."

"Grandpa told me to take it to Friar Brendiwald in Newridge before... before he died."

"I know," Juniper told her, laying a hand on her shoulder and giving it a squeeze. "And I know this has been hard on you. Brendiwald is closer to the heart of this and I think he'll have some real answers for you. Your Grandfather had the right of it and you two should get to Newridge as fast as you can."

"We've been trying to stay off the roads," Gerold supplied.

"That was good, but I think you should just get on the road and go as fast as you can. Stop only when you have too and don't look back. The people chasing you aren't thrown off by you being in the woods and they move faster overland than you do."

Gerold and Epiphany both nodded.

"Now you need to get moving. They weren't all that far behind me when I got here and I'm sure they haven't stopped for a cup of tea while we were chatting."

"Alright," Epiphany agreed, pushing herself to her feet. "Which way is the road?"

Juniper pointed off into the trees. The line of his finger

followed a gentle down-slope.

"It's about half a mile that way. Just keep moving and you should make it before the hour is out. Like I said, once you're on the road don't stop for anything."

"Thank you Juniper." She stepped in and gave him a hug.

"You're not going to come with us?" Gerold asked hopefully as the two men shook hands.

"No, I'm going to stay here and see if I can buy you some time before our friends get back on your trail. Now go!"

Without further ado the pair set off down the mountain at the fastest pace they dared. The slope wasn't steep, but the ground was covered with loose scree and gnarled roots that thrust up like grasping fingers. Juniper watched them go for a few moments and then turned his attention back to the area around him.

Juniper thought about trying to hide the trail and lead the trackers away, but they had stopped falling for his false trails and redirects. Instead he looked farther up the mountain for some sort of cover. He scrambled up over the big boulders until he found one with a deep cut behind it. He tucked himself down behind the stone, with his back against its cool flat expanse. Then he listened.

Juniper didn't expect to hear much. The men he was waiting for were very good at what they did, but unfortunately for them he was just a little better. As he waited he slipped the heavy revolver out from under his jacket. He flipped the cylinder open though he knew what he would find. The gun could hold six bullets, but he had only four. Guns weren't common anymore, and the farther you got toward the coast the less common they became. You'd find a few on farms but those were usually shot guns or single-shot riffles. Pistols were almost unheard of and bullets were reasonably hard to find.

Juniper snapped the cylinder shut and focused his attention on the area around him. He had grown up in the woods, spent most of his life in the woods, and felt best in the woods. Each sound he heard was familiar to him and any change would be noticed. That was how he caught them. They didn't make any noise as they crept toward the small shelter where Juniper had talked with the other two, but the birds moved away from them leaving a pocket of silence. It was subtle, but it was enough.

When he was reasonably sure they were directly below him he rose slowly from behind the rock. He crept up so only his eyes were over the stone. He could see them there, all three of them looking at the tracks, learning what happened in the meeting, determining where everyone had gone. Juniper knew it wouldn't take long and he lined up the gun quickly, bracing his arm against his sheltering stone.

As he'd expected, it didn't take one of the trackers long to find his trail going up the mountain. The man's gaze followed the sloppy trail upward. He reached the end of the trail and found himself staring down the barrel of Juniper's gun. Juniper didn't give the tracker time to react. He squeezed the trigger and the gun coughed out a sharp report. The shot wasn't perfect, but it was good enough and the man pitched over with a part of his face missing. Juniper held his second shot as the other two men dove for cover. He didn't have enough rounds to waste them rattling off quick shots.

Instead he watched their dives and lined up a second shot on the rock where one of them had gone to ground. He braced himself again and tried to find an angle where he'd be sheltered from the other remaining man in case they were also armed. He didn't have to wait long. The man he was watching popped a head covered by close-cropped brown hair over the lip of the rock, he was there for only a moment but Juniper fired. The shot ricocheted off the rock and spun harmlessly off into the woods. Juniper cursed and thumbed back the hammer for a third shot.

The crunch of stone to his left alerted Juniper to danger and he rolled to the side as the final man came over the top of the rock beside him. The man had a short curved dagger in his hand and murder etched in his brown eyes. He lashed out at the rolling mountain-man, but the strike came up short. Juniper tucked the pistol in close to his body and fired.

The bullet took the man low in the stomach. It wasn't an immediately fatal wound, but the gun was a high enough caliber that it put the man to the ground hard. Juniper spun back around to find his previous target charging up the hill toward him. He leveled the pistol and fired, but the man's irregular path fooled Juniper and the shot went wide. He growled and dropped the gun, pulling a wide-bladed survival knife off his belt.

The man was closing fast and Juniper moved up to the edge of the rocks where he could meet his assailant before the man was coming down from the high ground onto him. They came together hard and fast in a tangle of bodies and flashing steel. It didn't take Juniper long to realize that he was outmatched. He was a skilled woodsman, and knew how to fight, but the man he was facing had been trained to combat and it was quickly making a difference.

The man's knee thumped solidly into Juniper's abdomen and the old mountain-man barely managed to fall to the side before a swipe of his opponent's knife could open his throat. There was no pause to the action. Before Juniper could regain his feet a kick connected on the inside of his knee. He heard something pop. He tried to rise again, but the leg wouldn't take any weight and he flopped around on the ground like a landed fish.

His opponent stood over him, safely outside the reach of his flailing knife and watched his struggles.

"You put up a good fight old man, but it's over. Now tell me where they're going and save me the trouble of tracking them. If you tell me what I want than this can all be over quickly, otherwise I'm just going to hurt you until you tell me."

Juniper spat at the man as best he could from his prone position. The man sidestepped the glob of phlegm easily enough, laughing as he did so.

"I have to give you credit for mendacity old man," the other told him. "I almost hate to have to torture you, but a job is a job you know."

"I don't give you much credit for anything," Juniper growled and lobbed another ball of spit. Again the other man easily sidestepped the gesture.

"Alright, now you're wearing on me. The first time it was determination, now it's just futility."

"No," Juniper corrected. "The first time it was spite, this time it was a trick."

Before his opponent could consider his words Juniper lashed out with his remaining good leg. The other man was too far away to kick, but Juniper's boot connected with a jagged bit of shale sticking out of the rock face above him. With a crack the loose flake broke free, and with a shuddering boom the face above it came free as well. The other man would have been well beyond the reach of the rock fall if he hadn't stepped toward the face to avoid Juniper's salivary assault. As it was the first chunk of rock took him in the shoulder and spun him. The second clipped his temple and took him to the ground. The rest of the rockslide crushed him into the earth.

Juniper gritted his teeth against a cry of pain as the miniature avalanche that had felled his foe buried him from the waist down as well. He could feel things break, and in several places the warm seep of blood where sharp rock had torn flesh. The pain threatened to steal his consciousness away, but he fought to keep his eyes open. Juniper knew he was probably going to die on the side of the mountain, half buried in a landslide he had caused. It was worth it. He had stopped the pursuit and bought the fleeing pair all the time he could give them, but just because it was worth it didn't mean he was going to sell his life easily.

With trembling hands Juniper began to move the rock away from his crushed and broken legs.

~ ~ ~

"That was gunfire!" Epiphany insisted turning back toward the mountain again.

"How would you know what gunfire sounds like," Gerold insisted, taking her by the arm and trying to steer her toward the road. She pulled away from him and kept her feet firmly planted.

"My Grandpa had a gun and he showed me how to shoot it once; and anyway, what else could it be?"

Gerold shrugged, standing a few feet down the slope from Epiphany.

"What does it matter? Juniper told us to make for the road as fast as we could and not stop for anything no matter what."

"But what if he needs help?"

"He's helping us Epiphany," Gerold reminded her. "It won't do him any good to have us come back up there when he's doing everything he can to give us time to get down here."

It was hard to leave the old man behind. He'd always seemed so befuddled and helpless, but Epiphany knew now that had all been an act. That didn't make it any easier for her to abandon him to his fate. Still, they had to get away.

"Sorry, I know," she told Gerold, moving down the hill to join him. "Let's go."

They continued their mad dash down hill toward the road, moving as fast as they safely could; maybe a little faster than that. There were more cracks of gunfire then silence. The silence was worse than the gunfire and Epiphany had to again fight the urge to stop and turn back. Then there was a deep rumble that shook the mountain beneath them.

"What was that?" Epiphany asked.

"I don't know," Gerold admitted without stopping. "Rock slide maybe?"

"Should we-"

"No," Gerold answered before she even finished the question. He reached back and caught her hand and drew her on, not giving her the chance to consider turning back.

Then they were out of the trees.

This far up in the mountains the road was not wide, nor was it well maintained. It was little more than a dirt track, just wide enough to run a cart, with two deep furrows where years of wheels had dug for traction. The ever present rain of the past few days had turned the road into a morass of mud and deep puddles and Epiphany's first step found her ankle deep in the stuff.

"Ugh," Epiphany grunted as she extricated her foot from the mire. "Is it really going to be all that much faster slogging through this mess?"

"Stay up here on the foot path instead of down there on the cart path and it will."

Gerold held out a hand to her and Epiphany noticed that he was standing on a narrow strip of raised earth that ran along the edge of the road. That narrow strip was still muddy and slick, but it was free of the puddles and thick slurry that covered the cart road. With a deep sigh she took his hand and let him pull her up onto the embankment.

"Newridge is this way," he said, gesturing up the mountain. Ahead she could see a cleft between two of the peaks. It looked like in some long forgotten age a giant hand struck the mountains apart with an ax and they were about to pass through that cut. Behind her she could see the steeps falling away behind them. There was no sign of anything she recognized. They were too far inland to have any hope of seeing the Waters now.

The slate gray storm clouds seemed darker toward the coast, but Epiphany didn't know if that meant the storm would get worse, or if they had left the worst behind them.

"How far are we?" she asked.

"If we'd been on the road the whole time we'd be two days out of Seacliff now. We're about a day from the pass, and two days beyond that to Newridge. That's traveling normally of course. If we push it we can be there in probably about two days total. Of course that means eating on the move and not stopping much to sleep."

Just hearing the idea said aloud made Epiphany tired, but Juniper's insistence on haste was still fresh in her mind, as were the echoes of gunfire.

"That's what we'll have to do," she admitted with little zeal.

"No time like the present," Gerold replied, doing his best to give her a reassuring smile. With the dark rings of exhaustion around his eyes it looked more like a corpse grin, but Epiphany fell into an uneasy stride behind him, and the pair began the long climb up the mountain to the giant's ax-cut pass.

14

ELLIS' HEART SANK with every mile they drew closer to the town. The images of the slaughtered family from the farmhouse were burned into his mind and he couldn't help but wonder what horrors they were about to unleash on a new clutch of unsuspecting victims. Tsayyadiel had been like a statue the entire ride. He hadn't spoken or moved except to nod sharply whenever Ellis would request a stop so he could void himself or inhale a small portion of the dry hard bread that served as their only rations. Ellis' grim companion had allowed no longer breaks for sleep.

Their destination sat at the bottom of a gentle sweep of hills, nestled like a sleeping baby in its mother's arms, and just as defenseless against what was coming. It was much as Ellis had told Tsayyadiel it would be, a small cluster of buildings, interspersed with muddy streets. The buildings were made mostly of salt stained wood. Ellis could just hear the rumble of a generator over the soft patter of the drizzling rain. Again Ellis found himself longing for inland comforts.

Tsayyadiel barely seemed to notice they were nearing their destination. His expression didn't change at all, he just kept riding with fixed determination. As they neared the edge of the little hamlet Ellis could see people dashing about in a fervor. His heart sank further.

He hadn't hoped that they would get through the town unnoticed. He might have, but Tsayyadiel was still wearing his stark white robes and with his height and jet hair was hard to miss. Ellis had only hoped they wouldn't become the center of attention, maybe minimize the damage. That chance was fading with every passing moment as a small crowd of gray clad figures broke from the edge of town and headed for them on foot.

It didn't take them long to reach the group, and the seeming leader – a big man puffing like a steam engine – stepped forward to address them.

"I am Magis Lubb, head constable of Seacliff. What is your business here?"

Tsayyadiel dropped lightly off the horse and hit the ground in stride. Ellis drew his horse to a stop and began a clumsier dismount.

"Where is the Bearer?" Tsayyadiel asked, his voice cold and flat. Several of the officers with Lubb took a step back at Tsayyadiel's swift approach, but Lubb stood his ground.

"I don't know who you mean, however, we have had quite enough with strange visitors and if you know what is best for you, you will remount your horse and turn back the way you came; or continue on past for all I care, but you will not enter Seacliff."

Tsayyadiel let Lubb finish the statement, but the man was dead seconds after. Ellis was still struggling off the horse, one foot up in the stirrup when it happened. As soon as Lubb had finished talking Tsayyadiel surged forward, his silver dagger suddenly in his hand. Lubb let out a soft gurgle as Tsayyadiel slipped the knife back out of his throat.

The group exploded into motion as their superior pitched to the wet grass. Two of them dashed for the supposed safety of the buildings behind them. One young man with lank blond hair and a ghost of a mustache stood stock still with his mouth flapping open and closed. The last two, a man and a woman both drew wooden batons off their belts and leapt toward Tsayyadiel. His hand flicked out, faster than sight and opened a red line across the woman's throat. The angel wove back out of the way of the man's sweeping baton. With his empty hand, Tsayyadiel caught the man by the chin as he moved past, and with a sharp twist and a crack of bone broke his neck.

Ellis assumed that Tsayyadiel would go after the two that had fled, or at least kill the last of the group, but instead he tucked the knife back into his belt. He stepped up face to face with the gaping youth and set a hand on his shoulder. In other circumstances it would have seemed a comforting gesture, but now it was pure threat.

"Where is the Bearer," Tsayyadiel repeated his question.

"I don't know who that is," the young man squeaked. "Please, a girl left town a few days ago after hurting a priest, is that what you mean?"

"Where is the priest?"

"He's in the infirmary," the young man whispered. He licked his dry lips, coughed and repeated, "In the infirmary."

"Come," Tsayyadiel said glancing back at Ellis. The angel moved past the young man, leaving him where he stood. As Ellis moved to catch up he could smell the distinct reek of urine wafting off the youth.

They passed between two low wooden structures and into what appeared to be some sort of town square. It wasn't much to see, just a patch of mud with some flagstones set in the middle and a ring of modest buildings around the edge. The square was alive with running people. The two constables must have raised the alarm, because the townspeople were scattering like sheep before a pack of wolves.

With two long strides and a quick grab Tsayyadiel caught a man that was coming out of what must have been a general store. A bag fell from the man's hands as he was yanked from his feet by Tsayyadiel's fierce grip. The bag hit the ground and the thin fabric tore, spilling fruit across the muddy ground.

"Where is the infirmary?" Tsayyadiel asked, giving the man a sharp shake.

The man let out a string of inarticulate panic-stricken noises, but he leveled a finger across the square to a one-story structure that had spent years fading from white to gray. Tsayyadiel tossed the man aside with casual disregard. He struck the wall of the store with a wet thump and dropped to the ground with the same looseness as his fallen bag of fruit. Ellis couldn't tell if he was dead. The alchemist turned his attention from the fallen man and rushed to catch up with Tsayyadiel who was already striding across the square toward the infirmary.

The angel pushed open the door and strode through straight into the brunt of a shotgun blast. The cough of the weapon was deafening inside the building, and even outside the doors Ellis jerked when it went off. Tsayyadiel lurched back with the impact, but quickly righted himself.

"To Hell with you!" roared the old woman behind the counter as she tried to fumble more shells into the gun with trembling fingers.

"No, not Hell," Tsayyadiel told her as he slipped inexorably forward. "I am an angel of the Lord your God."

"Not my God," she growled as she finally slotted the shells and snapped the gun shut. Tsayyadiel slapped it from her frail hands before she could fire the second load and with the same casual flip of his hand battered her back against the wall. Ellis could hear bones crunch as she hit, and this time he had no question if she was dead.

Tsayyadiel moved past the counter she'd been hiding behind and through the next door. Ellis followed at his heels, dazed by the sudden outpouring of violence. The Crone had told him that they had need of soldiers, but with weapons like Tsayyadiel in their arsenal it was hard for Ellis to imagine that he had much to offer the war effort.

In the next room they found their query. The priest was dressed in a white cotton robe rather than his usual vestments, but he had the smug well fed face that Ellis had come to associate with the clergy of the High Church. He was sitting up in his bed, his eyes wide and afraid, clearly rousted by the gunfire. When he saw Tsayyadiel his eyes widened farther.

"I need information on the Bearer and I need it now," he told the priest.

The man blinked a slow, dumb blink and seemed to reconsider Tsayyadiel.

"You are with us," he said with a sigh. "Thank our Lord!"

"I am not with you," Tsayyadiel told him. "You are with me, and you will tell me what I need to know."

"Of course. Of course," the priest told him, holding up fat fingered hands in a calming gesture. "My partner and I were sent here to find the Bearer and the artifact. We traced it to an old man and his granddaughter. We went to his house to try and find it, but the old fool jumped us. We hurt him and decided to dig in and wait for the granddaughter, but she got the drop on us. She hurt me and killed Father Presscot. They say she skipped town, but I don't know where she's going."

"Can you find her again?" Tsayyadiel asked turning back to Ellis.

"Scrying is a slow and imperfect process," he told Tsayyadiel. "There are ways to make it faster, but they come at a cost."

"What are these ways?" Tsayyadiel asked.

"You say that this girl attacked you after you killed her grandfather?" Ellis addressed the question to the priest in his bed.

"She did, thought she'd killed me at first, but I was able to crawl away. I felt it was too important to get the report to whoever came next to let myself get killed trying to keep fighting her."

Ellis ignored the last part, talking over the priest's excuses.

"That kind of high emotion, that kind of anger leaves a mark on everyone it touches and it can act like a lodestone to help give a spell bearings."

"And?" Ellis could tell Tsayyadiel was getting impatient and that was never a safe thing.

"And," Ellis swallowed hard. "We need his intestines, at least some of them."

Ellis pointed to the priest whose face went white as the robe he was wearing. A pang of guilt shot through the alchemist. He knew what he was doing, that he was condemning the priest to death, but Tsayyadiel was growing impatient and if Ellis didn't give the angel answers than he would be condemning himself to death. Ellis was far more a coward than a humanitarian.

"What?!" The priest blurted as he tried to push himself from the bed.

He wasn't fast enough. Tsayyadiel had him pinned in an instant, one firm hand on his chest. The worst part was that he looked the priest right in the eyes as he did it. The angel plunged his hand, fingers like a spear tip down into the man's belly. There was a terrible ripping sound and the priest started to scream and thrash. A wash of crimson started to spread quickly out from where Tsayyadiel was doing his grisly work. He pulled a loop of intestines out in his hand and began to wind them around his fist, drawing more and more entrails out of the screaming man.

Ellis turned to the wall and retched. He'd had almost nothing to eat for days and so it was a thin string of bile and spit that drizzled onto the floor, but his body continued to convulse trying to expel his horror.

"We need ..." Ellis coughed and spat out a thick glob of phlegm. "We need to know where they lived."

"Where did they live?" Tsayyadiel asked conversationally as he continued the work of disemboweling the man. There was no response, only continuing screams.

"I said where did they live?" There was a sharper, shriller scream and Ellis was glad that he wasn't watching.

"Up the hill!" The priest's words were almost unintelligible with his agony, but he managed to squeeze them out around ragged breaths. "A house that looks like it was made of other houses."

"Thank you," the angel said. Ellis couldn't say why, but that thank you was the worst part of the whole thing.

Answering Tsayyadiel's question took the last of the priest's strength and his ragged screams faded to shivering sobs. There was a wet, fleshy tearing and a grunt and then footsteps.

"Is this enough?" Tsayyadiel held out a mass of intestines wrapped around his fist. Ellis could only nod.

"I wish the Devil had just killed me," the priest whispered to no one in particular. The statement was like a whip crack to Tsayyadiel and he shot bolt upright and spun to face the dying man again.

"What did you say?" he asked, his voice a dagger thin hiss.

The priest was delirious with pain and blood loss, but he managed to turn his head toward the sound of the angel's voice. From the glazed look in his eyes Ellis was certain he couldn't actually see them.

"I wish the Devil had killed me, I think he would have been gentler."

Tsayyadiel crossed the room and caught the priest by

the front of his robe, dragging him into a half sitting position. The man groaned and his head lolled loosely on his neck.

"There was a Devil here? Not a monster, or a vampire, or a wicked man; but a true Devil?'

The priest might have nodded or his head might have simply flopped forward. He was fading fast.

"Did he come seeking the Bearer?"

Again that maybe nod.

"How long?" The priest made no reply.

"How long?" Tsayyadiel roared into the man's face, but the priest was gone; if not completely dead than well beyond the reach of Tsayyadiel's questioning. With a howl he yanked the body off the bed and hurled it across the room. It left a trail of torn guts across the floor and a dark smear where it hit the wall. Tsayyadiel rounded on Ellis, that cold fury still in his eyes and for a moment the alchemist was certain he was about to die.

"We have to go. Now," Tsayyadiel told him. It seemed Ellis had been granted at least a few moments of clemency. Tsayyadiel grabbed a bucket from beside a wall and, dropping the intestines unceremoniously into it handed it to Ellis. The alchemist fell in behind Tsayyadiel again as they headed back to the exit.

As Tsayyadiel drew open the door he grabbed Ellis and shoved him to the ground near the counter. Ellis cried out in shock and pain as his elbow struck the edge of the counter and it was only by luck that he didn't upend the grisly contents of his pail all over the floor. He was about to ask what was happening when the door exploded inward in a blast of buckshot. More bullets cracked through the wall, leaving thin lances of gray sunlight in their wake.

With a cry Ellis crawled quickly around the end of the counter and in behind it. The old woman's body was still there, but Ellis had seen enough death that he was willing to sit next to it as more gunfire poured in through the wall of the infirmary. Ellis was amazed at the amount of firepower that was being brought to bear against them. Guns were uncommon in the extreme, especially this far toward the coast. The High Church tried to limit the power of the people beyond its easy reach and the townspeople must have spent years saving up all the bullets that were being shot at them now.

Tsayyadiel leaned over the top of the counter. As Ellis watched a bullet passed through his cheek, but before the wound even started to bleed it was closing back to leave Tsayyadiel's face perfect and unmarked.

"Stay here."

Ellis didn't have to be told twice. He kept his head low and waited.

He heard Tsayyadiel go out the door and the gunfire intensified. There were cries of alarm and pain, punctuated by more gunshots. Then there was quiet. Unnerved by the quiet Ellis reached over and picked up the shotgun the woman in the infirmary had loaded but never had the chance to fire. Ellis had never fired a gun at all, but the cold, heavy metal made him feel safer.

"Ellis Carter."

Ellis let out a shrill scream, and if the safety had been off on the shotgun he would have blown a hole in the wall. Tsayyadiel stuck his head over the edge of the counter.

"It is safe now. Come I have found the house of which the priest spoke."

Ellis pushed himself unsteadily to his feet. The adrenalin combined with the lack of food and rest was making him dizzy. He knew better than to complain to Tsayyadiel however, so he gathered up the bucket, and after a moment's consideration tucked the shotgun under his arm. He came back around the counter and followed

Tsayyadiel into the square.

Tsayyadiel was unerringly violent, but he was precise and tidy about it. There were bodies all around the square. Ellis could see six with a casual glance, and each of them had been killed with a single perfect knife stroke. Some had a straight puncture wound through the chest, others had slit throats, but none of them had taken more than that single strike. Their guns lay in the mud next to them as if they'd just lain down and wanted to keep the weapons close for when they woke. Ellis thought for a moment about trying to collect another weapon, or even more ammunition, but the idea of scavenging the corpses turned his already roiling stomach.

"This way," Tsayyadiel told him simply before setting off through the town, following a wide mud avenue up a gentle slope toward the forest beyond. The streets were empty as they went. Ellis knew that there must have been other people in Seacliff, but clearly they had learned their lesson and were staying out of the way. Tsayyadiel showed no interest in anyone else and the few times Ellis suspected he did see a person watching them from a partly shuttered window or a dark corner Tsayyadiel didn't even seem to notice.

Once they were past the rest of the buildings in town Ellis could see the house. The priest's description had been perfect. It looked like a house made of other houses. In some ways it reminded Ellis of his little hovel lashed atop the bridge span. That too had been made from pieces stolen from other buildings, though the house seemed a great deal more secure and definitely more air and watertight.

Tsayyadiel lead them up the hill and pushed his way through the front door of the house. Ellis was grateful to be back out of the rain again, but feared what he had to do next.

"What do you need?" asked Tsayyadiel as if reading his thoughts.

"I need a big room, probably the biggest in the house. I need a bare floor, and I need time."

"I will find you the first two. You do not have the last. The Devil has been here; the race is begun."

"Who is this Devil?" Ellis finally asked the question that had been plaguing him since the priest had brought it up at the infirmary.

"He is one of the Named. I do not know his true Name, but we called him the Devil in Red long ago. It matters not; your task is the same, Ellis Carter. Find me the Bearer."

With that Tsayyadiel was gone, moving deeper into the house in search of a suitable room. Ellis fought a shiver and clutched the shotgun closer to his chest. The thought of meeting the red-coated Devil again terrified him. Something else the priest had said came back to him.

'I wish the Devil had killed me, he would have been gentler.'

Ellis had been invaded by the Devil, had his inner most thoughts torn free and rummaged through with abandon. Even so, having seen Tsayyadiel's ways he wasn't sure he could disagree. There was nothing to be done about it. This bed had been made a long time ago. Ellis could only wait for Tsayyadiel to return and hope that when all of this madness was over he could return to the College and his life of peace. Perhaps then all this would be worth it.

He hoped.

15

THE LOCATION WASN'T ideal, but few things had been ideal in the last half a millennium. Crafter used a gloved hand to brush aside the deep cushion of fallen leaves that coated the forest floor. The rich earthy smell of dirt, moss, and rain leapt up to fill his nose and he breathed deeply. Some things may not have been ideal, but he treasured such small moments and they reminded him that not everything about being trapped on earth was bad.

He settled down into a cross-legged sitting position beside the little bowl of dirt he had cleaned out and drew open his coat to retrieve the golden cube. He laid it gently in the dirt, folded his hands in his lap and waited. The waiting wasn't easy. Time was even more precious than he'd known.

His trap on the Waters had slowed the Crone down, but he'd underestimated how quickly she'd be able to mobilize forces once she got the information they'd both been after. The fact that the two priests had already been in Seacliff was shocking. It showed a degree of preparedness that he hadn't credited to his opponents.

Then there was the woman he'd fought in the morgue. It had been coincidence that she'd been in Seacliff. The High Church had agents seeded everywhere and she had lived side by side with the Bearer for years without either realizing. Once the secret was out she'd been told to keep an eye on the Bearer's family and wait for the priests to come and secure the artifact. After the priests were killed and the Bearer escaped her job changed. Now she was to wait and make sure no one else was giving chase. That was why she'd attacked Crafter. She'd also told him, not willingly of course, that a hunter was coming. Crafter had a sinking sense that he knew who that would be and if he was right than he might already be out of time.

Rushed or no, the grandfather had done nothing wrong and Crafter would not treat him poorly. So he watched the cube, letting it settle into the dirt and grow accustomed to it's surroundings before he reached out and laid a hand on it. He whispered a few soft words and the cube came to life, golden light beaming out of its surface.

"Where... where am I?" The voice sounded far away, and it was full of echoes and static.

"You are in the forest near your home," Crafter responded, opting to begin with the more comforting answer.

"I was dead." It was a simple statement and Crafter was impressed with the strength those simple words showed. Most souls struggled to come to terms their mortal passing, but the old man accepted it as a fact already.

"How long have I been dead?"

"Three days."

"It seemed so much longer than that." There was a quaver to the soft voice. "So very much longer. It was dark and quiet and seemed to go on forever."

"The Gates are closed," Crafter told him. "There was no where for you to go."

"I heard whispering, terrible whispering. It told me that I didn't have to be alone, that there was a place for me, but I was afraid of those voices."

"You were right to be. Not all doors are shut to human souls. Hell is still running at full production, and those souls that lack the gravity to sink to that place on their own are often coaxed out of the dark to burn in the crucibles. Some hold out for mere hours, some for centuries, but most eventually give in and sink down rather than linger on in the dark of transition."

"And where am I now? I don't mean in the woods." The grandfather's voice took on a stern tone as if he was scolding a willful child.

"I know you don't. You are in a Soulforge. It is a device of my own making, and a tool of Hell. There are many forms the Soulforge can take, Strider, Seeker, Snare but all are powered by the souls of humans. As a tool of Hell the Soulforge is usually reserved for the wicked, and the more wicked the soul the more powerful the Souldforge it can fuel, and the longer it can serve as a power source. I always thought it was rather ingenious. It is just a smaller variation on the crucibles of Hell, and instead of the soul being purified over time through raw suffering, they instead are purified through service."

"So I am now bound to serve you?"

"No." Crafter paused. "No you aren't. I confess I've never freed a soul from one of my Forges before and I don't know if it can be done without burning the soul out first, but I didn't put you in the Forge for purification, because your soul is not wicked. In fact I was barely able to get you in it at all."

"Than why am I here?" Crafter expected more anger from the old man's spirit, but he seemed utterly resigned to his fate.

"I needed to talk to you. There are other ways to do it but they are more complicated and take a great deal more time and time is off the essence."

"Epiphany."

The old man's proclamation took the devil off guard.

"I'm sorry, what?"

"You want to find Epiphany. She's my granddaughter.

She's the Bearer now."

"Ah. Then yes, I want to find Epiphany, and it is crucial that I find her quickly. If my suspicions are correct than there is something terrible on her trail."

"I will help you find her."

"Thank you, though I'm surprised that you trusted me so easily."

"I've spent time inside this machine of yours, this Soulforge. I assume you have never been in one, but for as much as it may be a tool to purge a soul of debris there is kindness here. It is a comfortable place to be and full of light. I don't know if that was your intention, but it is clear to me that the hands that made this were good hands engaged in good work. I cannot image that sort of care coming from the Lie and its followers."

Crafter, for all his eons of work with the Soulforges and their passengers had never asked what it was like for the souls trapped within. It was true that he had built them to cleanse a soul with service rather than suffering, but as one of the Named of Hell he had always just assumed the suffering was part and parcel. Looking back over the years it did explain the loyalty of souls like Aleister despite their essential slavery.

"I am glad of it then," Mephistopholied decided. "I bear you no ill will, but I do need to find her and I need you to help me with that. Once that is done I promise you that I will find a way to set you free."

"No."

Again Crafter was taken aback by the old man.

"No," the grandfather repeated. "I was alone in the dark and now I am surrounded by light. I have the chance to serve the cause again rather than sit out the fight. You will hold me here at least until the War is won and I have somewhere to go."

"It will be as you wish," Crafter said with a nod. "What

is your name?"

"Thadius, but you can call me Thad!" The joviality was infectious and Crafter found himself wishing they'd met under different circumstances.

"What's your name?"

"I'm-" Crafter hesitated. It was unwise to give out your Name, but something about Thad put him at ease and it had been so long since he'd had a confidant. "– Mefistofolies."

There was a long silence.

"A Named."

It was a statement, not a question.

"Yes, though for obvious reasons I go by Crafter."

"It is a great trust you have put in me," Thad said softly, with reverence in his voice.

"I think you deserve it. Plus you're stuck in a tiny box, what are you going to do with my true name!"

He laughed quietly, though a corner of his being trembled at the knowledge of how very much could be done with that name, even from inside a box.

"I will do nothing with it. I swear it will never pass my lips... if I still had any!"

Now they both laughed. It felt good to laugh, but there was still work to be done. Crafter pushed himself to his feet and reached into his coat again.

"Aleister, to me," he intoned. He drew the strider out of his coat in cube form and set it on the ground a few feet from Thad. The cube began to unfold, slowly at first, but than with increasing speed until it hung a few feet above the forest floor, it's sweeping wings almost touching the trees around the clearing.

Crafter lifted the Soulforge that held Thad and stepped up onto Aleister's back.

"I hope you had a good rest Aleister," he told the craft, "for we have need of great speed now. Up."

He pointed to the crack of sky between the arching boughs of the trees. The craft responded immediately, leaping upward with a sharp jerk. It slipped through the tops of the trees and hung just above the leafy canopy. The strider couldn't fly outright, but as long as there was anything at all beneath it it could travel easily.

"So Thad, where is your granddaughter going?"

"Newridge."

"Very well." He leveled a long finger inland. Aleister began to accelerate quickly, skimming over the tops of the trees toward the sharp mountain peeks that lined the distance. Crafter carefully set Thad down in a groove along the spine of his craft so that the Soulforge wouldn't fall free during the journey, and sat down beside it. The wind whipping at his salt-and-pepper hair was cold and refreshing, and the rain had died down to a soft mist that coated his cheeks.

"You will feel her when we're close," Crafter told his new companion. "I will rely on you to guide us."

"I will do my best," Thad replied. His voice had grown stronger and clearer the longer they had talked.

The pair rode in silence for a time, the world passing below them in a green blur.

"You are truly one of the Named," Thad ventured, a note of awe in his voice.

"I am," Crafter confirmed, thought the other man already knew the answer.

"I didn't think any of the Named had... is it still called falling?"

Crafter couldn't help but laugh again.

"Rising would be more accurate I suppose, but there isn't a name for it that I know of because I'm the only one that ever has. There are others from Hell that resist the Plan, but they are mostly lesser demons and the like. All my true brothers and sisters remained behind."

"All the same I am glad you are with us, or perhaps that I am with you."

"It's been difficult, but I am glad of my choice. I've learned much being in the world. The purpose of the whole thing makes so much more sense when you have seen it from here then it ever did when I was locked away below."

"Soon maybe things will be back the way they're supposed to be."

Thad sounded hopeful, but not completely convinced.

"Perhaps," agreed Crafter.

"Do you want it to be?" Thad asked.

"What do you mean? I am fighting this War as well," Crafter asked, though watching the world whip by in a dizzying blur of color he suspected he knew what Thad was asking.

"If it all went back to how it was before, would you be locked away in Hell again? Would you want to be?"

Crafter thought about it for a long time. It was something he'd thought about before, but not something he'd ever discussed with anyone. When you are the lone rogue devil of Hell who do you talk to?

"Things must be restored to balance," the devil finally said. "I know that within that balance I have a role to play. It would be lovely to say that I could stay in this world and enjoy its pleasures, but that is not my role. I don't relish the thought or returning to Hell, nor of the reception I'll receive there, but this is about something bigger than me."

"Perhaps there will be another way when the time comes," Thad ventured. Crafter smiled wistfully.

"Perhaps," he said again. He knew it wasn't true though, the Machine was righteous, but it was not always kind.

"We have to find Epiphany though," Thad said. "Whatever is to come we have to find Epiphany."

"No," Crafter corrected. "We don't just have to find

Epiphany, we have to find her before everyone else does."

~ ~ ~

"You will work faster."

It was not a question, nor was it encouragement. Ellis knew a threat when he heard it, and from what he had learned in their time together, everything Tsayyadiel said was a threat. Ellis was full of responses; that this was a delicate work; that it had taken him almost a year to find the Bearer the first time; that if he rushed and did it wrong it would take even longer to start over; but he was also full of the sure knowledge that if he did anything other than what he was told he would be dead before the echo of his words was gone.

He did his best to put the looming threat of the angel's presence from his mind and focus on his work. He'd been at it for almost an hour and much of the room was already covered in glyphs and symbols. When they'd first arrived at the hodge-podge house Tsayyadiel had moved into one of the large rooms and proceeded to throw the furniture against the wall and tear up the carpet. Once the room was nothing but smashed wood and bare floor he'd stepped back and gestured for Ellis to begin.

In the center of the room sat the pile of intestines Tsayyadiel had torn out of the unfortunate priest. Ellis had worked with caustic chemicals for years and his sense of smell was poor, but the reek of it still turned his stomach. The sharp copper smell of the blood he was using to write with didn't help. His hands were sticky with the stuff, but he tried not to think about it.

When he'd begun he'd used a wadded up shirt found on the back of a chair as a brush, but it was too clumsy and the symbols unclear. He'd had to resign himself to using his fingers to trace out the careful sigils. He was close to completion, but this was also the most delicate phase. Each of the characters had to be drawn in the right order.

Crafting a spell was like writing a story, and to put the symbols in the wrong place or write them in the wrong order would be like taking a story and jumbling the words together and trying to read it. The difference was a jumbled story couldn't go horribly wrong and kill the writer.

Ellis stilled his mind, letting go the thoughts of his vicious companion, or the consequences of error. He went through the motions with a careful precision. He had been a scientist once, then an alchemist, and over time had learned the way of workings and spell craft. It was all its own sort of science, each simply requiring a knowledge of a different set of rules. The precision and care that went into each was the same and he had been raised on such things. Thinking of his father created a dull ache in Ellis' chest so he pushed those thoughts aside as well.

He lost himself in the work, in each careful sweep and exacting angle. He fell into a rhythm, moving quickly around the room, stepping carefully over the work he'd done previously. Soon there was hardly enough blank space on the floor to walk and only then did he set down the jar containing the blood and move to the center of the vast circle he had made. Near the wall Tsayyadiel started to move but Ellis held up a hand.

"Only I can be at the center." He was afraid to give the angel something that could even resemble a command, but what he said was true whether Tsayyadiel liked it or not. For a moment he thought Tsayyadiel might object, but then he leaned back into his place by the wall to wait. Ellis let out a breath he'd been holding.

Ellis positioned himself above the coiled pile of entrails and stretching his arms out to either side he began to intone the words he'd been taught. His voice was neither deep nor rich, but it did the job and as he spoke the symbols around him started to smoke and smolder, leaving patches of carbon black in the wood around them. Soon the whole room was filled with a sizzling hiss and the air was clogged with dank smoke.

He bent forward at the waste and took up two handfuls of the intestines. With a shiver and a flick of his wrists he flung them forward. When they hit the glowing sigils they began to pop, hiss, and leap around like bacon thrown into a hot skillet. Each time they touched one of the symbols they would snap back into the air and twist almost like they were a still living thing. Ellis waited, his hands back out to his sides and his nasal voice continuing to drone.

This sort of working was notoriously inaccurate, but the man who'd sacrificed his insides for the spell had not only been around the intended target, but had been wounded by her while she was in a heightened emotional state. That connection would hopefully be enough to give the spell more focus.

The whipping intestines started to settle. They were still crackling, and a charred meat smell filled the room but they weren't jumping anymore, just twitching on the floor. Finally they came to rest in long coils. Even when they were completely still Ellis waited, continuing his chant. With a loud pop a part of the fallen guts burst outward, spraying a wash of gore across a section of boards. Only then did Ellis let his hands fall to his sides and his voice fall silent.

"It's done," Ellis said, glancing back to where Tsayyadiel was leaning against the wall.

"What does it mean?" the angel asked, pushing himself upright and moving toward the alchemist.

Ellis pointed to the point of burst entrails.

"That's where we'll find her."

"And where is that?"

Ellis crossed to his bag and drew out his maps of the

coastline. He flicked through them, pausing to compare the drawn layout to the shape of the intestines across the floor. Finally he found one that matched. The spell caused the entrails to create a makeshift map, and if you knew the general area it was depicting the caster could often find a specific location within it. The issue always came when you didn't know the area you were starting with. Luckily in this case Ellis did.

He held the map up, comparing it to the bloody mess on the floor. His eyes flicked back and forth, determining where on the map the exploded portion would fall. When he was certain, he tucked the map under his arm.

"She's on the Inland Road making for Ridgeway Pass."

"Show me," Tsayyadiel said gesturing to the map. Ellis drew it back out and pointed on the parchment to a point along a wide line that marked out the main road into the mainland. "This isn't accurate enough to tell you exactly where she is, but we have a general area, and if we start moving up the road I expect we'll come across them."

"Good," Tsayyadiel said with the feral growl of a predator circling for the kill. "Than we go. Now."

The angel didn't wait for a response, just swept out of the house with Ellis dashing along behind him.

"We should get new horses!" Ellis exclaimed, puffing along in Tsayyadiel's wake. "We'll move faster on fresh mounts."

"We will not be riding. The devil is ahead of us and we do not have time to lag on such a weak thing as flesh."

"Than how-" Ellis didn't get the chance to finish the question. Tsayyadiel reached back and latched on to the alchemist's collar. He bent his legs and leapt. Ellis was jerked from his feet. His guts felt like they stayed behind as the pair rose upward. He expected to start falling, but instead they continued to rise. Ellis looked up to see four black wings stretching out above his head.

He glanced down, but only for a moment. The ground was spinning away below him and rushing by faster than seemed possible. He couldn't fully strangle a cry of terror and he wrapped his arms around his chest. Tsayyadiel let out that cold, killer's laugh and all Ellis could do was squeeze his eyes shut and wait for the flight to end.

16

TIRED WAS A SMALL WORD. It was a tight, simple word and it was utterly inadequate to describe how Epiphany felt. She ached down to the depths of her bones and she hadn't known before that the simple act of walking could take every ounce of willpower. It could though. Epiphany tired not to look ahead, tried to keep her eyes on the ground and off the endless stretch of road that lead to the pass. That cleft of rock, touched by the last dull light of the rain laden day seemed no closer than it had when they'd started walking that morning.

The rain had been as persistent as the distance. There had been patches where it had lightened to just a faint mist, but it had never let up completely. Epiphany and Gerold both had coats and good shoes, but those could only provide so much protection. Epiphany was soaked and had been most of the day. The water made her clothes and shoes into soggy, leaden weights and created relentless chafe points that she feared would be bleeding by the time they were done walking.

Gerold insisted that they were 'almost there' but they words sounded empty to Epiphany. That might have been Gerold's fatigue coming through in his tone. He was trying to put on a good face and keep Epiphany's spirits up, but she could see he was as dead tired as she was. His rounded shoulders were slumped and the deep bags had settled under his eyes. It was strange to look into those eyes and see the web of lines that orbited them now. She wondered how much his suddenly advanced age was playing into Gerold's weariness.

Epiphany didn't like to think about what had happened in the cave, or what Juniper had said when they'd emerged. Angels were real and they were walking around in the world and sometimes killing people; like her parents. Magic worked. It was all tied up with some grand plot that her family had been a part of for generations, at least since her grandpa's time. It hurt Epiphany's head to think about it, but what hurt worst of all was that she'd been lied to her entire life.

Her grandpa had told her stories, mythologies of the past, but they'd always seemed like stories to her, and he'd never made any effort to make her feel otherwise. He'd let her continue to believe that he was just an eccentric old man. Her parents never said anything at all. Their mysterious trips made more sense now. They'd spent so much time away and never once said that it was for anything more important than business, or idle curiosity. Juniper had known. It made her wonder how many other people knew.

Her tired mind started building a conspiracy where everyone in town played a part. Jacob of course was there to give her daily menial work at the tailor shop and keep her from asking too many questions. Lucy, her friend from the grocers would often talk with her about how foolish the older generation was with all their stories and legends. Lucy was always too ready to agree when Epiphany would proclaim that you didn't need magic to explain the world. Of course Lucy knew the truth and was just feeding Epiphany what she needed to hear to keep her in the dark.

On some level Epiphany knew what she was thinking was crazy, and that none of the people in town had known any more that she did. It gave her something to occupy her mind though and distract her from the burning bottoms of her feet. It also made the lies hurt less. If everyone had been in on the plan to keep her ignorant than it wasn't all her parents fault. She could be angry at everyone and not just at them.

"I think we should stop," Gerold's voice snapped her our of her theorizing. She'd gotten so caught up in her web of deceit that she'd completely lost track of the trip, which was a blessing in its own right. She looked up from her shuffling feet to find Gerold stopped a few feet ahead of her. He'd turned around to face her and was pointing a little way up the road.

On the other side of the narrow track was a plaster-fronted building. The pale blue facade was splattered with mud and cracked in several places, but it looked more like heaven than anything Epiphany had ever seen before. One thought made her heart sink.

"Juniper said we shouldn't stop," she told Gerold.

"I know," he said nodding. "If we don't stop and rest though we're both going to collapse and than whoever's looking for us can just pick up our bodies from the side of the road without much of a fight."

Epiphany wanted to protest, to insist that they had to keep moving no matter what, but she knew Gerold was right. She was amazed she'd made it as far as she had. Epiphany had spent days hiking before, but never without any break, even to eat, and never all up hill. The grade wasn't significant, but it was steep enough to burn.

"Maybe we should stop, but should we stop in such a public place?"

"I don't know. I knew this place was here so I've been thinking about it. On one hand it is way more public, which means more people, will see us. On the other hand it's more public so maybe it'll be harder for anyone to try anything while we're there."

Gerold sounded less than sure, and Epiphany was

181

even less so. It didn't seem like the people that were after them were the types to be put off by a crowd and the inn didn't look particularly busy.

"Anyway," Gerold continued. "We can try to get some bad rest in the rain and the mud on the side of the road and then have to rest again a few hours later, or we can get some real rest here, maybe even a decent meal and then hit the road with full steam. We don't even have to stay the whole night."

Epiphany still wasn't sure the logic was solid, but it sounded wonderful and she was all out of will to resist.

"Let's do it," she told Gerold, gesturing up the road at the inn.

Inside they found a small vestibule with a narrow counter and a sleeping clerk. The light from a sputtering lantern danced on the top of his bald pate and his contented snores rumbled against the varnished wood of the counter.

Gerold coughed gently, then harumphed a little louder, but the man didn't stir. Finally Epiphany reached out and shook the clerk by his shoulder. The man sat up immediately, a wide smile on his face and his eyes sharp and alert.

"Good-" the clerk glanced out the window beside his counter in an effort to judge what time of day it was, but the gray wash of rain made that impossible. He finally ventured a guess, "-evening?"

"Yes, good evening," Epiphany replied. His smile widened.

"What can I do for such a lovely young couple?"

"We need a room for the evening and a hot meal," Gerold told him, stepping forward.

"I can half help you," the clerk told them. "You and I are the only ones here so I have plenty of rooms, but we're the only ones here so I don't have anyone to cook. You're welcome to go into the kitchen and fend for yourselves, but the provisions have been a bit short of late so I won't promise you'll find much to excite you."

"I'm sure we'll make due," Gerold responded.

"Alright, we'll put you up in the master sweet. No one else here, so no reason not too. As for the kitchen, there'll be no charge for that. I can't bring myself to charge for making folks do for themselves. All told the two of you can stay for ten certs."

Epiphany stifled a gasp. The trade certificates – certs – that made up the backbone of the inland economy were hard to come by in the best of times. Many people on the coasts lived by barter with their neighbors and wouldn't see a real cert even once in their whole lives. Even families that took their business inland like Gerold's or Epiphany's when her grandpa would go in to trade the curios he found at sea would come back with maybe one or two of the valuable currency. Ten seemed like a kings ransom for a simple room.

Gerold didn't even flinch. He reached into his bag and drew out a thick leather wallet. He pulled out ten leafs of the paper money and laid it on the counter. Epiphany could see a thick stack of the certs still in the wallet as Gerold flipped it shut.

"Been keeping secret accounts from the misses?" the clerk joked as he took the certs from the counter top and tucked them into a drawer in front of him. Gerold didn't reply, just gave him a tired smile.

"Room is at the very top of the stairs and the end of the hall," the clerk told them, drawing a key out of a different drawer and handing it to Gerold. "Kitchen is through that door. I'll be here until a bit after dark at what time I lock the door and turn in myself. If you need anything there's a bell pull by the door you can ring, otherwise help yourself."

"Thank you." Gerold took the key and shouldered his bag.

"Thank you," echoed Epiphany as she followed Gerold up the stairs.

Every step felt like a cliff she had to climb, and her legs throbbed all the way. She was grateful when they reached the top and even more grateful when Gerold unlocked the door and stepped aside to let her enter their room.

The master sweet was a grandiose name for the room. It was small, with a writing desk by one wall cramped against a large bed with a quilted mattress. There was a small stove in the corner for warmth, but the grill was cracked and rusted. The floor was bare wood, loosely covered by worn rugs and the paper that had been glued to the walls was torn and sagging in a few places. There was a small door near the bed and when Epiphany pushed it open she found a small porcelain bathing tub. Epiphany knew she should probably be glad to get a chance to sluice the mud off, but after a day in the rain the idea of more water didn't appeal to her.

Instead she dropped onto the wooden chair by the writing desk and started wrestling her wet shoes off. She had to peel her socks off slowly, like peeling a piece of overripe fruit, and as the cloth came away it took some of her skin with it. There were large blisters across the edge of her feet and the back of her heels. Several of them had already burst and were weeping clear fluid. Gerold cringed when he saw.

"We need to clean that. I brought bandages and the like, but they're all soaked right now. I'll go down and see if the clerk has any here we can buy."

Epiphany nodded and let him go. She leaned back in the chair and let her eyes slip shut. If she'd thought her feet hurt in her shoes she'd been totally unprepared for what they'd feel like out of them. It was as if the shoes had some how kept the pain pressed in small, but now that it was free it was running wild. It didn't stop with her feet either. Her whole body hurt. Each pulse of her heart sent an aching wave through every muscle. Even with the discomfort Epiphany started to drift. She considered moving to the bed, but that would require putting weight on her feet again, so she settled deeper into the chair and let herself go.

~ ~ ~

She was dreaming of her grandpa. It was a strange dream though because he was trying to wake her.

'Epiphany you need to wake up, there isn't much time,' dream grandpa was telling her. Even stranger was the fact that in the dream he had a halo. It made his white hair look golden blond, which she'd heard it had been when he'd been very young. He was smiling, but there was a sternness in his eyes.

'Epiphany, you need to wake up right now,' he told her again. This time she obliged.

Epiphany didn't know how long she'd been asleep. She didn't think it had been very long, but it was long enough for all her tired muscles to turn to stone. She groaned, everything pulling and stretching as she shifted upright in the chair. She blinked a few times to clear her head.

When she'd drifted off there had been a faint light still crawling in through the round window at the end of the room. That faint illumination was gone, leaving the room dark; so dark that it took her a long moment to pick out the tall figure standing by the foot of the bed. For a moment she thought it was Gerold, but the proportions were all wrong, this person was taller and far leaner. In the shadows she could see that he was dressed in a floor length coat but not much else.

There was a scream somewhere inside Epiphany, but it was locked beneath a paralyzing fright and all she could do was stare and tremble. When the man saw that she was awake he held up his hands slowly. It could have been a gesture of reassurance, but in the dark room it looked ominous.

In one hand the man held something, though Epiphany couldn't make out what. Suddenly the item flared into light, casting a warm amber glow through the room. By the light she could see that the intruder was an older man, with short salt-and-pepper hair and a long crimson coat. It might have been a trick of the light, but his eyes looked to be the same shade of red.

"Who... who are you?" Epiphany finally managed to squeeze out through her trembling lips. She could still feel the horrendous pressure of the scream down inside her.

"I am a friend," he told her in a softly accented voice. "You can call me Crafter, a mutual friend does."

"Mutual friend?" Epiphany looked around the room for Gerold, but he was nowhere in sight.

"Epiphany." It was her grandpa's voice. Epiphany looked frantically around the room again. Maybe this had all been some cruel joke and he was still alive. Then he spoke again and as he did the lights around the box Crafter held pulsed with his words.

"Epiphany I know this will be hard to understand, but you need to listen to Crafter. I brought him to you because he is here to help."

It was all too much and the scream that had been trapped and building finally broke free. She shrieked and tried to put distance between herself, the glowing box, and the strange man holding it. She didn't have anywhere to go and managed only to crawl half way up onto the desk.

"Please," both Crafter and the box spoke in tandem. Crafter fell silent and let her grandpa speak.

"Epiphany, I know this is strange and frightening, and I know things have been happening very fast but you have to calm down and listen. We probably don't have much time."

"How is this even possible?" Epiphany half asked, half shouted.

"I did die Epiphany, but Crafter is holding my soul in this box so that I can help him... and you."

Further explanation was cut short when Gerold burst through the door, a piece of firewood held in his hand as a makeshift club. He scanned the room quickly, saw Epiphany perched on the edge of the desk confronted by the tall stranger. To his credit he didn't hesitate. Gerold charged across the room, the cord of wood hefted above his shoulder.

"Gerold no!" Epiphany cried out, but he was committed to his attack and didn't listen. Crafter snaked out a hand and caught the wrist with the club. He twisted quickly but gently and brought Gerold to the ground at his feet. Epiphany was worried her friend would come to some harm, but he seemed more startled than hurt.

"Gerold, wait. I think they're here to help us," she told him. This time he heard her.

"They?" Gerold whipped his head around.

"Hello Gerold," her grandpa's voice drifted out of the box. Again Gerold looked around the room.

"It's the box," Epiphany said, pointing at the glowing cube. "His soul is in the box."

"What?" Gerold gasped. Crafter let go of his wrist and Gerold climbed to his feet. He moved quickly beside Epiphany and regarded the man and his cube with open suspicion.

"I'm sorry. I understand this is a both a strange and important meeting, but we really don't have time for this. We should have moved already," Crafter said.

"He's right Epiphany," her grandpa's voice told her.

"I – we will explain more as we travel," Crafter told

them. "For now you need to know that we're here to help you. There are forces after you, powerful forces that you cannot hope to face. I have a way of traveling more swiftly than on foot but we must go now."

"I don't know," Epiphany said, laying a hand on Gerold's shoulder for both support and comfort.

"Epiphany please, you must trust us," her grandpa's voice urged.

"What was my first word?" Epiphany blurted.

"What?" Crafter asked, his eyebrows bunching together.

"Not you," she told him, pointing at the glowing box in his hand. "I'm asking my grandpa. If it's really my grandpa he'll know."

"It was goat," the voice told her. "I had an old wooden statue of a goat I'd found in a house on the bottom of the Waters. None of us knew why but you were obsessed with it when you were a baby. Your first word was goat."

"Let's go," Epiphany said without pause.

"But-" Gerold began, but Epiphany rounded on him. She wasn't angry with Gerold, not really but all the tension of the past days had been forged into a hard spike by this new strange twist and it had to go somewhere or it would kill her.

"All of this is strange Gerold. None of it makes sense. We were almost killed by an angel yesterday, and you're still... who knows how much older. Now my dead grandpa's soul is in a box being carried by a..."

"I'm a Devil," Crafter supplied.

"... by a Devil," Epiphany continued with a surrendering shrug. "Why should that seem any stranger than the rest. If they say we're in danger I believe them. We already knew that. If they say we have run I believe them, because we already knew that too. If my grandpa says they're here to help us than I believe him and they said we have to go now."

Gerold didn't offer any further argument. He gathered up his bag, slung it over his shoulder and waited. Epiphany set about the painful work of getting her shoes back on her feet. She would have liked to clean and bandage the blisters, but that would have to wait until they were moving. Once she was shod Crafter held out the box toward her.

"Would you like to carry him for now?"

Epiphany hesitated. She was thrilled to get to talk with her grandpa again, but the idea that he was a little box now still hadn't fully settled in her mind. It was better than nothing though, so she reached out and lifted the cube from Crafter's open palm. It was heavier than she thought it would be and subtly warm against her skin.

"It is wonderful to be near you again Epiphany," grandpa told her.

"I'm glad," she told him. She wished she could reply in kind, but it was too soon. He didn't seem to notice.

"This way," Crafter motioned toward the round window in the far wall. For the first time Epiphany noticed that it was slightly ajar. The group moved to the window and Crafter pushed the window all the way open. Without waiting for the rest he leapt out into the dark. With a panicked start Epiphany leaned out the window, expecting to see the Devil three stories below, but instead found him only a few feet down standing astride some strange craft that was hovering in midair. He motioned for her to follow, and she tossed her bag down to him and made the leap.

Gerold followed and when their bags were stowed in concealed hatches across the craft's surface Crafter spoke softly and it started away. It accelerated smoothly, climbing until it was gliding along the tops of the trees.

"This is Aleister, my strider," Crafter told them both.

He had to shout slightly to be heard above the wind whipping past them. Thankfully the rain had stopped, at least for the moment.

"He will carry us to Newridge. You can rest."

Epiphany couldn't imagine a better idea.

17

IT HAD TAKEN the tornado a long time to pass. The Crone had done her work well when she'd crafted the windstorm and it had lingered in the area far longer than any natural storm would have. Even after it passed violent gusting winds continued to lash the skies, scattering clouds and turning falling rain into wild skirls of swirling water. The three angels ventured out of the battered farmhouse as soon as the greatest brunt of the storm had passed, but they were forced to continue traveling on foot for several hours more before the winds died enough that they could fly.

Impatience ruled them, and even when they did take to wing they were tossed and buffeted like leaves on a roiling river. Much of their energy was spent just staying both aloft and together. Reaper, with his four great black wings took the lead, cutting the air for the other two, who followed along in his wake. Fist staid close to Heart, her black wings brushing tip to tip with his softer gray as they soared through the tumultuous skies.

They pushed hard inland, knowing that they were behind in this race already. Before they'd left Heart had suggested abandoning their plan to go to Newridge. It would take them too long, and too far out of the way to go that far inland only to have to turn back toward the coast, but Reaper had been firm. They didn't know where the Bearer was, and though they could try to follow the signs it was too great a risk that they might be mislead. They could waste more time searching than they would simply going and asking.

So they made for Newridge.

It chaffed at them all, but at Reaper more than the rest. He could feel Tsayyadiel moving, feel his hatred and his rage like a lighthouse across midnight waters. There was a physical pull toward the other angel, but he resisted it. As much as he wanted to kill Tsayyadiel there was a bigger game being played and Tsayyadiel was not the only piece the enemy had on the board. It would be too easy to send Tsayyadiel off to some corner of the map to draw the Three away while the Crone or some other agent snatched up the Bearer.

Tsayyadiel's time would come, but it wasn't come yet.

Once they crossed over the mountains the winds calmed and they could make swifter progress. Before long the first signs of the older inland civilization began to appear. Roads went from mud to broken asphalt, and the buildings beside them were of stone and concrete instead of wood. There were more electric lights as well, glowing like fireflies far below the flying angels. In the distance they could see the wash of light off of Newridge.

Newridge wasn't the biggest inland city to survive the coming of the Waters, but it was big enough to have a real presence, as well as a still functioning electrical grid run off the two flowing rivers that raced past the urban sprawl. The trio swept past the outlying districts that were made up mostly of houses and a few small shops and toward the bustling heart of the city. They started a curving decent that drew them like water down a drain toward a tall stone cathedral that stood astride two great flag-stoned squares near the city center.

Their final decent was a headlong plunge to earth, wings tucked and ground rushing up to meet them. The thunderous decent would minimize the chance some aimless passerby would note their coming. If someone did see them it could start a panic; flying people dropping from the skies! Worse, they could be seen by an agent of the High Church. The three angels were pressed for time and couldn't be stalled by either dodging tails or fighting.

They dropped into a narrow alley several blocks from the cathedral. They ducked down and folded their wings away before moving out of the alley and into the narrow street beyond. It was little more than an alley itself and butted up against the back of a row of shops in the square. Still glancing furtively around they moved up to one of the buildings and knocked at a dirty metal door set under a tin awning.

After a long moment a bolt flipped in the door and it opened a crack.

"Tell Brendiwald the Three are here. Tell him we must speak with him now," Reaper commanded.

The door snapped shut and the bolt flipped back into place.

"The problem with not coming here more often is that no one ever recognizes us and we always get left standing on the stoop," Heart said with a grin, as he scratched his thick beard.

"The reason we don't come here more often is so that no one will recognize us," Reaper countered, gesturing toward the city.

Further argument was forestalled by another loud click of the bolt and the door swinging open. A cherubic young man stood framed in the doorway. His cheeks were flushed red and his breathing rapid from rushing to deliver the visitors message, but he was smiling. He waved the trio in the door and closed it behind them.

"Father Brendiwald is eager to see you!" he declared, motioning them deeper into the building. They passed through the small closet that doubled as an entryway and out into a hallway painted a pale shade of institutional green. The young man pushed past them and lead them down the hall to a door near the end. He knocked lightly.

"Enter," a voice called from inside.

The youth pushed the door open and again stepped aside. The angels moved into the room, a wide office lined with tall bookshelves and dominated by a dark wooden desk. Heavy drapes were pulled across the windows and candles burned in sconces on the wall to hold back the dark. The building could have run electric lights, but the High Church ran the city and by extension the power. Brendiwald and his followers didn't want the High Church to know they were in the building so they relied on candles and lanterns for light.

Behind the desk, his craggy face cast in flickering shadows sat Father Bruce Brendiwald. The left side of Brendiwald's head was a gnarled mess of scar tissue where a gunshot had torn his ear off, and taken a sizable chunk of cheek with it. The tight white tissue pulled at the side of his face and gave him a constant growl. He was a tall, broad, and fierce man in every aspect; every aspect except for his character.

Father Brendiwald had begun his career of faith as a member of the High Church. He had been the leader of the small congregation of a village high in the mountains even farther inland than Newridge. He had distinguished himself as an orator and a leader and he hadn't staid in the mountains for long. The farther he was drawn into the higher orders of the Church, and the more he learned about the true nature and mission of that institution the less he wanted to be a part of it. He was promised wealth and power, access to arcane sorceries that could prolong his life, but unfortunately for the High Church Brendiwald proved to be one of those rare souls who was actually concerned about the salvation of his fellow man.

His discomfort didn't go unnoticed by his superiors, nor was it missed by members of the resistance. When the time came that Brendiwald could take no more everyone was ready except maybe Brendiwald himself. On his way from a High Mass back to the mansion the Church had built him the resistance made their grab. Brendiwald went willingly, but his handlers managed to keep his ear. Father Brendiwald had fled the High Church because he was a gentle and compassionate man, and even with his scaring and the constant struggle of the following years he had only grown more meditative and kind.

When the trio of angels walked through the door a wide smile turned up the right side of his face.

"Welcome my friends it has been too long!" he exclaimed.

"It has," responded Heart with equal enthusiasm. "But better late than never!"

"We don't have time for this," growled Fist.

"Indeed," agreed Reaper. "Do you know where the Bearer is right now?"

"In Seacliff where they ought to be I would expect," Brendiwald said, his eyebrows beetling down over his nose. "You have too much presence to go near the Bearer without putting the secret at risk however."

"It is not secret anymore," Reaper told him.

"The Word has found the Bearer," Heart supplied. "He has sent Tsayyadiel to retrieve the artifact."

Brendiwald was on his feet, eyes wide and glimmering in the candlelight.

"What? Are you certain?"

"The Crone attacked us on our way here. She spoke of the Bearer. We are sure," Fist confirmed.

"What are you going to do?" Brendiwald asked them.

"We came here because we guessed that the Bearer would flee this way once they were out of their hole. We hoped they would have contacted you and from that we could get to them more swiftly," Reaper told him. "We are ready to move, but first we need to know where to go."

"Seacliff," Brendiwald told them with an exasperated shrug. "The Bearer lives in Seacliff, and as far as I know they are still there."

"They are not," Reaper told him.

"What else can you tell us?" Heart inquired.

"The artifact has been in the care of a family called Gale, though I don't know which of them currently has it. I've corresponded most with the elder of the family, a man named Thadius, but he has a son and a granddaughter."

"We make for Seacliff then. We will look sharp and find whoever has the artifact on the road."

Reaper nodded to his siblings and they started for the door.

"If we come here we may need shelter. Have someone on the road to Seacliff waiting to hide the Bearer once we reach the edge of the city," Heart instructed as they filed out the door past the round-faced man, who was still waiting in the hall.

"I'll see to it," Brendiwald called after them.

Outside the three angels moved back into the narrow alley where they'd arrived. They huddled close together to confer before setting out once more.

"Do we fly?" Fist asked.

"It would be faster," Heart suggested.

"But we would have to stay low and risk being seen, or stay high and risk missing the Bearer," Reaper countered.

"We are beyond the point where being seen is our greatest risk," Fist said.

"There is still some continuing benefit to secrecy," Heart insisted.

"No," Fist growled, "we are beyond that."

She dashed down the alley in a sudden rush. The other

two were caught off guard, but had worked with their sister long enough to trust her instinct and they ran after her. The man skulking at the end of the alley didn't react as swiftly. Fist had him by the lapels of his raincoat with his feet dangling above the ground before he managed to turn to run.

Fist hauled him back into the alley and out of sight of any passersby on the street. He struggled against her grip, but lacked the strength to resist the powerful angel. He opened his mouth to cry out, but she slapped him hard across the cheek and he was shocked back to silence. Once they were deep enough into the cover of the alley she shoved him up against the wall hard enough that his head snapped back against it with an audible thump. His eyes rolled in his head for a moment before refocusing.

"Gently Sister Fist," Heart urged. "If you break him too soon we can't question him."

Reaper slid up next to the man, his face only inches from the lurker. Reaper looked down on the man, even with Fist holding his feet above the ground.

"Who knows we're here?" he snarled at the man.

Dull gray eyes flicked back and forth between the three angels and he licked his lips with the tip of his tongue, but said nothing.

"This hurts a lot less if you answer the questions," Fist told him.

"Who knows we're here?" Reaper repeated.

The man seemed inclined to keep his silence so Fist punched him in the gut. The man let out a deep grunt of pain and a spray of spittle flecked off his lips. Reaper reached up and wiped the clinging drops from his cheek. Fist hit him again without waiting for her brother to offer another question. This blow came higher up on the man's body and was accompanied by the crunch of cracking ribs. The man's eyes rolled again, but Reaper seized him by the chin and forced him to focus.

"Who knows we're here?" he asked again.

"No one," the man coughed out. A long line of drool fell from his slack lips.

"Who sent you to watch us?"

"Not you," the man groaned.

"What?" Reaper prompted when the man didn't continue.

"I wasn't watching you, I was watching the building."

"Do you always have someone watching the building?" Fist asked. When he didn't answer right away she hit him again; another shot low into his stomach. "Do you always have someone watching the building?"

"Yeah ... yes, sure," he sputtered.

"He's lying," Heart said flatly. "You can see it in his eyes. He's lying."

"But if you weren't watching us, why would you be watching the building today?"

Reaper was moving before the answer came.

"Kill him," he shouted back over his shoulder as he dashed back toward Brendiwald's hideout.

The man opened his mouth to object but before he got a sound out Fist's blow crashed into the side of his head, collapsing his skull. She dropped his limp body and turned to follow Reaper. Heart dropped in with her.

"What's going on?" he called out to Reaper who was rounding the corner into the street a dozen feet ahead of them.

"They're going to attack Brendiwald!" Reaper called back. "They're watching the building because they're going to attack it and they want to make sure he's inside. They're trying to cut off the Bearer's escape."

"You have to admit it's admirably thorough," Heart said as they charged into the street.

They were met by the sound of gunfire. There were

two men in dark coats dead by Brendiwald's door, their blood splattered across the wall behind them. Reaper was making a line for the door, his heavy pistols in his hands. The door was already open and he dashed through without slowing.

"Go with Reaper," Fist told Heart as she broke off and headed for the corner.

Heart followed his brother through the door. Inside he found the cherubic acolyte slumped against the far wall. The young man had been shot in the chest. He was still alive, though his breathing was faint and his eyes were fluttering, half open. Heart dropped to his haunches next to him and took one of his hands between both his own. The youth's hand was ice cold and covered in a sheen of sweat. When Heart touched him his breathing softened and the pain that clenched his face eased.

"It is time for you to move on," he said. From farther into the building came the chatter of gunfire, rapid cracks of automatics followed by the deep boom of Reaper's pistols. Heart ignored them all, focusing his attention on the dying boy at his feet. "You have served a noble cause, and though this life is at the end this is not the end for you. There is a great kingdom waiting beyond the veil and though you may have to wait to reach it we will see you safely there. Sleep now my child, you are a beloved of our Prophet."

He brushed his hand down over the young man's face. When his hand passed the boy's eyes, they slipped closed and one last breath eased out between his lips. Then he was gone. Heart pushed to his feet and moved into the building, following the sounds of fighting. The exchange of gunfire continued to echo through the hallways, punctuated by cries of pain.

The door to Brendiwald's office at the end of the hall had been torn from its hinges and laid askew against the far wall. There were three men dead in the hallway. One wore the same heavy coat as the men Reaper had shot outside, but the other two were in casual clothes; presumably members of Brendiwald's sect.

Heart hurried to the door, fearing the worst, but the office was empty. A door across from the office was open revealing a stairwell. Heart could hear more gunfire, and a deep throated roar echoing down from above. He ran through the door and with a single leap bounded to the landing above. At the next door there were two more of Brendiwald's people laying dead. One had been shot through the head, but the other looked like something had torn her open. Long claw marks swept down from her collarbone and ended near her hip.

Heart stepped over the bodies and found himself in another hallway of the same quiet green. The hallway was anything but quiet however. The dead were strewn about like tossed jacks. They were both the High Church's long-coated thugs and the more day-to-day seeming members of Brendiwald's sect. The walls were riddled with bullet holes, rent by deep gouges, and splashed with sprays of blood. Heart was amazed that so much carnage was possible in only a few moments.

When he looked to the end of the hall he could see why. Someone had summoned a demon. Oily smoke rose off the things rubbery, black skin in curling clouds and its steps left charred patches on the tile floor; signs of the heat of it's own realm still clinging to it. The beast had four long arms that ended in wickedly curved talons and a slavering mouth full of thin needle-like teeth. It was a soldier demon, a mostly mindless machine of violence and death. They weren't good for much else, but if killing needed to be done there was little better.

It was locked in combat with Reaper, who was ducking and weaving around the sweeping claws and firing a tidal wave of bullets into the bulk of the beast. The demon was no match for Reaper and the outcome of the battle was inevitable, but Reaper wasn't the thing's target.

Brendiwald was pressed back into the corner of the hall. His arm was held close to his body and Heart could see that he'd been shot through the shoulder. The wound was bleeding freely and the angel knew that if they didn't get the priest help soon he'd bleed to death. He was flinching and shivering each time the long claws of the demon lashed out, trying to reach around Reaper. Reaper was able to turn the attacks aside, but each one was getting closer as the four arms of the monster began to out pace his efforts.

It was a race, a war of attrition. At some point Reaper would miss one of the demon's attacks and Brendiwald would be dead, the question was could he kill it before that happened. The problem was that killing a soldier demon was not a simple thing. They didn't always have brains, or hearts that could be broken or stopped. If you took out their eyes they had other senses that let them continue the fight. Killing a demon was a matter of damage, pure, overwhelming damage. If you could hurt it enough it would die.

Reaper was doing all he could, his guns roaring in an almost unbroken chain, but the soldier wasn't slowing. Heart rushed forward. He was no warrior, but he might be able to buy Reaper the time he needed to finish the soldier demon. Swift as he was, Heart knew he wouldn't be in time.

As he watched one of the four limbs snaked down and caught Reaper by the ankle. The angel stumbled only slightly before a withering fusillade of fire took the hand off at the wrist, but it was enough. While his attention was focused low two of the beast's other talons swept over the top and down toward the waiting Brendiwald. To his credit the old priest brought up a wooden cudgel he'd been using to defend himself, but it was a gesture of empty defiance.

That was when Fist came through the wall. She was tucked up into a ball and blasted out in a spray of wood dust and plaster. She hit the demon in the flank hard enough to rock it back and its claws tore harmlessly through the wall above Brendiwald. It roared its frustration, the sound rumbling the whole building. It tried to move back in for a second strike, but if it had been outmatched by Reaper, now it was hopelessly outnumbered as well.

Fist was on her feet in an instant, raining blows into the things body even as she shook dust from her eyes with a sharp shake of her head. Reaper followed her lead, redoubling his efforts against the beast. With the more physical angel to take on the bulk of its attacks and the terrible toll of Reaper's guns the soldier demon finally began to falter. As it backed away from Fist's vicious assault one of its legs buckled beneath it, bringing it down to one knee.

Heart knew how the story would end and didn't wait to see the rest. He dashed past the embattled group and moved to Brendiwald. The priests face was ashen and the whole sleeve of his jacket was soaked in blood. He looked up as Heart approached and with a smile finally let the cudgel slip from his weakening fingers. He started a slow slump down the wall, but Heart caught him under the arms and propped him up.

"Oh no you don't," he told the old priest. "You're not done yet. We need to get you somewhere I can lay you down and work on you."

Brendiwald nodded and pointed across the hallway to another door that was still closed. As he half lead, half carried the man across the narrow gap he glanced back to the fight between his siblings and the demon. It was all but over. Reaper was standing beside Fist, his eyes panning back and forth looking for additional threats while she crouched over the demon pounding the last vestiges of life out of it. Fist liked her work and Heart knew she could be at it well after the ghost had fled the monster's flesh.

He kicked open the door and brought Brendiwald into the room beyond. It was a bedroom, monastic and austere, but there was a thin bed that would suit his needs. He laid Brendiwald down on the hard mattress and quickly tore a wad of fabric from the man's shirt. He had the priest use the wad of fabric to apply pressure to the bullet hole in his shoulder.

"Firm, constant pressure," he told Brendiwald. The priest nodded and did as he was told, though his hand was shaking.

"Always thought you'd be able to heal," Brendiwald said, his voice raspy and dry.

"I can," Heart replied as he felt around the back of the other man's shoulder for an exit wound. He found none. "But as I suspected the bullet is still in there and unless you want me to heal your tissue around it and just leave it as a souvenir we need to get it out."

"There are implements in one of the rooms downstairs," Brendiwald informed him.

"No time," Heart replied.

"Than how?"

Heart didn't reply. Instead he laid his hand gently on Brendiwald's sweat slicked forehead.

"Be at peace," he intoned softly. "Be at peace and know only joy."

A golden light flowed around Heart and when it brushed over Brendiwald's twisted features his face went slack and his eyes empty of awareness.

"I'm sorry about this," Heart said. He drew the wadded cloth away from the wound, and with a soft pop and tear of flesh plunged his fingers into the hole left by the bullet.

18

ELLIS CARTER KNEW EXHAUSTION in a way he had never known it before. Even on the long overland ride with Tsayyadiel he'd been able to drift into his thoughts, but as they soared over the land for the greater part of a day there was no respite. Tsayyadiel had seized him by the back of his coat and hadn't shifted his grip. Ellis had been hanging from the arms of the coat the whole flight and though his arms were completely numb he kept them crossed tightly across his chest for fear that if he relaxed them he'd slip out and Tsayyadiel wouldn't bother to catch him. He couldn't feel his hands at all and his neck and shoulders were cramped and aching from the effort.

It was with great relief that he felt Tsayyadiel dive toward the earth. He could see lights below them, though they were still too high to make out what it was they were sweeping towards. Ellis didn't care, as long as he could put both feet on the ground. As they got closer Ellis could make out a square building huddled on the side of the highway, some sort of inn or restaurant.

It was only at the last moment that Tsayyadiel pulled out of his vertigo-inspiring dive, but Ellis was beyond the point where he could feel afraid, so he simply waited until Tsayyadiel set him on the ground and released him. Ellis hadn't realized his legs had gone as numb as his arms and he collapsed in a heap as soon as Tsayyadiel let him go.

"Get up," Tsayyadiel told him, settling gently onto the ground and folding in his four midnight wings.

To his credit Ellis tried. He tried to push with his arms, but they wouldn't move from their death grip around his chest. He tried to dig with his legs but they only twitched in the dirt. He tried again, but to no greater effect.

"I can't," he finally admitted. Tsayyadiel grimaced and crouched down next to him. Ellis expected that was the end of his life. Tsayyadiel had made it clear how he felt about delays. Ellis felt strangely numb to his coming demise.

With firm hands Tsayyadiel drew Ellis' arms away from his body. Ellis cried out in agony as muscles that had been frozen for hours were pulled back into motion and a rush of blood hit his hands with burning pins. Tsayyadiel began to rub them briskly and Ellis cried out again as the burning tingle became a raging bonfire.

"Be still Ellis Carter," Tsayyadiel told him dispassionately. Ellis bit his lip and obeyed.

When there was a measure of feeling back in Ellis' hands Tsayyadiel moved on to his legs, giving them same aggressive rubbing treatment. Ellis flexed his fingers and found that he again had control of his extremities. When Tsayyadiel was done with Ellis' legs he stood back up and looked down at the little alchemist.

"Now, get up."

It was not a swift process, but this time Ellis was able to get to his feet. Once he was up Tsayyadiel moved away without another word. Clearly his kindness had limits. Ellis followed along, but not quickly. Tsayyadiel did not wait. Ellis could catch up in his own time.

By the time Ellis made it up the short flight of steps to the inn's front door and into the anteroom the clerk was dead. He was slumped forward over his narrow counter with a pool of blood spreading out beneath him. The lantern light glimmered in the cooling vitae. Ellis found he was no longer shocked by death, or Tsayyadiel's brutality. He started for the stairs at the end of the room, assuming that his new master had gone to the upper floors, but before he made it far Tsayyadiel came back down.

"This place reeks of demon," the angel growled as he stormed past Ellis. The alchemist turned to follow him back outside. He was starting to get back full function and was able to better keep up with Tsayyadiel.

"They are not here?" Ellis braved a question.

"They are not," confirmed Tsayyadiel. "They were, and the scent is still fresh. They are not far ahead of us."

"We're going to fly again?" Ellis felt sick to his stomach and the muscles in his shoulders gave a sympathetic twinge.

"We are," Tsayyadiel confirmed. "I am going to bear you differently however. You will be no good to me if when we arrive to a fight you are crippled by the journey."

Tsayyadiel drew a folded sheet out from under his arm and unfurled it out across the damp grass.

"Sit," he instructed Ellis.

The alchemist did as he was told, settling himself onto the sheet. He could feel the moisture from the grass quickly soaking through the thin cloth and into his clothing, but if he didn't have to get carried by his scruff like an unruly puppy the momentary discomfort was worth it. Tsayyadiel quickly wrapped the sheet up around him like a giant sling, and when he was satisfied knotted it above Ellis' head and took a fistful of the cloth.

"Hold on."

That was all the warning Ellis got before the ground dropped out from beneath him. He let out a sharp cry and clutched the edges of the sheet in desperate hands. As they rose upward Ellis allowed himself to relax and settle into the cradling embrace of the cloth. It wasn't a featherbed, but it was more comfortable than he thought it would be, and infinitely more tolerable than his last ride through the sky. He even found himself looking over the side of his makeshift seat and marveling at the rush of landscape below.

The clouds were still dense above them, but fingers of orange fire shot through them as the sun began to dive below the distant horizon. The rain continued to hold off, but he could see a thick mass of dark clouds farther to the south that was rushing across the sky like a crashing wave. Before they caught their prey he suspected they would be in a deluge again. Somehow that seemed fitting.

"You have them," Ellis shouted to be heard over the wind.

"I do," confirmed the angel without looking back at his cargo.

"Why do you need me?" Ellis hesitated to ask the question, afraid that he would bring his uselessness to Tsayyadiel's attention and the angel would simply drop him.

"I have been told you still have a part to play in this," Tsayyadiel replied simply.

"Will this be a battle?"

"I expect it will. The devil will not part with the Bearer easily and we cannot know what other allies they have rallied around themselves."

"I am not a soldier," Ellis insisted. The Crone had not listened, but perhaps the angel would.

"You are a soldier if you must be Ellis Carter," Tsayyadiel told him. It was so close to what the Crone had said that he wondered if there was a script.

"I don't understand!" Ellis insisted. Now the angel glanced back and Ellis knew he was out of questions.

"Your understanding has never been necessary alchemist, only your obedience. The Word has wiser servants than you to handle understanding. You have done well thus far. You have aided my quest and sped my journey. Do not waste all of that now by questioning your appointed task. When the time comes simply know that you will be ready."

Ellis sighed and laid back into his sling. There was so much more that he wanted to know, but he knew that to ask would put him in direct danger so he held his tongue. Despite the vast space below him, and the lingering fear of a fall, the gentle sway of flight stole over the little alchemist. It mixed with his fatigue into a powerful soporific, and as his silence settled over him Ellis slept.

19

BRENDIWALD CAME ABOUT with a start. He jerked forward and immediately dropped back onto the pallet behind him with a dull groan. His hand crept up to his shoulder and gingerly probed the area. He grimaced and drew his hand away.

"I know," Heart said with a sigh, from where he sat beside the injured priest. "It was a rush job. Normally I'm much better, but we had to get you stable and get you moved in case they came back."

Brendiwald nodded and looked around. He and Heart were in the cramped confines of a carriage, and from the gentle sway he could tell they were moving. The interior was hot and dark and a thin sheen of sweat coated his face and arms.

"Where are we going?" he asked the angel.

"I honestly don't know," Heart shrugged. "After we killed the soldier demon," there was a soft cough from outside the carriage, "-sorry, after Fist killed the soldier demon we were able to find a few members of your order who had avoided the High Church hit squad. We told them it was imperative to get you to a safe location. They brought us to this hidden carriage and said there was a safe house near the edge of town. One of them is driving right now while I tend you and Fist walks guard outside."

"And Reaper?" Brendiwald asked of the most grim of the trio.

"They first suggested that you had a car we could use

to transport you; much faster, but also much more visible."

Cars were not unique in the inland cities, a few had survived the coming of the Waters and a few of those had been maintained well enough to survive the coming centuries. A few people even still built the metal monstrosities, though it was a real luxury not only for the car itself, but to afford the fuel to run it. Still, they were far enough between that to see one rolling down the road caught eyes and turned heads, the last thing they needed while trying to escape. It was a little surprising that Brendiwald had one, but it was one of the things he'd managed to escape with when he left the High Church where power had visible privileges.

"Yes, we have a car, and I agree it would have been a disastrously visible way to travel. Oh..."

Heart nodded.

"Reaper took your car on a little distraction tour around town while we slipped you out the back. It might be too obvious to really fool anyone, but we had to try something and Reaper seemed eager to shoot more people so no one tried to talk him out of it."

"They attacked us because they know the Bearer is coming didn't they?"

"That's what we suspect. They're coming at this from both ends. They have someone, or maybe more than one someone chasing the Bearer, but they wanted to cut off escape on this end as well."

"We are nearing the end of this aren't we?" Brendiwald asked, turning sober eyes on Heart.

"I believe we are," the angel replied with a soft smile.

Brendiwald studied his companion. Heart's appearance hadn't changed at all in the years Brendiwald had known him, his copper hair and beard hadn't even change lengths.

"How old are you?" Brendiwald asked.

Heart's smile widened a bit.

"You're not the first person to ask me that," the angel told him, "but I've never been able to answer it. I existed before time so it's difficult to gauge."

"How is it possible to exist before time?" the priest asked, propping himself up on his elbow. He grunted as his weight shifted against his injured shoulder.

Heart pursed his lips, considering his answer.

"What you understand as time is not really a 'thing'. Time is more a way of ordering events so that you mortals can easily understand. Let me explain it this way. When we were first building the world someone made trees. Trees were a grand idea; create oxygen, prevent soil erosion, provide shade – you get the idea. To keep trees going however they needed to be self-sustaining; they had to be able to self create. Someone had to go back before there was tree and create the acorn. If time was linear then there would be no way to create the acorn before the tree and so no way to have a tree, but if there was no way to have the tree first we wouldn't know what we needed when we made the acorn. Does that make sense?"

Brendiwald thought for a moment and then shook his head.

"Not really, but I get the impression that it's not supposed to make sense to me."

Heart chuckled.

"There are not many with the wisdom to recognize what they are not intended to know, not even among my kind."

"Thank you. If you can't tell me how old you are, how long has this war been going on?"

"A hundred human lifetimes," Heart told him, shaking his head sadly, the smile falling from his face. "Longer than it should have been. Now, finally after so much pain and death it is finally drawing to a close."

"Do you think we will win?" Brendiwald asked the question hesitantly. The priest was made of stern stuff, and put on a good face for his followers, but here in the confines of the carriage with only the mighty angel to see him he let his guard down.

"I like to think that we will," Heart said, his wistful smile returning. "I cannot say though."

Brendiwald nodded, then his lips pursed and his brow beetled down.

"Is there anything else you would ask?" inquired Heart, seeing the look.

Brendiwald thought for a long moment.

"Does Reaper know how to drive?" he finally asked.

"You know... I don't honestly know."

The car slewed wildly around the corner, wheels squealing across the uneven flagstones of the road. Reaper's hands were white knuckled on the carved hardwood of the wheel and he kept his foot crushed onto the break pedal until the small vehicle slid to a complete halt. He took a deep breath and glanced around. The sounds of pursuit were not far behind and with a growl he shifted his foot over and slammed the gas to the floor. The tires spun on the wet stones and his growl grew louder. He eased off the pedal and then pressed it more slowly. This time the tires caught and the car pulsed forward.

The car was newly built rather than antique, one of the recreation cars that were built for the richest and most powerful. Like most of those cars it was a heavy steel frame wrapped in elaborately enameled metals and wood; a lumbering monstrosity that built momentum slowly and turned poorly. It didn't matter, Reaper didn't need to win any races, just keep the High Church hit squad busy long enough for his siblings to get Brendiwald to safety.

A gray truck swing around the corner not far behind

him. If the car Reaper was in was a luxury, the one chasing him was pure function, an old horse cart that some inspired craftsman had jury-rigged with an engine. There were two men riding in the back, with guns braced against a long bar that ran above the cab. As the truck leveled out and dropped in behind Reaper's car they started to fire. The uneven flagstone road combined with the wooden wheels on the truck made it hard for them to draw a steady aim and most of the shots went wild, but a few slammed into the body of the car. Reaper gritted his teeth and focused on the road. He understood the concept of driving, and knew the basics of how a car functioned, but he'd never actually driven a car before and it was taking all his considerable concentration.

People along the side of the road leapt and ran as bullets bounced off the buildings around them and the cars screamed past. Some simply stood and stared. To see two cars locked in a chase must have been like seeing two unicorns dueling with their horns. Luckily there weren't that many people out and they were able to get out of the path of Reaper's headlong rush. Trying to keep the car straight was enough effort, if he had to weave around obstacles he would probably be better off just getting out and surrendering.

At least the gambit was paying off. As soon as he'd exploded out of the garage where Brendiwald had kept the car secreted away the pursuers had been on him. At first it had been another car, but he'd been able to fire out the window as he went around a corner and kill the driver. The car had careened into the side of a building and shortly after this truck had dropped in behind him.

He slowed and rounded another corner, this one he was able to manage a little better and the car was still moving after the turn. The driver of the truck was a more skillful hand however and they didn't have to slow nearly as much. They closed ground through the turn until they were near enough that even with the bouncing of the truck their shots were getting more accurate. A bullet zipped through the back window of the car and out the front, crazing the glass and missing Reaper by scant feet.

He had to open up the distance, so he mashed down the accelerator again. As he did, a small horse drawn buggy swung out of a side street ahead of him and started down the road. Reaper cut the wheel, trying to go around them, but he wasn't used to guiding the car with gradual motions and he turned too hard. The back of the car went out from under him, whipping around in a wide arc. He tried to turn back the other way but the car was beyond his control by that point, gliding on pure momentum. The truck was still closing in, its passengers keeping up a steady stream of ineffectual fire. People on the sidewalk were diving out of the way of the uncontrolled spin.

The chase was over. Reaper would just have to hope he'd lead them far enough and offered a visible enough target to have given his siblings a fair lead. He pushed open the heavy door and stepped out of the still spinning car. He rolled with the momentum and came up guns in hand.

His first two shots clipped off the two gunmen in the back of the truck, silencing their riffles. The driver saw the danger, but rather than trying to weave out of the way he jammed the accelerator to the floor and rushed toward the waiting angel. Two more shots ended both him and his passenger. Reaper slid out of the road to let the cart rush past when he heard a cry of terror from behind him.

He spun to see a man and his daughter wide-eyed in the street. They'd been running for cover and managed to get clear of his own vehicle, but the man had caught his foot on a paving stone and gone to the ground. His daughter was desperately tugging at his arm, but she was young – no more than six or seven – and had no hope of getting the big man to his feet. The father for his part was trying to shove the girl out of the road, but it was clear to Reaper that neither of them was going to get out of the path of the driverless truck in time.

"Dammit," he grumbled under his breath as he stepped back out into the road. He stepped one leg back behind himself to brace and unfurled his four great wings. As the truck rushed on he tucked his shoulder, gave a single powerful flap and lunged into the front of the truck.

The impact was tremendous; a sound like an explosion that bounded and ricocheted off the buildings around them. The front of the truck folded in around the angel. The wood body cracked and splintered, but the heavy engine hit him square on, the metal deforming around him. He was pushed back, but dug his toes into the ground, tearing up stones and leaving long furrows as he slid. Finally the tangled wreck came to a halt a dozen feet from the father and his child.

His breathing coming in ragged gasps, Reaper dug himself out of the wreckage of the truck. There was blood dripping from his scalp where a piece of metal had torn into his skull and his left arm hung limply by his side. He took a few limping steps away from the truck and folded his wings away before anyone else had a chance to see them.

"Thank you."

He turned to find the father gazing up at him with wide, tear filled eyes. Reaper shrugged. The daughter, a dirty girl with tangled blond hair and blue eyes like twin lakes reflecting the sky pulled away from her father's hand and wrapped her arms around the angel's legs. He stood still for a moment, caught off guard and then let a hand come to rest on top of her head.

"You are loved child," he told her, his voice far softer

than most would ever hear it. "You are loved by your father, and by this universe and all that it is. Remember this moment, and remember that love is a moment of sacrifice without thought."

She let go of his legs and smiled up at him, simple and without guile. He returned the smile earnestly.

"Thank you," her father repeated.

"Raise her well," Reaper told him before he turned and hobbled off the street. He had to get back to Brendiwald now. The Bearer was still on the move and they still had to get to them before someone else did. He had an inherent sense of where his siblings were and could get there quickly enough if he flew, but after the recent attack he needed to draw as little attention to Brendiwald's new location as he could. He would have to run, but he was hurt. It was hard to kill and angel, but hitting one with a truck could certainly slow them down.

He started trotting down the street, favoring his right leg. There was no strength in it and he leaned against a wall for support. Like it or not he didn't have the time to wait and heal, nor did he have the time to try and hobble all the way to the others. Brendiwald was important, but the Bearer was more so. He would have to fly close and hope he could pass unnoticed.

Reaper pushed himself away from the wall, and with a great leap, took to the air.

~ ~ ~

"You look terrible, what happened to you?" Fist asked when Reaper pushed through the door of the little house that had become Brendiwald's new hiding place. Reaper was still limping, though he has started to regain some use of his arm. The wound on his head had closed, but his face was caked in dried blood.

"I got hit by a truck," Reaper replied.

"Impressive!" Fist nodded.

"Where is everyone else," Reaper asked her.

She indicated a back room with a tilt of her wide chin.

"There's a trap door in the floor of the next room. It goes down to an underground bunker. They're all down there right now. I'm keeping watch."

"Brendiwald?" he asked the question that had been plaguing him. It had almost nagged at him enough to throw caution to the wind and fly all the way to the safe house, but wisdom had ruled the day and he'd landed a mile from the little two story stucco and come the last stretch on foot.

"A little worse for the wear, but he's alive. Heart is good at what he does."

"We all are," Reaper told her, laying a hand on her bare shoulder as he moved past. She reached up and squeezed his hand for a moment. They broke contact and Reaper moved through a wooden door painted with a woodland scene of flowers and animals. The next room was a small dining area, but the table had been turned up on its edge and pushed against one wall. In the center of the room a section of floor had been lifted up to reveal a narrow set of stairs that led down under the house. He took them one at a time, favoring his leg on the decent and using one hand against the packed earth wall for balance.

The stairs opened onto a midsized chamber of the same packed earth, shored up by wide oak timbers. Around the edge of the chamber were six small rooms with basic living necessities, beds, chamber pots, and jugs of water. The center of the room was dominated by a large table covered in maps and papers. Brendiwald, Heart, and two of Brendiwald's acolytes were gathered around the table talking quietly. They looked up when Reaper came down the stairs.

Brendiwald's eyes widened when he saw the injured angel limping towards them.

"Clearly he does not know how to drive," Heart said with a grin.

"What?" Reaper asked with a glower.

"It's nothing, just answering a question from earlier," Heart told him.

"Is this location secure," Reaper asked.

"To the best of our knowledge. I don't believe we were followed, and though we've had this safe house for some time, we've never used it before so I have no reason to believe the High Church would have been watching it."

"That will have to do," Reaper replied.

"For what?" Heart asked.

"We are bringing the Bearer here, and we are doing so right now."

"But you're injured," Brendiwald said, concern written clearly across his face.

Reaper just shrugged.

"I have been hurt before, and I will be hurt again. Someday I will be killed. In the mean time we have a purpose to serve and right now that purpose is to get the Bearer safely here."

"Why not stay here and act as guard?" Heart suggested. "Fist and I-"

"No." It was whip crack sharp and Heart stepped back from the fierce expression on his brother's face.

"No," Reaper repeated. "If he might be there than that's where I'm going. Fist can stay here as a guard."

"If he's there than you're in no condition to fight him," Heart objected.

"Than it's a good thing you'll be with me."

"You know I'd be no help against him!"

Reaper wasn't listening though, he was already on his way back up the stairs. Heart growled in frustration.

"Make the safe house ready. The Bearer is coming," Reaper called back over his shoulder.

"Get ready, we may be coming in with friends," Heart added as he hurried after his stubborn brother.

"We'll be ready," Brendiwald promised.

Heart hurried up the stairs to find Fist and Reaper already making plans.

"– and watch over Brendiwald. Make sure no one is watching the house. The last thing we need is to bring the Bearer all this way only to lose them here," Reaper told the other angel.

"I will," Fist assented. "Though I hate not being there to face off against him."

"I know," Reaper laid his hand on her arm again. "We need this house safe though and there is no one better than you to see to that."

She smiled at him, a thin sharp smile.

"Flattery doesn't suit you Brother Reaper, but I will be here when you return, and so will Brendiwald and a safe location. Go with His Grace," she told them both.

"Thank you Sister Fist," Heart told her, squeezing her shoulder as well. He wondered for a moment if this would be the last time they'd see each other. It wasn't impossible. He and Reaper were off to face one of the most dangerous foes in all of existence and Heart was no warrior.

He'd just have to have faith.

"Come," Reaper said when they were both outside. "They have been talked about enough, it is time we finally go and meet this Bearer."

20

AT FIRST EPIPHANY had been afraid of the strider and its inexplicable flight over the trees. The longer they had gone however the more she started to enjoy it. The gentle rocking of the craft had a lulling quality and the cool wind whipping through her hair made her feel more clear headed than she had in a long time. Gerold remained close to the center of the flat surfaced ship, but Epiphany had moved up to the very edge of the bow. The subtle sense of vertigo as the world slid by below her was strangely exciting.

Partially she sat at the front of the craft watching the earth and sky so that she wouldn't have to ask the questions that were churning in her disquiet mind. She wanted the answers; wanted them desperately, but she was afraid of what they would mean. Her whole world had been turned on its head, and she was spinning in a way more fundamental than simple vertigo. The worst was her grandpa.

She hadn't had the chance to mourn him, and now he was returned to her, but not as himself. Instead he was a voice locked away inside a magic box carried by a demon. He knew things only her grandpa could know, and he sounded like her grandpa, not only his voice, but his tone and the things he said, but she was terrified to believe. Too many things had been taken away from her in the last few weeks, and she didn't want to try to hold on too hard.

She could hear Gerold talking quietly to the other two

passengers, but over the wind she couldn't make out what they were saying. As the night wore on she was finally overcome by her curiosity and Epiphany rose carefully to her feet and moved to where Gerold and Crafter were sitting.

Gerold looked green at the edges and kept both hands planted firmly on the carved metal surface of the strider. Crafter by contrast seemed utterly at ease. Between them sat the glowing golden cube. As she approached Crafter looked up at her and smiled. It was a kind enough expression, but the golden light glittering in his blood colored eyes made him seem terrible and sinister. She just had to trust that what her grandpa told her was true and he was a friend.

She settled herself on the deck beside Gerold.

"So, what have I missed?" she asked them.

"I wouldn't even know where to begin," Gerold told her, shaking his head and motioning to Crafter.

"Honestly there is no good place to begin," the Devil told her. "I'll do my best however. The truth is that it has gotten harder to explain all of this over the centuries because most people don't even remember the world as it was when the War started. What you need to know is that the world once had many gods, or at least thought it did. They used many names: God, Allah, Buddha, Kali, and on and on and on. But they were all actually the same god, appearing to different groups in different incarnations and creating competing sects. He would tell them they alone were right and that they had to drive out all the false gods from the world, thereby setting them at war with each other."

"Why?" Epiphany cut in with the question.

"That is a question that has plagued many of us for a very long time. The easy answer is so that he could keep control. There is something that we eternals – angels, demons, and the like – call the Machine. It's more than I can easily explain right now, so just trust me when I say that the Machine is all of creation and it is all about progress. What you know now as the God, or the Word was a servant of the Machine, but he got tired of being the servant and wanted to be the master. The easiest way to do that was to sabotage the Machine. The easiest way to do that was to stop progress in the human race, and the easiest way to do that was to keep you full of hate and seeking war."

"I can see that." Epiphany nodded. "Grandpa told me stories sort of like that when I was young. I never believed them of course, just thought he was crazy."

"Not so crazy now eh?" her grandfather interjected with a laugh. Epiphany cringed. She'd forgotten the box was there when she'd talked about her grandpa.

"You're right grandpa," she told him softly, trying to get over her resistance to his new form.

"Either way," Crafter resumed his story, "one of the agents of the Word realized what was happening and decided to try and stop it. We call him the Prophet and he came time and again into the world and tried to infuse love and forgiveness into the Word's divisive sects. Just like the Word he took different forms to fit with each of the sects, but where the Word taught fanaticism, the Prophet taught acceptance. The Word finally caught him on Earth in one of his incarnations. Using members of the very sect the Prophet had come to teach the Word had the Prophet killed by the local rulers. That would have been the end of the uprising, but somehow, three days later he was brought back to life."

"What do you mean 'somehow'? Can't some of you bring people back to life?" Epiphany asked, thinking of her grandpa.

"Certainly," Crafter agreed. "People. Humans have

souls that can be lost, gained, and moved around. You can be restored to life if the body can be salvaged, and saved in other ways if it cannot."

Crafter waved a gloved hand at the box sitting between them.

"The same is not true of eternals," he continued. "We don't have souls. We are what we are and if we are destroyed, especially on Earth, then we simply cease to exist."

"But not this time," Gerold supplied.

"Not this time," Crafter agreed. "Somehow the Prophet was restored, and that's when the War really started."

"So the war you're talking about, it's a fight between the Word and the Prophet?"

Crafter nodded.

"Basically. There are beings that have sided with each. We have been fighting for a very long time. The flood – the coming of the Waters – was the Word's attempt to kill off most of us who oppose him here on Earth."

"So much was lost." Her grandfather's voice was full of wistful sadness.

"Indeed it was. It was an act of desperation because the Word was loosing, but it turned the tide well enough. We've been stalemated ever since." Crafter's voice was grim.

"Alright," conceded Epiphany, deciding to just trust that what she was being told was the truth. "What does any of this have to do with me or with my family?"

"Long ago, even before the Waters our family was given a great calling," her grandpa explained. "We were entrusted with a powerful artifact and tasked with guarding it until a time when it became necessary."

"The box," Epiphany guessed.

"Yes, the box," grandpa confirmed.

"What's in it?" she asked.

"I don't know," grandpa admitted. "None of us have known for a long time. I think maybe the first members of our family to receive the box might have known, but that knowledge has been lost in the time since then. Now we just know that we have to keep it safe."

"Do you know what's in it?" she asked Crafter.

"I don't," he told her. "There are rumors of course. It is whispered that it was, at least in part how the Prophet was resurrected. There are also those that believe it has a far more critical role in the end of the War."

"What is that?" Epiphany was caught up in the myth now despite herself.

"When the Word sent the Waters he slammed shut the Gates of his kingdom and locked them tight. We have been unable to get in to attack him for all these years. Whatever is in the box, it said to be a key that can open those doors."

"Why haven't you used it before now? Why have you forced Epiphany's family to hide it and suffer?" Gerold's question caught Epiphany off guard. It seemed to catch Crafter off guard as well because he took a long moment before answering.

"The truth is we aren't winning this war," the Devil finally said. "There is no reason for us to storm the gates because we'd be thrown back and defeated. We were trying to marshal our strength enough to make a proper attack before we drew the Bearer out of hiding. Of course, it might not be the key at all."

"So are we to go back into hiding now?" Epiphany asked. She wasn't sure which answer she'd prefer. Part of her wanted to return to her quiet life, free of angels and excitement, but another part of her knew that too much had happened for her to settle quietly back into anything.

"No, I think not," Crafter said after a further moment of consideration. "I think things are in motion now. For better or worse we are moving into the end and we will just have to hope our forces prove adequate to the task."

"Ummmm ..." Gerold waved his hand distractedly at the group.

"What is it Gerold," Epiphany asked him. He pointed off the back of the craft. Behind them there was a thick bank of dark clouds that rippled with seething bolts of lightning. It was racing over the forest and gaining quickly on their swaying craft.

"That storm has been gaining on us really fast," Gerold said.

Crafter spun in his seat.

"Damn that hag!" he snarled, surging to his feet. His long coat flapped around him in the strong wind skirling across the deck and he pulled it tight around him. "Faster Aleister!"

He moved to the back of the strider and watched the storm, his eyes darting back and forth, though Epiphany couldn't tell what he was looking for. He turned back to them, his lips squeezed into a tight line.

"Epiphany, get your grandfather and keep him close. No matter what happens don't get involved."

"What's going on?" Gerold asked, his voice quavering.

"That is no natural storm," Crafter told them both. "There is a terrible creature known as the Crone. She is the Witch of the Winds and she is no friend to us. I don't think Aleister can outrun her, and I suspect she will try to bring us down."

"Can she do that?" Gerold's voice jumped up a few octaves and his fingers turned white where they were pressing against the deck of the strider.

"Yes, unfortunately she can," Crafter replied.

As if summoned by their talk a tongue of purple lightning leapt out of the bank of clouds and whipped past the strider. The following clap of thunder shook them all, and Gerold cried out and fell to his side. The air was thick with the tang of ozone.

"Down Aleister, now!" Crafter shouted. The strider dove toward the earth, but the decent wasn't quick with all the trees blocking the way.

The second bolt of lightning clipped the wing of the strider, and fingers of electricity danced across the deck. It lurched violently to the side and Epiphany made a desperate diving grab for her grandpa. Her hand came down short and time seemed to slow as the glowing box tumbled across the deck toward the listing edge. Gerold let go of his flat-palmed death grip and shot out a hand to arrest its fall. Epiphany let out a ragged breath of relief. Gerold gave her a wan smile and drew the box in close to his chest.

Another bolt slammed into the deck, this time only a few feet from where Epiphany was sitting. The concussion threw her backwards with the force of a tidal wave. She felt the metal deck go out from under her, and then she was falling. She had the terrible sense of empty space looming below her, and this time the sense of vertigo was not thrilling. A strong hand seized her wrist before she could plunge into the waiting trees. She looked up to meet Crafter's crimson eyes. One gloved hand was wrapped around her arm and the fingers of his other hand dug into one of the grooved symbols that covered the strider.

With a grunt he pulled her back onto the deck, but before either of them could get stable a fourth bolt cracked into the reeling ship. This one hit close to the bow and the great manta shaped turned sharply downward. Crafter drew Epiphany close to him, wrapping his arms protectively around her. His coat was soft and smelled faintly of cinnamon. Gerold flattened himself against the deck as they dropped through the top of the trees.

Branches cracked like bones against the hull of the plunging strider, and leaves whipped against Epiphany's face, twigs leaving long scratches on her cheeks and exposed arms. Part way down they hit the trunk of one of the trees. The strider won the contest and the thick bole snapped across the swept wing, but the impact also started a slow rotation. When Aleister finally hit the ground the ship was sideways to its path of travel.

Epiphany and Crafter were thrown from the deck and even with the Devil's cushioning embrace the impact knocked the breath out of Epiphany. They rolled across the uneven ground, roots and stones hammering at Epiphany and leaving aching bruises all over her. When they finally came to a stop Crafter was on his feet almost immediately, his eyes scanning through the dark wood. Epiphany came up more slowly, pushing herself up on arms that trembled with the overload of adrenalin hammering through her system.

The first thing she did was look around to find Gerold. At first she couldn't find him at all in the shadows under the trees, but then she saw a glimmer of motion and a soft golden light. As she watched Gerold unfolded himself slowly from around her grandfather's cube. He sat up, his free hand going to his head.

"Gerold, are you ok?" she called out.

"For the moment," he replied. "I don't think we're safe yet though."

"He's right," Crafter confirmed. "Both of you get under Aleister and stay there. He may be down, but he can still offer you some cover."

Epiphany went to Gerold first, helping him to his feet. He didn't seem much worse for the wear, though there was a quickly darkening bruise at the corner of his eye and a trickle of blood running out of the sleeve of his jacket. The pair leaned on each other, Gerold still carrying the cube and they moved quickly toward the fallen strider. The craft had stayed where it had hit, it's starboard wing dug into the soft earth and the other wing thrust up toward the sky. They moved into the shadow of the swept wing and crouched down to wait.

Then the rain came. It didn't start gradually and build, but rushed over them like a wall of water. One moment the forest was still and silent, the next it was blanketed in pounding drops that thundered against the canopy and drowned the ground. In moments thin streams were running over the soil and small lakes were starting to form in the hollows between the trees. The strider offered some shelter from the sudden deluge, but the rain came with fiercely gusting winds and Epiphany and Gerold were quickly soaked despite the cover.

The rain crushed all visibility beyond a few feet and try as she might Epiphany couldn't see Crafter out amongst the trees. Even though Epiphany was looking for the Devil she still cried out in surprise when he emerged from the wet darkness beside the strider. He leaned down, one hand on the craft above him and looked in at the huddled pair of humans.

"Stay close, she's coming," he said.

Crafter hadn't even finished standing up when the lightning bolt took him in the chest. With a crack he was thrown backward off his feet. He hit the edge of the strider and the metal hull rang with the sharp impact. He bounced once off the ground and spun away into the dark.

A soft, dry cackle drifted out of the darkness beyond the edge of the strider. Epiphany squinted out into the shadows and curled closer to Gerold. He put an arm around her shoulders and drew her close to him.

"I'm afraid," she whispered softly.

"It will be alright Epiphany," her grandpa replied. For the first time Epiphany wasn't put off by him being a box. She was just glad to have him there.

"He's right of course," a croaking voice called out to

them. "Everything is going to be alright."

A dark, hunched shape shifted out of the confines of the rainstorm and hobbled into the arched shelter beneath Aleister. The rain drew back from the figure and the wind died down, leaving Epiphany and Gerold in a clear patch. The figure shuffled closer, but with the storm clouds blocking out any light from the night sky Epiphany still couldn't tell anything about it.

"Stop there," Epiphany barked. "Don't come any closer."

The figures stooped shoulders bobbed and shook with another bout of crackling laughter.

"You have no power to command me child," the Crone told her, continuing the slow but inexorable approach. "But you also don't need to fear me. You are not what I want, and if you will relinquish your terrible burden to me than I will simply set you free. How much pain has your burden brought you? How much has it brought to those you love? I can make all that stop child, just let me take that weight from you."

Epiphany had to honestly consider her offer. For all she knew Crafter was dead already and if the Crone could control lighting there was no way Epiphany could fight her. Epiphany also had to admit that the wizened woman was right, the box had brought her nothing but pain. Out of the corner of her eye she saw the soft pulsing of golden light. Her grandpa had died to protect this burden, who was she to give it up so easily.

How could she hope to protect it though? She was dealing with powers that she didn't even start to understand; which made her meager strength inconsequential. In the end she did the only thing she could think to do, she lied.

"I would give it to you if I could, but I don't have it, at least not here."

The Crone's shrouded head tilted to the side as she considered Epiphany's words.

"I think you lie to me child. That is a dangerous choice."

"I'm not lying," Epiphany said with a shrug. "Why would I keep it with me? It's the only bit of leverage I have. If I had it with me you could just kill me and take it. At least this way I have some room to bargain."

The Crone's head swayed back the other way and Epiphany was put uncomfortably in mind of a wolf considering its prey.

"Say I believe you," the old woman-thing hissed. "Where is it?"

"I left it in a cave, back on the other side of the mountains," Epiphany told her, thinking on the fly. She suddenly became aware of movement behind the Crone, almost invisible fingers of black on black creeping out of the rain fogged dark.

"I think I know of this cave," the Crone told her, taking a lurching step forward. She reached out a knobbly fingered hand toward Epiphany. "Come girl, we can be there in mere hours and we will see the truth or the lie of your tale."

"What about my friend," Epiphany asked, gesturing to Gerold. She didn't really want to draw the Crone's attention to him, but she was desperately trying to make more time.

"Him I have no need of," the Crone said with a sharp laugh as punctuation. She raised a hand to her shoulder and the smell of ozone trebled. Epiphany let out a strangled gasp and threw herself in front of Gerold.

Before the Crone could unleash the building energy however those crawling fingers shot forward. One wrapped around her legs, another around her hand that was poised to strike, and one last around her throat. At the same moment the night exploded with crimson light.

Crafter stood back amidst the trees. His coat was drawn open in the front and a vortex of pulsating black smoke curled and roiled where his body should have been. It was out of this writhing cloud that the dark fingers had come. The light came from his eyes, which burned like twin red suns. Epiphany couldn't be sure through the dark and the rain, but it looked like they were actually smoking.

"This meeting is long over due witch," he said, his voice a bass rumble.

"Indeed it is Devil," she spat. The building energy around her hand leapt to the tentacle holding her wrist and raced up the smoky mass. Crafter let out a grunt and for a moment the dark tentacles shrank back leaving the Crone free.

It was only a moment before Crafter's dark appendages were surging forward again, but a moment was all the withered woman needed. Despite her hunched form she moved with shocking swiftness and before Epiphany could even blink the old woman was behind her, a withered claw wrapped around her throat. The black tentacles came to a stop, hovering in the air and weaving back and forth like vipers waiting to strike.

"So we find ourselves at an impasse Devil," the Crone said with a cackle. "I have a solution however. Perhaps I'll just kill you all and then tear your craft apart. I suspect despite this one's charming tale I'll find what I seek within. The only question is who do I kill first."

That wicked hand began to tighten on Epiphany's throat.

21

GEROLD KNEW he had to do something. He looked around the ground for any sort of weapon. There were broken branches everywhere, but none of them seemed to have sufficient heft to be used as a club. He knew he would only get one swing. Then he noticed the cube in his hand. It was heavy; heavier than it should have been and all the corners were sharp and unyielding. He debated for a moment if it was all right to attack someone with Epiphany's grandfather, but only for a moment. Epiphany was in danger. Gerold had to do something.

It wasn't hard to close on the Crone. She didn't consider him a threat so she wasn't paying him any attention. All her focus was on the Devil and his dancing black arms and flaming red eyes. Gerold couldn't blame her, but he would still take advantages where he could. He crept as close to her as he quickly could and then lunged the last stretch between them. He had the cube clutched in one fist and he swung it in a wide horizontal arc with all the force he could muster.

Gerold wasn't a fighter, and he wasn't a strong man, but he was a big man and when the cube connected with the mass of lace and hair that covered the back of the Crone's head it had all his weight behind it. It hit with a wet crunch and the hag reeled to the side, her hold on Epiphany slackening. Epiphany pulled away, diving to the side, but as she did she cried out and clutched at her neck.

Gerold was shocked by the success of his attack, but

pressed forward, swinging at the Crone again. This time she saw him coming and managed to get an arm up, but there was still a satisfying crunch of bone as the cube slammed into the spindly limb. She cried out, but it was more than pain that came out of her mouth. Her shout had the force of a hurricane wind and Gerold was thrown away from her. He slid across the ground and came to rest against the base of a tree. The cube lay several feet from him, pulsing with its amber light.

"Well done Gerold," Thad told the young man softly. "Now, quickly, get to Epiphany."

Gerold shook his head to clear it from the blow. Epiphany was between him and the Crone, still clutching her neck. In the glow of her grandfather's housing and the burning shine of the Devil's eyes Gerold could see blood trickling out between her fingers. He threw himself forward onto all fours and started crawling quickly toward her.

The Crone had seen her as well and threw herself toward the downed girl. Crafter's swirling shadow arms swept back and caught her again, lifting her off the ground and holding her spread eagle.

"That was a good trick," he hissed, fury boiling off him in palpable waves. "You won't manage it again."

The old hag just laughed.

"It's too late Devil. Too late for you all!"

"I am not afraid of your bluster you withered bag of air," Crafter told her, tugging at her limbs. She cried out in a moment of agony, but then started to laugh again.

"It's not me you should fear foolish creature," she said, one of her bony fingers stretching toward the sky. "He is here."

Even with the wind and rain whipping into his face and forcing him into a perpetual squint Ellis could see the fiery red glow in the trees below them. Tsayyadiel circled once and then pitched into a sweeping dive.

"Get ready Ellis Carter," the angel shouted over the whistle of wind. "When we are close I will let you go. You will have to roll the best you can, but we are out of time."

Ellis gritted his teeth and waited. Trees whipped by him lightning fast on either side and the ground was rushing up fast enough to make his guts crawl up into his throat. At the last moment Tsayyadiel pulled up his decent for the briefest of moments and let go of Ellis' cradle. The alchemist hit the ground and tucked as best he could. The impact was not gentle, but neither was it unbearable. He tumbled across the loamy ground and finally came to rest in a tangle of roots.

What he found when he sat up was a scene from his worst nightmares; all of his tormentors drawn together in one place. The red Devil stood with his back to Ellis, a fierce crimson glow shining around him and dark tendrils of smoke pulsing out of his coat. Two of those tendrils had been cut and lay on the ground, writhing and dissolving into smoke.

Tsayyadiel stood in front of him, silver knife glittering in the Devil's ruddy glow as if coated in a thin sheen of blood. Tsayyadiel's wings were thrown wide and his body held tense and ready. Behind the angel the Crone hunkered down near the ground. Her veil was pulled back to reveal her empty eye sockets and their eternal storms. A thick line of black ichor ran down her face from a deep wound in the side of her head.

"You have troubled us long enough Devil," Tsayyadiel said. His voice was quiet, but it cut through the thunder of rain a surely as his knife had cut through the Devil's smoky arms.

The Crone let out a long tittering laugh, like fingernails being run over rough glass. The sound made

Ellis' skin crawl.

"Finish brimstone's bastard quickly, our prize is within our grasp," she said, sweeping a boney arm behind her. For the first time Ellis noticed the other humans in the area. There were two of them, a man and a woman and they were huddled low under a strange metal overhang. The man was doing something to the woman who seemed to be hurt. A thrill of anticipation ran through the alchemist. If what the Crone said was true then one of those two people were the Bearer.

Ellis started forward, moving around the edge of the confrontation in order to reach the other two humans. If he could be the one to catch the Bearer, the one to secure the prize than it would prove his worth to those he served. Perhaps then they would send him back to the College, or at least take him out of the hell that his life had been since he'd left the bridge.

As Ellis crept through the trees Tsayyadiel made his move. He leapt forward, his wings giving him extra distance and lashed out at the Devil with his long knife. The Devil weaved away from the slashing blade and darted deeper into the trees. His lashing tentacles snapped in at Tsayyadiel, but the angel dodged out of the way or cut them down with ease. He continued his push, driving the beleaguered Devil farther and farther away from the rest of the group.

The Devil may have been powerful, but it was clear he was no warrior and faced against the murderous angel he was terribly outmatched. Still, he was putting up a good fight, keeping Tsayyadiel at bay well enough to drag out the fight. The Crone for her part was crouched low on her haunches and tittering madly. She was wringing her hands together eagerly as she watched the combat draw ever closer to its inevitable conclusion.

She was so focused on the two combatants that she

failed to notice the long ribbon of shadow that had been oozing toward her. Like a coiled snake it struck, wrapping her ankle and jerking her off her feet. It yanked her upward and dashed her against a tree hard enough to crack the trunk.

"Epiphany run!" the Devil cried out as he slapped the Crone into another thick tree. Ellis turned to see the girl under the ledge. She was wide-eyed and staring, but suddenly free to escape with the Crone's lurking presence gone. With a curse Ellis dashed toward her.

~ ~ ~

Epiphany heard Crafter's cry; watched as he dragged the Crone away so that they could escape. She also saw what it cost him. The shift in focus had allowed the four-winged angel with the wicked knife to finally close ground with the Devil. The knife rammed home into the side of the crimson coat and Crafter cried out. The smoky arm holding the Crone aloft evaporated immediately and she dropped unceremoniously to the earth. The angel yanked the knife free and shoved Crafter back against a nearby tree.

Epiphany could see where the knife had sunk into the Devil's coat. She wondered if it could even hurt him since he seemed to be nothing but smoke and shadow under the thick velvet, but then she saw the silver fire beginning to crawl across the dark fabric, eating the hole wider and wider. Crafter cried out in agony and clutched at the spreading tear.

The angel laughed, a short cruel sound and stepped in for the kill, his white robe swirling around him in the storm winds.

Epiphany wanted to cry out, but when she had pulled away from the Crone the old hag had snagged her with cruel nails. It had only been a small cut, but Epiphany hadn't been able to get it to stop bleeding, and now it felt like her throat was trying to close.

"Epiphany we have to go!" Gerold was tugging at her hand, but she couldn't reply, and she couldn't look away from the moment of finality drawing closer between the angel and the devil. She hardly knew Crafter, but he seemed like one of the few friends she had in this upside-down world and he was about to die.

"Epiphany!" Gerold was screaming, practically spitting in her face in his desperation to use the moment Crafter's ploy had bought them.

The silver knife rose up for a final fall.

The new angel hit the ground with a force like a landslide. The earth jumped and shook. The angel with the silver knife was thrown back from the impact, though he twisted in the air, his wings pulsing and landed on his feet. The new angel rose to his feet as well and turned to face his knife-wielding foe.

"Acaphiel," the knife wielder said, and though his back was to her Epiphany could hear the cruel smile in his voice.

"Don't call me that," the newcomer snarled, his own four wings flaring in anger. Epiphany couldn't help but notice that though they were dressed utterly differently, one in white robes and the other in a voluminous black coat, the two angels looked almost identical, with the same narrow cheeks, long nose, and jet black hair.

"Why shouldn't I call you that Brother?" the white angel asked. "It is your name, as you have been called since the beginning. You were made to be the Reaper of God, and so you have been called."

"I have not served your false god for a long time Brother Hunter. It's just Reaper now."

There was another figure beside Epiphany, one that had not been there a moment before. Epiphany turned to find a handsome man, with short red hair and a thick coppery beard to match. His eyes were depthless blue and full of kindness. Epiphany knew she should be startled to find him there, or continue her escape, but there was a sense of peace that came with the man and she couldn't find her fear. So calmed was she by his presence at her side that it took Epiphany a moment to notice the pair of soft gray wings folded behind his shoulders.

"I am Heart," he told her, "and we have to go. Now."

Epiphany gestured to her throat. He laid a hand on top of hers and suddenly the pain was gone and she could breath again.

"Alright, but there's something I have to get first," she told him. He seemed hesitant to delay, but he nodded and motioned for her to lead them.

"Have you come to kill me," she heard the white robed angel, the one that had been called Hunter ask.

"It has been long overdue," Reaper replied. "You have a debt to pay brother."

Epiphany was trying not to be distracted by the two angels as she scrambled across the ground beneath the fallen strider. She had to get on top of the craft and get the box. All this was about the box and she couldn't leave it behind.

"Gerold, bring my grandpa," she said as she moved past her friend. Before she could go farther however the Crone was there in front of her.

The old hag looked worse for her confrontation with Crafter, one of her arms was twisted around at an unnatural angle, black ichor was flowing from multiple wounds, and if it was possible she was standing even more hunched than she had before. She still exuded a sense of deadly menace however and Epiphany pulled up short.

"Not so fast child," the witch tittered at her. "You and I have not concluded our business."

"I think you have," Heart said, sliding in front of

Epiphany and spreading his wings across her protectively.

"Ah Heart, the soft, weak core of the Three," she said, offering a mocking bow. "I will sweep you aside with a single blow and have the girl. Stand aside and save me the trouble."

"You will not find me so weak as you seem to believe," Heart responded, setting his feet in a fighting posture.

"Ellis Carter," the Crone called out, looking into the darkness beyond them. "Ellis Carter your lord and master had need of a soldier."

~ ~ ~

Ellis froze when he heard the Crone call his name. A soldier? What did she expect him to do, run out of the night and with his bare fists lay into the angel guarding the girl. He was willing to serve, and even to fight if he had to, but he was in no hurry to commit suicide. He wished he hadn't dropped the gun he'd taken from town, but somewhere in the long numbing flight it had slipped from his fingers. Now his only real weapon was surprise and the Crone had ruined that for him.

Then there was a sharp, burning pain in his chest. He cried out and clutched at the area, wondering if some hidden assassin had shot him through the heart. He found no wound, but pulled his hand back with a yelp when it touched something coal hot beneath his shirt. He pulled the fabric up to find the strange medallion the Crone had given him glowing a bright cherry red. He could feel the heat from it starting to blister his skin. He leaned forward so that it dangled away from him.

He moved to take it off, but before he could it leapt towards his chest with a will of its own. When it struck, the skin began to blacken and cook immediately and Ellis let out an agonized wail. He clawed at the smoldering metal, but it was burning deeper into his skin and he couldn't pry it loose. With wide-eyed terror he realized that the skin the medallion had damaged was not just blackened, but was beginning to change. What had only moments before been charred flesh was becoming smooth black scales, and worse yet, the change was starting to spread.

"What have you done to me?" Ellis screamed at the Crone, but her only reply was a shrill cackle.

He could feel the scalding metal of the amulet moving through him, and with a final jolt he felt it eat its way through into his heart. Then the changes came much faster. Ellis' bones broke and reformed with such brutal speed that he dropped in and out of consciousness with each shift. His skin was almost completely covered by the black scales. He could feel his mind beginning to go as well, felt cold reptilian thoughts of blood and murder creeping into his brain. He tried to cry out to the Crone again, demand that she stop what was happening, but all that came out was an ululating hiss.

"Now you are the soldier we need Ellis Carter," the Crone sighed softly. "Be a good boy and kill them."

~ ~ ~

The Crone was a dangerous opponent, and Heart was not a warrior, but he knew he had the strength to hold her long enough for the girl and her friend to escape. He wasn't so sure that he could hold the Crone and whatever this new horror she had conjured was. He had heard stories of mortals being used as gateways to bring in hell spawned monstrosities, but to see it happen in person had turned his stomach.

"Reaper!" he called.

"Yes Reaper," Tsayyadiel snarled. "What will you do? You might have been able to face me down, though you are wounded, but you can't fight me and them at the same time."

Reaper's answer, as it so often did, came in the form of violence. He leveled his guns and fired. One shot was at

Hunter, the other at the quadrupedal snake creature the simpering human had become. Hunter leaned out of the way almost casually and the other creature leapt forward, devouring ground between it and its prey and leaving the shot behind it.

Reaper's attack hadn't been entirely wasted however. The first shot had never been intended for Hunter, but the Crone who stood behind him. The shot hit the Crone without her even knowing it was coming.

The bullet hammered into her face, right between her empty eyes and erupted out the back of her head in a spray of puss and gore. With a dry rattle she pitched to the ground dead.

"Well played Acaphiel," Tsayyadiel said with a thin smile and an admiring salute. "You're still wounded and have to face me however."

Tsayyadiel surged forward, but was met by a swirling wall of black that deflected him to the side and sent him reeling into a tree.

"He may be wounded, but he is not alone."

Crafter stepped out of the woods. His eyes no longer burned with the furious fire and only a listless trickle of black flowed out between the buttons of his coat, but he stood straight and ready beside Reaper. Heart would just have to hope the pair could handle Tsayyadiel, because the snake was almost on them.

"Run," he told the girl, giving her a hard shove the direction she'd been going before the Crone had appeared. She didn't have to be told twice and took off at a sprint with her friend in tow. The snake-thing tried to weave around Heart and give chase, but he flicked out the tip of one of his wings and caught it in mid-stride. The blow took it off its feet and it rolled across the uneven ground. Heart was disappointed to see that it had its feet back under it before it even finished the slide.

He was more disappointed to see that he had not captured its attention. Even as it was righting itself it was reorienting on the running pair of mortals. With a soft curse Heart dug his toes into the dirt and took off at a run, hoping to intercept the creature. The thing was wickedly fast and Heart had to use his wings to get the speed to start closing ground.

Ahead he could see the pair of mortals climbing up onto the grounded craft. The monster rushed past them and spun, crouching low on its haunches to leap. Heart knew that was the one chance he would get. As the creature pushed off so did he. He hit it in mid-air, his shoulder catching it in the underbelly. They tangled together as the force of the angels push threw them back from the craft and the fleeing pair.

The thing was attacking him before they'd even hit the ground. It's sharp hind claws raked at his lower abdomen and legs and he could feel countless wounds opening and blood beginning to flow. The pain was immense. Heart ignored it. He wasn't a warrior, but he was strong and he was tenacious and as the tangled combatants hit the ground he wrapped his hands around the monsters sinewy neck and began to squeeze. He could feel its muscles bunching and straining against his strangling grip and it redoubled its efforts to eviscerate him. It snapped frothing jaws down at his face, but he had too firm a hold on its throat for it to land a bite. He was grateful for that as he could see thick drops of poison glittering on its fangs.

They slipped and slithered through the mud and the rain, each fighting for more purchase. Heart wasn't sure how much damage the creature had done to him, he'd gone numb below his chest, but he continued to squeeze, refusing to let go. The creatures muddy brown eyes were bulging from its skull and he could see the panic there. With its front legs it tried to pry him off, push him away, but the angel was the stronger and he held on with all he had.

With an almost listless motion it reached out and swept a claw across his face. He could have blocked it, but he would have had to let go of its throat so he let the attack land. He felt his cheek tear open and his left eye burst as the claw sliced through the juicy orb. He gritted his teeth and felt bare muscle flex in the wind. He squeezed harder still.

There was a sudden pop, and the creature spasmed once, twice, and then was still. Even after it had stopped moving Heart didn't let go in case it was some sort of trick. He couldn't have gone anywhere anyway, there wasn't enough left of his legs.

22

EPIPHANY SCRAMBLED over the steeply canted hull of the strider. With the sounds of battle still behind her she had to move more slowly than she would have liked, but the rain was still coming down and the metal was slick and treacherous. She just had to hope that Heart was winning and that she had time to do what she had to do.

She reached the part of the deck where they had stowed her bag, but could find no obvious seems or latches. She ran her fingers over the metal. There were well-defined grooves where the symbols were etched, but none of them seemed to correspond to any sort of door nor handle. Gerold dropped down next to her and started searching as well but with no more luck.

"Gerold we have to get the box out of here," she told him. He knew that of course, but speaking out loud, connecting to her oldest friend seemed a thin rope of sanity amidst the madness of the last hour.

"I can't find the door though," he told her.

"Are we in the right place?" she asked, though she was sure they were. Gerold nodded.

"Epiphany," grandpa's voice cut in to her frantic searching.

"Grandpa?"

Gerold had set the cube next to him when he'd started looking for the hatch. It was propped against his foot so it wouldn't slide down the deck and pulsed with light each time Thad spoke.

"Aleister isn't a machine Epiphany, he's like me."

"What?"

"I don't fully understand it," he told her, "but Crafter creates devices that are powered by souls. Aleister is one of them. If you need the door open ask."

Epiphany took a deep breath and laid her hands flat against the metal.

"Aleister," she spoke softly. "Aleister, I need to get into the hatch, can you open the door please."

There was no response.

"What if he's ... I don't know... dead? Can he die?" she asked, looking alternately between Gerold and her grandpa. Gerold just shrugged. Grandpa was little more help.

"I don't know," he admitted. "When Gerold used me to hit the witch I was shaken a bit, but I didn't feel like I was in danger, but it also wasn't a direct attack against me."

"Epiphany! Look!"

Gerold was pointing excitedly at the decking between her hands. Spider webs of blue tracery were glimmering to life and then dying away.

"Aleister?" Epiphany ventured hopefully. "Can you open the door?"

A fearsome quiet had descended over the forest and the rain had eased, but Epiphany didn't know if any of that was good.

"We need you Aleister."

The light grew between her hands, and with a soft hiss the hatch popped open.

"Thank you!" Epiphany gasped gratefully as she snatched her satchel out of the open hole and rummaged out the box. She almost expected to find it missing, somehow stolen by their enemies, but the dark lacquered wood was tucked deep beneath her clothes where she'd left it. She turned it in her hands to check and then shoved it back in the bag.

"What now?" Gerold asked. Epiphany hadn't thought that far ahead, hadn't really planned beyond getting the precious box.

"We have to at least start back the way we came. It's the only way down unless we want to jump and I don't relish that idea in the dark and the wet. We'll go slowly and carefully."

Gerold took his bag from the hatch and after a soft word tucked Thad's cube into it. The pair slipped across Aleister's deck toward the low edge, their ears straining for any sound. There was none.

When they got to the lip they found Crafter and the dark angel that had called himself Reaper standing over the fallen form of Heart. Epiphany couldn't stifle a gasp when she saw the terrible damage that had been done to the kind angel's body. His face was a mess of blood and torn tissue and everything from navel down looked as if it had been run through an over-sized cheese grater.

Both the angel and the devil turned at the sound of her gasp. Upon seeing them the angel turned his attention back to his fellow, but Crafter motioned for Gerold and her to come down and join them.

She slipped off the lip of the strider and dropped the few feet to the ground. Gerold thumped down next to her and side-by-side they went to join the other two. Up close the damage to Heart was even worse than it had seemed, and she was surprised to find him still breathing.

"He's still alive," she gasped.

"Oh I'll live," Heart burbled out around a mouthful of blood. The fallen angel even managed a week smile, though with his face in ribbons it was a grim sight.

"My brother may not be a warrior, but he is mighty," Reaper said. His voice was choked.

"No tears for me brother, though it cheers my heart to

hear you speak of me so. I did as I had to."

He waved a hand weakly beside him and Epiphany noticed the body of the snake-thing that had been chasing them laying a few feet away. Its black scales had almost completely hidden it in the mat of black dirt. Epiphany could see that it's neck was twisted at an odd angle and that's its claws were stained with blood.

"Thank you," she said, kneeling down beside Heart and laying a hand on his shoulder. "You saved our lives."

Heart smiled at her again, and even with the ruin of his face the warmth that came from his one remaining eye almost moved Epiphany to tears.

"It is right brother," he said turning back to Reaper. "She is the right one. Can't you feel it?"

"I can."

"As can I," Crafter agreed. "I got a sense of her from Thad, her grandfather, but once I actually met her I knew."

"What do you mean?" Gerold asked.

Heart laughed, a thick wet sound, but full of happiness.

"Even you can feel it young man. That is why you are here in the woods instead of home with your mother and brothers. There is something about her. She is the Bearer and I think she was even before she took this form in this world. She will be the one there at the end of the War."

Epiphany didn't like being talked about in such grand terms.

"I don't know about all that," she told them, from where she hunkered down with Heart. "But I do know that we probably shouldn't stay here."

Suddenly she looked around the dark forest with a rising panic.

"He's gone," Reaper told her, seeing her frantic searching. "He couldn't fight both the devil and myself and he fled once his allies were destroyed. You are right though; we should be off before he returns. Brother Hunter is not known for his forgiving nature, nor for giving up easily."

Crafter turned to look behind him at his fallen strider. He considered for a long moment and then shook his head.

"Aleister has completed his service and flown his last. If you can you should carry both your brother and the girl. The boy and I will walk from here. We will meet you when we can."

"I cannot carry Heart," Reaper told him. "He lives yet, and may recover-"

"I'll never dance again," Heart interjected.

"– but he is too weak to be carried as I fly. The strain would finish him."

"Then take the girl and the man and I will build a litter and carry him," Crafter offered.

"I'm happy to help," Gerold volunteered, stepping forward.

"Wait!" The voice was muffled from inside Gerold's bag.

"My grandpa is ... well I don't know how to explain it, but he's in a cube in Gerold's bag," Epiphany explained as her friend dropped his pack and drew out the glowing cube.

"If the strider is a Soulforge, can you make me into a strider," Thad asked once he was free of the bag.

"The life of a strider is hard work, and you have done nothing to deserve such harsh service," Crafter said shaking his head.

"I'm volunteering," Thad insisted. "I am not out of this fight, and if I can help than I will. That angel saved my granddaughter's life, and if I can help save his I will."

"Are you sure?" Crafter asked. "I can only move you from a simpler Forge to a more complex one, so once I put you into the strider I cannot draw you back out, and you will have to serve because here in this realm I don't have the means to make a new one."

"I'm in this to the end Crafter," Thad said with a fierce determination. The light around his cube pulsed brightly. "Do it."

"Very well. Wait here."

Crafter moved away from them the short distance to the strider. He laid a gloved hand gently on the side of it and leaned in close. He spoke softly, and Epiphany could only make out some of what he said.

"... served me well ... to go ... this ... sleep now ... nowhere ... to go ... earned ... over we ... each other ..."

He raised his other hand to the side of the craft and began to chant. A blue light grew around the ship, shimmering and throbbing like a great heart beat. It built until it was so bright that it was almost unbearable. There was a single, starburst flash. When Epiphany's eyes cleared the ship was gone and Crafter was holding one of the small metal cubes in the outstretched palm of his hand.

"Is that ...?" Gerold asked.

"The strider? Yes. All the Soulforges share a basic shape; it is what they can become that differs. Are you ready Thad?"

"I am," Thad replied with no hesitation.

Crafter held out a hand and Gerold offered him the second cube. Before they could make the exchange Epiphany snatched the golden cube from Gerold's hand.

"I love you grandpa," she said, pressing her lips to the warm metal.

"I love you Epiphany. I am so proud of you," he replied.

"I'm proud of you grandpa."

Epiphany handed the cube to Crafter. He was smiling

at her as he took it, and the soft lines at the corners of his eyes made those bloody orbs seem not so terrible. She returned the smile and stepped back to let him work.

He held the cubes in opposite hands, and slowly moved them closer together as he chanted softly. The cube her grandfather was in began to glow more brightly, taking on that same heart beat pulse they'd seen in Aleister's final moments. Sparks of golden electricity started to crackle between the two cubes and slowly runes on the inert cube began to light. As Crafter continued the light in the first cube started to dim and the pulsing throb shifted to the new cube. There was another bright flash and now the second cube was glowing a bright golden and the first was a dark block of metal in the devil's hand. He tucked the old cube into his coat and set the new one on the ground in front of him.

"This will be strange the first time Thad, but it is time to spread you wings," the devil said. He rejoined the group and motioned everyone back several feet.

"The first time a new strider opens it can sometimes get a bit chaotic," the devil explained. They all stepped back and waited.

Bright amber light flowed across the surface of the cube in growing waves and what happened next was anything but chaotic. The cube began to unfold in impossible ways, plains opening out of smaller spaces, each step building on the last until it was like a liquid wave of burnished metal surging outward. It was beautiful.

It took less than a minute. When it was over the glow dwindled and then died, leaving the familiar manta-like shape of the strider hovering a few feet above the ground. There were subtle differences between this strider and Aleister. This strider seemed broader across the bow like powerful shoulders tucked to charge, and it swept back to a gracefully thinning tail where Aleister had simply rounded off. Crafter nodded in approval.

"Grandpa?" Epiphany asked hesitantly.

"I'm still here Epiphany." If his voice had seemed distant and frail in the first cube, that was all gone now. His voice had a deep rumble as it rolled out of the body of the strider. It sounded strong and fearsome. Epiphany imagined that if she had known him as a young man this is how he would have sounded.

"Are you alright?" she asked.

"Honestly? I haven't felt this good in half a century. I should have died and been turned into a devil's flying machine long ago!" A laugh boomed out of the ship with enough force to shake collected rain off the leaves above them. It hammered down across the strider's deck with a crash like a hundred hammers.

"That was odd though," Thad confessed.

"You'll get used to it," Crafter told him, reaching out to pat the flank of the hovering ship. "Reaper, help me get your brother on board."

The two leaned down, and Gerold moved in to help steady the wounded angel. Working together the three got Heart up onto Thad's broad back and everyone else climbed aboard.

"Where are we going?" Crafter asked, looking to Reaper.

"I'm looking for Father Brendiwald," Epiphany interjected before the angel could answer. He smiled at her.

"That is good child, because he's looking for you as well. There's a house at the edge of Newridge. Brendiwald and my sister are hiding there waiting for us. It is also where Heart can get the care he needs."

"All I need is a good nap," gurgled Heart. He was still smiling but Epiphany could tell he was getting weaker.

"Do you know how to get to Newridge from here?"

Crafter asked, leaning down to speak to Thad through the deck.

"Follow the road. Not a tough trick."

"Indeed," Crafter laughed. "Keep a bit off the road though. Stay low above the trees so we are less likely to be seen in our approach. When we get close we'll figure out how to actually get there without being spotted."

"Alright," Thad said. "Everyone hold on!"

The strider shuddered once and then began to sweep up toward the top of the trees. Once it had cleared the canopy it surged forward. Crafter laughed again, pulling his coat tight around him as the wind whipped past.

"You're faster than Aleister was!" he said. "I should have started using the righteous a long time ago!"

Reaper gave him a sidelong glance.

"I jest," said the Devil holding up a hand in truce.

"Who was that other angel back there in the woods?" Gerold asked.

"Tsayyadiel, the Hunter," Reaper told them. "He is a cruel and vengeful creature and a loyal servant of the Word."

"He," Epiphany hesitated, not sure if she was stepping into dangerous territory. "He looked just like you, or at least almost."

"They're twins," the answer came from Heart. Reaper gave him a look that Epiphany couldn't read, but either he couldn't see it with his damaged eye or he chose to ignore it.

"It is a rare thing for angels to be made twins, but Reaper and Hunter came into being together. They were two halves of the same being, the hunt and the kill. The search and the find. One was the answer to the question that was the other."

"So he is your brother as well?" Gerold asked.

"Indeed he is young man, as is Reaper, and Fist who

you will meet soon enough is our sister."

"What happened?" Gerold pressed. "Why is he fighting you?"

"Family spat," ventured Heart.

"He betrayed us all," snarled Reaper. He said it with such fury that Epiphany worried that he was going to lash out at one of them. He held the trembling rage in however, and continued.

"When we saw what the Word had become we met as a family. We made the decision to break with the Word; to fall. We were going to come here and serve the Prophet in his War against the Lie."

Reaper stopped, his hands balled into white knuckled fists.

"Hunter was at that gathering. He agreed to join us; at least he did in word. Secretly he didn't want things to change. He liked the unrest. He liked being unleashed on the humans. He never had any sympathy for your kind, but he didn't share this with the rest of us. Instead he went to Enoch, the seneschal of the Word. He told him of our plan and said he was still loyal, but the Word wanted proof."

"What?" Epiphany had a terrible feeling that she already knew the answer.

"He had to kill us all," Reaper answered simply.

"Indeed," continued Heart. "He had to kill us all, but he failed. He knew that in the moments before we fell we would be distracted and easier to kill. It was his only chance. There was no way he could kill us all otherwise. So we gathered to make our break. He was there, but as we prepared to go he attacked."

"But you got away," Gerold said, gesturing to the two angels on the strider with him.

"Not all of us," Reaper again interjected.

"The first one he attacked was our sister, Silence. She

was the most powerful of us so he knew if he didn't kill her first he wouldn't be able to beat us all even in our disoriented pre-fall trance. He struck her down, but as he did she cast out the other three of us and held him there. We fell, she died, he stayed."

"I'm so sorry," Epiphany said. She could hear the sadness in the angel's voice and it broke her heart.

"Not as sorry as he'll be when our reckoning finally arrives," Reaper growled.

"I believe that," Gerold told him. Reaper gave Gerold a soft chuckle.

"It is one thing to frighten a human boy," he said. "It is quite another to strike down Tsayyadiel, the Hunter of God."

"Tsayyadiel," Epiphany rolled the name across her tongue. "He called you something."

Reaper shook his head, but Heart spoke up.

"Acaphiel. It means Reaper of God, We all have true angelic names, but that was part of our pact when we fell. We no longer served the God for whom we'd been named so after the fall we chose to go simply by our titles; Reaper, Heart, Fist."

"Silence," Reaper added.

"Silence," echoed Heart. "It is an old story, and a sad one. It makes me tired. I'm going to sleep now. Wake me when we get there."

The angel let his remaining eye slip shut. Epiphany was afraid he was dying, but his slow labored breathing continued unbroken and Reaper seemed unworried.

"I will fly ahead and make sure the way is clear," Reaper told them. Epiphany could see that the recounting had worried an old wound and the angel was troubled. He pushed himself to his feet. His black coat flared out behind him, flapping in the wind and his long, dark hair whipped around his face. He flexed his shoulders and four soot black wings rolled out from his back. He spread them wide, letting the wind catch and lift him off the back of the strider. For a moment he dropped behind the speeding craft, but with a single mighty flap he shot ahead of them and disappeared into the night.

"I might be fast," her grandpa's voice rumbled from the deck beneath them, "but clearly I'm no angel."

"None of us are my friend," Crafter said laying a hand on the deck. "None of us are."

23

THEY HAD LANDED the strider a few miles outside Newridge. Reaper had returned and told them that everything had been prepared and guided them to a meeting place. When they set down in a small grove of apple trees there was a two horse carriage waiting. The driver was a young man in a plain blue coverall who seemed unsurprised to have a flying craft land in front of him and drop off two angels, a devil, and a pair of filthy humans.

The party carefully unloaded Heart, who had slept through the whole journey and continued to sleep as they settled him into the carriage. Reaper seemed unconcerned so Epiphany let herself believe that the angel was stable or even recovering. At least the bleeding had finally stopped, though how that was possible with the overwhelming damage done to his body she didn't know.

Once Heart was settled Crafter had Thad collapse back into his cube form. That transformation seemed to surprise their driver a little, but he kept his comments to himself. Once the shift was complete Crafter held out the still glimmering cube to Epiphany.

"It seems right that you should carry him with you," the devil said with a thin smile.

"Thank you," she said as she accepted the box. The metal was warm, almost hot to the touch and she pulled down the sleeve of her jacket to cradle it. She felt wrong about dropping her grandfather into a bag, even if he was a metal cube now so she carried it as she climbed into the carriage behind Gerold.

"I'm tired Epiphany," grandpa told her.

"Are you alright?" she asked as she settled onto the low wooden bench. Inside the carriage it was mostly dark, and the low glow from the cube made everyone look like they were gilded in gold.

"Yes," he replied. "Just tired. I'm going to sleep. You don't have to hold me, I'll be alright."

"Sleep well Thad, you did well," Crafter said as he climbed into the carriage with them.

The glow around the box pulsed once and then faded to darkness. Even if he was sleeping Epiphany still felt odd dropping him in a bag like a bit of tack, so instead she slipped the cube into one of the large pockets on the outside of her coat.

With a crack of reins the carriage set off along the bumpy road. This far out from the city the paving work was poorly maintained and on the hard wooden seats the ride was far from comfortable. The inside of the carriage was cramped for the five of them, especially with Heart sprawled out across the floor. It was also pitch black once her grandpa's light was gone. They all rode in uncomfortable silence until the carriage drew to a halt again.

The door swung open and Epiphany found herself face to face with a severe looking woman. It took Epiphany only a moment looking at her features to know she was related to the angels. She had Reaper's narrow, sharp features with a wild main or red curls that matched Heart's hair and beard.

"Fist?" Epiphany half asked.

"Yup," the woman grunted and offered her a hand down. They had been cramped long enough for Epiphany to get stiff so she gratefully accepted the hand and clamored down into the dirt. As Fist helped Gerold down Epiphany took a look around at her surroundings.

They were outside a small, but pleasant house. The area they were in had several other houses spread out along the road, but they were far enough from the city that they weren't close. In the near distance Epiphany could see a ubiquitous glow across the horizon. She'd heard that big cities put off so much light that they lit up the night sky, but to actually see it took her breath away. On dark nights Seacliff was almost lightless. To imagine that many lights was more than she could conceive. Closer still she could see clusters of houses, like herd animals nestling together for safety. Some of the little enclaves were bigger than her whole town.

Gerold was at her shoulder.

"We should move inside," he told her. "The others have already taken Heart."

She nodded. She was going to point out what she had seen to Gerold, but then she remembered he'd been here before. He'd been even farther into the city than they were now. She swallowed her words, not wanting to seem rural. Instead she just dropped into step with him and entered the house. As she came through the door she saw Fist and Reaper carrying Heart up the stairs.

There was a middle-aged woman slouched against the doorframe farther into the house. Her brown hair was cropped functionally close to her skull and her hands were tucked under her arms. When Epiphany came in the woman looked her up and down.

"We've been expecting you," she said. Epiphany was taken aback. She wasn't used to being the type of person who was expected.

The woman didn't wait for Epiphany to respond. She rolled off the jam and walked into the next room. Epiphany shrugged to Gerold and the pair followed. In the next room was a table tipped up and pushed against a wall to make room for a gaping hole in the floor. The woman stepped to the side and gestured to the trap door. Epiphany went through the trap and down into a wide dirt room.

It seemed to Epiphany everything that a secret hideout should be. It was a rough place, carved out of the hard packed earth, and spartan in the extreme. The only light came from a few flickering lanterns and the dancing light gave the room a ceremonial feeling. In the center of the room there was a wide, low table covered in papers that screamed importance.

She knew the man on the far side of the table had to be Father Brendiwald. Slate gray eyes gazed out of a careworn face with a mixture of kindness and determination. At first Epiphany thought he was scowling at her, but then she realized that the left side of his face was drawn tight by scar tissue where he was missing an ear.

"You must be Epiphany," he said. The earthen walls absorbed his voice, leaving him sounding small and flat. "Your grandfather told me a great deal about you."

"He never told me anything about you, at least not until he was dying," she replied.

Brendiwald's face fell, his lips turning down at the corners and his eyes partially closing.

"Thad is dead?"

"Yes," Epiphany told him. Then she reconsidered. "Sort of dead."

"What?" Brendiwald's craggy brown drew down over his eyes.

"I don't know if I can explain. Some priests killed him. As he was dying he told me to come to you. He told me to bring you this box that he had me get out of a secret compartment. Later I met a devil named Crafter and he'd put my grandpa in a magic metal cube. He's still dead I guess, but he can talk to us, and now he's some kind of flying ship."

It sounded insane when she said it all out loud, but it was the truth. Brendiwald, for his part took the whole story in stride and didn't seem surprised by any of it.

"Where is he now?" the old priest asked.

Epiphany drew the strider cube out of her pocket and laid it on the edge of the table. It was still dark and inert.

"I think he's sleeping. He carried us most of the way here and it made him tired."

"I imagine it would. I don't think I could carry a group of people any distance at all myself."

A wide smile opened up across Brendiwald's face. It was a generous and guileless smile.

"I suspect I owe you a great deal of explanation," Brendiwald told her, motioning to a chair across from him at the table, and then to a second chair for Gerold. "Do you have the box Thad had you get?"

Epiphany set her bag down and dug out the box. She set it on the edge of the table next to Thad and took the offered chair. Once she was settled Gerold sat down next to her.

"How much do you know?" Brendiwald asked, leaning forward and folding his hands on the table in front of him. His index fingers came together to make a little steeple and he propped his chin up on it.

"I guess I know a fair amount," Epiphany said, thinking back through what she'd been told. "I don't understand most of it, but I know that there is a war. I know that the war is between the Word and the Prophet because the Word tried to take over reality by making people fight each other. I know that you serve the Prophet and that your forces can't get to the Word to attack because he locked you out, and that whatever is in this box is maybe some kind of key to get you through the gate."

"That's probably the best and most concise summery I've heard of the whole mess. You've certainly got the core of it in hand."

"There's so much I don't understand though!" Epiphany pleaded, leaning forward across the table.

"There's a great deal that most of us don't understand. I might understand more than you, and the three upstairs might understand more than that, but what I've found is that the more you know the more questions it leaves you with. What I don't question is that the rule of the Word is a Lie and has to be stopped, and that his servants in the High Church are cruel and terrible. I know because for a long time I was one of them."

"You were ...?" Gerold queried.

"A High Cleric of the Church; yes I was. When I came to really understand what the Church was, and what it stood for I fled. Most of me made it out." Brendiwald gestured to his missing ear. "Still, it was worth it and I have never regretted the decision."

"So, do you know what's in the box?" Epiphany asked.

"It took us longer to get around to that than I thought it would," Brendiwald said with a smile. "I do know what is in the box, and not only will I tell you, but I'll show you."

He motioned for the box and Epiphany eagerly slid it across the table toward him. She was trembling and had to remind herself to breath as he slid he hands along the smooth surface of the wood. He played his hands back and forth until he found what he was looking for. He pressing his thumbs down together and a latch that Epiphany had never been able to find gave with a soft pop. The lid of the box hinged up on a well-concealed seam.

Brendiwald looked down into the box, a secretive smile playing across his face. Slowly he turned it around to show Epiphany its contents. The box was lined in a deep purple velvet that had worn smooth and gray in many places. Dust clung to the soft fabric and Epiphany had to wonder how old the box itself was. In the center of the box, held securely in place by a carved wood stand was a cup.

It didn't seem overly remarkable, simply a ceramic cup in an old box. The outside of the cup had been painted once, though much of the paint had flaked away to reveal the dull brown clay beneath. The scene might once have been an orchard, but all that remained were a few tree limbs and a daub of orange that might have been a fruit. The inside of the cup had been glazed and polished so that it shown softly in the cavorting light of the lanterns, as if it was still wet from a recent drink.

"What is it?" asked Gerold.

"There is a story that was told long ago, before the consolidation when the Word brought all his churches together in the High Church. The story is of a being, part man and part god who comes to earth to teach a new gospel of love and forgiveness. He had twelve followers, but at the height of his teachings one of the followers betrayed him and he was killed in gruesome fashion. Three days later this man-god rose from the grave, supposedly on the will of the God that had sent him, but before that, the night before he was betrayed he had a last meal with his followers, and at that meal he drank from a cup that would be famous for centuries after. They called it the Grail."

"Is that story true?" Epiphany asked. She'd never heard any story like that, but a lot of the old tales had been crushed out and lost when the High Church came to power. It didn't suit their agenda to remember that once there had been many faiths all with their own myths and histories.

"It has many elements of truth," Brendiwald said. "That man-god from the story is the Prophet. He did indeed come to earth, though it was not his first visit. He had been visiting the world in many forms for a long time, always trying to infuse the same message of peace into the Word's sects. He was betrayed by one of his followers, but it was not just to a civil government, but to the Word's agents who saw to his murder. I suspect he did have a last dinner, but that has little to do with the actual story.

What's important is that he did indeed drink from this cup, but it wasn't the night before, it was the night after, and for the two nights following that. This cup is a powerful artifact that has existed perhaps even longer than the Word and it has a great many gifts it can bestow. In this case drinking from it for those three nights, or more accurately to have water from it poured into his dead mouth, brought the Prophet back to life. It is because of this cup that we can even continue to fight."

"So that cup can raise the dead?" Epiphany asked.

"It can in some cases, though that is only one of the things that it can do. I don't know if anyone fully knows what it is capable of accomplishing."

"It has been said that it is the cup that held all of existence before it was poured across creation to make the world."

Epiphany turned to find Reaper coming down the stairs, his black coat brushing softly against each step as he descended.

"Heart?" she asked, rising to greet that angel.

"He'll survive," Reaper said, his eyes dark. "He'll loose the use of the eye and both legs."

"He healed me during the fight, can't he heal himself?" Epiphany asked, her hand rising to her throat with the memory of the Crone's terrible poisonous touch.

"To some degree," Reaper said, moving past her and taking a seat at the table. His eyes were fixed on the cup. "He lives only because he is an angel and we can all heal to some degree, but it was a magical creature that attacked him, and we are here on earth with the Gates sealed shut. We are cut off from our strength here and so our ability to recover is limited. That's why the Word sealed the Gates and sent the flood in the first place; because here we could be destroyed."

"I'm sorry," Epiphany said, resuming her seat and reaching out to Reaper. He didn't pull away, but didn't seem comforted by her touch either.

"It is no matter. We are angels. We are created to a purpose and Heart is filling his purpose. There is no sorrow in that."

Epiphany nodded, though she didn't really understand.

"What is our next step?" Reaper asked.

"Are we going to attack now that we have the key?" Epiphany joined the questioning.

"I don't know if we're going to attack. Though there are always those who join our cause, the years have not been good to us and our forces are scattered and few. I don't know that a direct attack would win us anything."

"I understand," said Epiphany crestfallen. She had been running for what felt like forever even though it had been a scant week. Now they were here, everyone together and the idea of doing something potent appealed to her.

"It's not for me to decide however," Brendiwald continued. "We need to take her to the Prophct."

"With as closely as they've been watching all of us do you think that's wise?" Reaper asked.

"I don't think we have much choice," Brendiwald replied. "We have the Bearer and we have the Grail. We have to go to him. Trust me, I don't like it either, but this is too big for us to decide. Anyway, she has worked hard enough, she should get the chance to meet the one she's working for."

Reaper considered it for a moment, pursing his thin

lips.

"Very well. I'll go tell the others. We should stay here the rest of the night and all of tomorrow and rest. We'll leave after dusk tomorrow."

"Agreed."

Reaper pushed back his chair and returned up the stairs.

"Reaper is right of course," Brendiwald admitted. "It is a serious risk to take you to the Prophet right now. He's been in hiding for years, dodging agents of the Word and the Church. They would love to get their hands on him and finish what they started, but I think this," he gestured to the Grail and to Epiphany, "is too important not to bring to him. We'll just have to be careful."

"Tsayyadiel, Hunter, he's still out there," Epiphany said. The though made her tremble. She hadn't had to face him directly, but she'd seen enough to be frightened.

"He is, and though he is one of the worst, and certainly mightiest things standing against us he is certainly not alone. Reaper told me you already saw the Crone."

"Yes, but she's dead," Gerold interjected. "Reaper shot her."

"We hope she's dead," Brendiwald corrected. "With things like the Crone it is never safe to assume. As you've seen with poor Heart, these creatures are not like us and they can survive things that you wouldn't think they could. Nonetheless, I too hope that she is gone. She was a terrible and vicious thing. I've lost many friends to her over the years.

Enough about terrors however, you need to rest and such talk is no way to prepare for sleep."

The idea of sleep hadn't occurred to Epiphany with all the running and excitement of the night, but when Brendiwald mentioned rest a wave of exhaustion swept over her and left her shaking and bleary eyed in her chair.

The priest could see it and he motioned for Gerold to help her.

"Rooms have been prepared for you down here," he told them, gesturing to the curtained off alcoves around the room. "I'm sorry it's a little monastic, but this is the safest place in here, so we think it's where you should stay."

"Thank you, I'm sure it'll be good enough," Epiphany told him. She meant it as well. She was certain that if she just slid off her chair and laid down on the dirt floor she'd be asleep in minutes.

Gerold helped her out of her chair and she leaned on him gratefully. The pair moved slowly to one of the alcoves and Gerold pulled the canvass curtain to the side. Inside was a small cot, a bowl of water, and a chamber pot. Brendiwald was right, it certainly wasn't glamorous, but at that moment the cot looked like a king's feather bet to Epiphany. Gerold set her down onto the hard pad and helped her get her shoes off.

"Thank you Gerold," she said warmly.

"It's no big deal," he replied rolling his shoulders in a shrug.

"No, not just for my shoes. Thank you for coming with me. I wouldn't have made it if you hadn't been here."

"Of course," he said. He drew her into a tight embrace. "I would never leave you to do this on your own Epiphany. We're friends."

She returned the embrace. When they parted she ruffled his hair the way she had when they were young.

"Go and get some sleep now," she told him. "You've earned it."

They said their good nights and Gerold left, drawing the curtain back across her little cell. She could hear Brendiwald talking to other people in the main room. At one point she was certain she heard Crafter, and perhaps even her grandpa, but all the voices blurred together into a white noise drone and Epiphany gave up on being awake.

24

TSAYYADIEL FURLED his wings at the last possible moment, dropping heavily onto the marble steps in front of the Cathedral. The first rays of sun were starting to burn away the morning's clinging fog. The Crone's storm had died with her and for the first time in a week the sky was beginning to clear. The light caught flecks of gold that had been pounded into the marble surface, and the swirled green and white stone looked like it was catching fire.

Tsayyadiel strode across it, unaware of the breathtaking vista the steps made, or even of the grandeur of the building they served. It towered over him, rising into the blue-gray sky like a single pointing finger, reminding everyone who they really served. The whole edifice shared the artifice of the steps, and glimmering gold leaf was lighting up with the coming day. The angel saw none of it. He had a mind only for his rage.

The Angel of the Hunt was not accustomed to failure, nor to having his prey escape his grasp. Yet that was exactly what had happened. The Bearer and the artifact had been at his fingertips and he was going to get to destroy the Devil in Red once and for all. Then his thrice fallen twin had shown up with their younger brother and it had all slipped away from him.

It was not entirely his fault of course. He'd had allies with him and they had failed even more utterly than he had. The Crone had died through nothing but her own negligence. It seemed so unlikely that Acaphiel could have felled her so easily, that when the storm had cleared Tsayyadiel had returned to the scene of the battle to look for her, thinking perhaps it had been a trick she'd pulled to avoid the more dangerous foes. She was gone though. All that had been left of her was a smear of dust and some tattered lace tangled through a knot of tree roots. Tsayyadiel did not mourn her. She was a foul creature, but it was not a good time for her to die.

Ellis Carter had proved an even greater disappointment. Tsayyadiel had been told that the simpering human would be a powerful aid in his quest to find and take the Bearer; moreover he had been told that when the time came the man had been hexed so that he might turn the tide in a battle. Though the alchemist had aided the angel in tracking the Bearer it had merely saved him a bit of time, and when the battle came the beast the man had become was felled by Tsayyadiel's weakest sibling.

The angel's hands curled into trembling fists as he replayed the ignominy of his necessary retreat. He was a great warrior of the Word, but his twin was a match for him, even injured and though alone Tsayyadiel could have destroyed the devil with little effort, the two together were too much. Tsayyadiel had taken to wing as soon as he'd seen Carter, in his altered form brought down. There had been a reason to fight before then. If he could keep the two powerful celestial busy than the creature could kill the Bearer and secure the prize, but with the creature dead Tsayyadiel would have been alone against all three of the others.

Now it was time to regather his composure and plan for the next phase of the hunt. They may have driven him off, but this war was not over and Tsayyadiel was far from done. He could not return to heaven. The Gates were closed to him as much as to anyone else. His only choice was to finish the task given him; not that he would have left the world before then anyway. He still had a score to settle with his betraying family.

He stopped before the towering doors to the cathedral. They were almost two stories each and carved of heavy bronze. The intricate artwork depicted scenes of war in which servants of the Word overcame hordes of infidel disbelievers. They were depictions of the time shortly after the coming of the Waters when the High Church had first moved to absorb all the individual sects the Word had created over the years. Many of the sects had resisted, clinging to the belief that their deity, their faith really was different than all the rest.

Tsayyadiel barked a short laugh. Human's were such foolish creatures.

There were heavy rings welded onto the doors where thick chains could be attached and gangs of servants used to pull the heavy doors open. Tsayyadiel dug his fingers into the carved bronze and pulled. The mass of the doors shifted slowly, but once the angel got them moving they swung easily enough. They parted with a sigh like the final release of a dying man.

Tsayyadiel stepped between them into the nave of the building beyond. The interior of the cathedral was no less ostentatious than the outside. The bulk of the building was made of the same veined marble, though the gold flecking was reserved for the exterior. Thin fluted columns rose out of the floor and spiraled upward into the shadowy recesses of the distant ceiling. The early dawn light shown through tall, thin stain glassed windows that showed various saints of the High Church in all their polychromatic splendor. The crimson cast of the early sunlight made them all look as if they were being martyred.

Tsayyadiel grinned a cruel grin. The image was appropriate to his purpose.

As he strode through the nave and into the sanctuary proper a robed acolyte ran up to the angel, his hands tucked into the sleeves of his black robe.

"I'm sorry sir, but the cathedral is not open to visitors at this time. If you'd like to-"

"I am not a visitor," Tsayyadiel cut off his nasal protests.

Tsayyadiel brushed past the low level functionary without another word. The man continued to stammer on behind him, but he didn't have the time to deal with it. Things were continuing at a pace that brooked no hesitations. The quick strike portion of this fight was past and it was a ground war now. It was not a type of fight the Hunter of God liked, but it was one he could do. He would need resources however; would need to know the disposition of forces and to gain access to more weapons. That meant he needed to talk to Enoch.

It was true that the High Church was fairly well organized and if he wanted to take the time he could probably get all the information he wanted from them, but the idea of trying to fawn his way through webs of banal human bureaucracy turned his stomach. It was far better just to go to the source for his information. Unfortunately Enoch was still beyond the Wall and that meant magic, and a costly sort at that.

Tsayyadiel moved up the wide steps to the pulpit, a monstrosity of sculpted gold and draped purple cloth and kept going past it to the altar. The altar was a simpler creature. It was a wide table of dark wood stained with years of spilled wine and smudging hands. The center had a draping of more purple cloth, but Tsayyadiel grasped a fistful of it and yanked it from the table. There were gold leaf inlaid symbols in each of the corners. He reached out and traced them with a fingertip. They tingled at his touch.

"Who are you to come and profane this sacred space?"

The voice was phlegmy and deep, full of recriminations and self-righteous fervor. The angel turned slowly from the altar to find a group of clergy assembled near the pulpit. There were six of them, all men. The oldest stood to the front, clearly their leader. Three jowly chins swing below an expansive jaw and his hands were folded over a rotund belly that was barely squeezed into his black robe. A heavy chain of office swung from his thick neck. There was a carved stone at the end of the chain that denoted his rank within the Church, but Tsayyadiel had never bothered to sort out their hierarchy.

"Sacred?" The angel laughed and spat onto the marble dais at the fat priest's feet. The assembled mob gasped in abject horror at the perceived profanity. "This is a building. It was built by meat and will be felled by time. It gives pompous fools like you a place to hang your pilfered wealth and nothing more."

"I am-" the fat man drew himself up as best he could, ready to lambaste Tsayyadiel with his rank and privilege, but the angel was getting tired of the drama.

"What you are," he cut the man off, "is a cog in a broken machine. Today you will finally get to fill a purpose however. Today you finally get to matter."

"Who are you?" one of the other gathered priests asked. He was a bone thin man with thick red lips and a wide nose mottled with the petechiae of the heavy drinker. His long fingers were fidgeting with the hems of his long sleeves.

"I am Tsayyadiel. I am the Hunter of God, He Who Finds, the Eyes of Night."

Tsayyadiel let his wings unfold behind him, four pitch-black streaks across the growing light of the church. The reaction was immediate but varied among the group. Some dropped to their knees, others simply stared wide-eyed; one fainted. The fat priest bowed his head and

275

pressed a hand to his lips as if in prayer.

"I am sorry my Lord, we did not know you!" he declared feverishly. With his chin pressed to his chest the man's voice was even thicker and harder to understand.

"What is the great purpose you would have of us Lord Tsayyadiel?" another of the priests asked. He was one that had dropped to his knees and his eyes glittered with tears.

"I have need to speak to my masters beyond the Wall. There are magics that will allow me to do so, but they are difficult and costly," he told them.

The leader bobbed his head, his chins waggling.

"Of course Lord, of course. We will do anything you wish to aid you, and certainly will pay any cost. As you can see we have no lack of funds." He waved a thick-fingered hand to indicate the obvious opulence of the palatial church.

"I had no doubt that you would pay my price for me, but I have no need of your riches."

"My Lord?" The fat man's eyes began to widen as he gleaned the angel's meaning.

"To speak beyond the Wall is blood magic," Tsayyadiel told them. "This will be an important conversation and I don't want it cut short, so I'll need plenty of blood."

They scattered like dust in a tornado. He let them all start running. He was a hunter after all, and he enjoyed it more when they were running.

~ ~ ~

The dark wood of the altar was quickly soaking in the pools of blood Tsayyadiel had poured across it, leaving darker circles on the already stained wood. The angel himself was covered in gore. His arms from hand to elbow were solid red and his face was streaked like warpaint. The bodies of the dead priests were in a heap next to him, tossed like unceremonious rag-dolls. As he'd killed each, careful not to spill too much of their precious life-blood

276

he'd gathered them up and brought them back to the altar.

Once he'd gathered them all he'd set to the real work of painting the sacred surface, the only thing with any real power or significance in the entire edifice. Once it was well covered he dripped more blood onto it to make sure he had plenty. He didn't want to be interrupted once he began. He laid his hands flat on the wood. The blood, still warm pooled around his fingers. His eyes slipped shut.

"Enoch," he called into the empty space. "Enoch."

He waited patiently. He was not a sorcerer, there were others with that gift but Tsayyadiel knew this magic well enough that he was certain it would work.

"They have eluded you." Enoch's voice drifted through Tsayyadiel's thoughts.

Tsayyadiel suppressed his irritation at the greeting. It was a true statement, but Enoch sounded subtly pleased at the other angel's failure as if it proved some long-standing point.

"The resources I was given were inadequate to the task," he replied sharply. "The Crone fell like a novice and the alchemist was next to useless in the end."

"So I have heard. You cannot return."

Another flare of irritation. His fingers curled into claws, digging furrows in the ancient wood of the altar.

"I have no intention of returning, whether I can or not. I have never returned with a task unfinished and this will be no different."

"Than what do you need?" Enoch sounded almost bored. Tsayyadiel gritted his teeth and took a long breath. He knew he was being bated. Enoch had always been attached to their master's side and because of that he had many privileges, but had seen very little actual glory in the years of the War. All he could do was pass on the edicts of their Lord and snipe at better angels.

"I need better resources. I believe that now that they

have the girl and the artifact they will attempt to return to the Prophet."

"The Prophet." Enoch couldn't quiet maintain his bored veneer. "He has been an even more closely guarded secret than the Bearer was. It has been centuries since we have seen any real sign of him."

"Not since the Waters I've heard."

"That is so," Enoch confirmed. "What makes you think after all this time he'll surface now? It seems they'd find it far too dangerous with you back in the world."

A thin smile twisted across his face.

"What choice do they have?" Tsayyadiel asked. "We have forced their hand; largely because I am here. My brothers and sister know me well enough to know that I will not stop until I have found the Bearer. They have to move forward, they have to go to the Prophet because to simply try to hide or run will keep them only so long. Eventually I will find them. They will go to the Prophet."

"Very well." Enoch was silent for a long time. "You are the best eyes we have there, what do you propose?"

"I can track them," Tsayyadiel began. "I can find them eventually, but when I do I cannot fight them all. I will need allies, and not of the paltry variety you gave me before. I need allies equal to the task ahead. I need allies who can face the Three and not falter. Only two of the Three were even present at our last encounter and they were still more than a match for everything you gave me for aid."

"Give me a few moments." Enoch's presence, a dull ache at the base of Tsayyadiel's neck was suddenly gone. The angel remained frozen, his hands steeping in the blood as he waited. As he did he considered what he'd told Enoch. If he could track his family to the Prophet than they could end this War once and for all. It would be a great victory, but it would require great skill on his part.

It would be easy enough to find his family again. They were drawn together like loadstones, but if he attacked them as soon as he found them they would lead him no where, and if they realized that he'd found them they wouldn't go anywhere near their precious, traitorous leader. He would have to locate them and then shadow them without their knowledge until the perfect moment to strike. When that moment came if he didn't have the resources he needed it would all be wasted.

"Very well," Enoch was suddenly there again.

"I will receive the aid I need; real aid this time?" Tsayyadiel had never doubted the answer. This was too great an opportunity for the Word to ignore.

"Of course, we always offer aid to those who call."

"Do we?" Tsayyadiel couldn't keep the jab out of his voice. Enoch had a tendency to use 'we' when he spoke about the Word's decrees. Enoch ignored the jab.

"Unfortunately more and more of our servants and angels are falling to the lure of the Traitor and his lies so our resources are limited."

"Don't tell me of limited resources Enoch," Tsayyadiel snarled. "I am stranded here trying to win a war and all you've given me so far is paper dolls. We have a real chance to end this here and now."

"I understand that. I was simply prefacing our situation so you would understand the decision that's being made."

A suspicion started to gather itself into an unruly tangle in Tsayyadiel's gut.

"What decision?"

"You are being given charge of some of the Adversaries minions."

Tsayyadiel turned his head and spat violently onto the floor.

"Demons," he snarled. "I want no truck with those foul

beasts. The Crone walked a line between our world and theirs and she was bad enough."

"I told you before you left this place Tsayyadiel, things are different. They are not the enemy any more. Your venom is misplaced. Your own family is now--"

"Do not finish that sentence Enoch," Tsayyadiel hissed, his voice deadly quiet. "My family is lost and fallen, but they will never be so low as that brimstone born brood. I will not--"

"You will." This time it was Enoch's turn to interrupt. "You will do what you have always done, and this is what you are told. This is not something that I have decided. You are right that we have a significant opportunity to change the face of this War and it cannot be ignored. You are right that you need allies up to the task. We do not have the force to spare to give you the strength you need, but the Adversary does. You will use the forces you are given. You will find the Bearer. You will follow her to the Prophet, and you will see to it that they are all destroyed. You will see to it that you do not fail again."

"I will not fail again." It was a whisper, a cold fury compressed into sound.

"We know. Go to the Cathedral of Equiter. You will find your lieutenant and connection to your forces there."

"It shall be done."

Tsayyadiel severed the connection with a violent wrench of his mind. It left a dull pounding in his temples, but he knew it did the same to Enoch and that was satisfying enough to make the pain worth it.

He stood slowly, letting his height unfold from where he knelt at the low altar table. He wiped his bloody hands clean on the front of his robe. The once white fabric was wildly stained. There was blood and dirt ground together, a caked on mixture that had been growing since he had arrived in the world. He would need a change of clothes.

Tsayyadiel moved to the pile of bodies and started sorting through them. The angel was tall and broad, but not inhumanly so and there had been one priest who came close enough. He only hoped that when he had opened the man up for the bloodletting he hadn't made too much of a mess of him. When he found the tall priest toward the bottom of the pile Tsayyadiel was gratified to see that his robe was only slightly touched by blood, his and his fellows and that the black fabric hid the stains well.

He dragged the body out of the pile and stripped the robe off it. It was made of a rich, heavy cloth and had a black on black brocade pattern across the chest. There were several pockets hidden around it, some inside the robe itself and one in each sleeve. It would serve his purpose very well.

Tsayyadiel quickly slipped off his own stained robe and threw it aside. He drew the new robe over his head and let it fall into place. It fit as well as he could hope. He took the gold rope from one of the curtains in the room and wrapped it around his waist as a belt. Once it was secure he shoved his knife through the impromptu belt and headed for the double doors which still stood ajar at the front of the cathedral.

Outside the sun had broken over the tops of the buildings. It spilled across the square in front of the cathedral in a warm wave. The first few parishioners of the day were making their way toward church. They would have a surprise when they got inside. Tsayyadiel saw no reason to wait until they got inside to surprise them.

He walked out of the shadow of the building so that the sun fell fully across him, glittering in his black hair and disappearing into the thick fabric of his new robe. A few of the approaching people took note of him, but most ignored his presence. There was nothing unusual about a priest walking out of the church. His thin smile returned.

He spread his arms wide and unfolded his wings.

Now they noticed him. The reactions of the people in the square were just as varied as those of the priests and he stood for a moment letting them reel in awe and terror. Then he bent his strong legs and with a powerful leap and a flap of his great wings he pulled away into the clear sapphire sky.

25

NIGHT WAS WELL on them when Reaper came back into the house where they were hiding. The angel had been out moving around the perimeter of the area making sure there were no spying eyes before they embarked on their journey to see the Prophet.

"We're clear," he told the assembled group in the kitchen. They'd closed the trap door and drawn the table back on top of it. Epiphany, Gerold, and Brendiwald were sitting at the table while Fist and Crafter stood near a side door talking quietly.

"Alright, no reason to hold off," Brendiwald said, rising to his feet. Epiphany and Gerold rose with him, shouldering their bags. Epiphany let a hand drop to her coat pocket. She felt the comforting weight of her grandpa; a soft warm buzz through the fabric of the jacket.

Reaper turned and went back outside, the rest of the group following. The sky was clear, though with the spill of light from Newridge so close by Epiphany couldn't see that many stars. It made her glad she didn't live in one of the inland cities. To be without the stars for long would drive her mad. Still she was glad to see that the clouds had burned away during the day.

The decision had been made that the journey to see the Prophet would be taken on foot. It would take longer, but it would attract less attention than using any of their swifter means of travel. They would be bringing one cart, but it was just an open wagon they could use for supplies and only one person could ride on it at a time. Either way the clear skies promised a trip without rain. After the last week that was a blessing.

The cart was already loaded, and had its one long-term passenger carefully ensconced in the back. Heart was going with them, but he was still recovering and even once he did he wouldn't be able to walk. As an angel he could still fly, but for the overland journey he would have to ride with the packs.

The genial angel seemed to be taking it all with a calm demeanor. He was all smiles and laughter and try as she might Epiphany couldn't see any falsity to it. He seemed genuinely at peace with his crippling. When they approached the cart he waved broadly at them.

"So," he called out. "Who gets the dubious honor of keeping me company and listening to me prattle for the first leg of the trip?"

"That would be me dear brother," Fist said, leaping up to the bench beside the acolyte who would be driving the cart for them. The driver for her part seemed happy enough to be transporting the two angels. She was a middle-aged woman named Stel with sandy hair and not enough chin to excuse her wide face, but Brendiwald said she was a fair hand with a campfire, a horse cart, and a billy club so she'd been drafted for the trip.

Epiphany tossed her bag into the back of the cart with the rest. Heart caught her with his soft blue eyes. Eye. One of the orbs had been damaged in the attack and though the eye itself had healed it was milky and empty.

"All of this is for the good Epiphany," he told her. "I see the looks of sorrow that linger around you when you think on me, or your grandfather, and especially when you're mind is drawn to your parents."

"How can you know when I'm thinking of my parents?" she asked.

A smile split his curly beard. The damage to his face was starting to heal, but there were still deep pink furrows through the rusty hair.

"I'm an angel child. We all have gifts. I am an angel of the Heart, and it is not hard to see what is weighing on yours. I just want you to know, all this is for a purpose. You might not be able to see it yet, but it is there just beneath the surface."

"Can you see it?" she asked, leaning on the rail of the cart.

He laughed, and even in his damaged state it was bright and full of joy.

"Of course not!" he proclaimed. "I can't see it any more than you can. The secrets of the heart are mine to peruse, but the greater plan... that is beyond even an angel."

"Than how can you be so sure that all this is happening for a reason. How can you know that you weren't maimed for nothing?"

Heart rolled toward her, shifting his weight up onto his elbow to more easily focus on her with his one good eye.

"It's faith Epiphany. For all these years you have lived without that simple thing, but that isn't how life is supposed to be. You aren't supposed to go through life laden only with doubt and fear, but that is the world the High Church is creating. In their world they tell you what to believe and what to expect. Faith isn't necessary.

For those that reject the High Church, they often don't find their own faith, they just reject faith entirely; like you. You believe nothing."

"I believe things," Epiphany protested.

"No, you know things," Heart corrected. "Some of the things you know don't seem completely obvious and so you call your knowing them faith, but in the end you just know them. In the dark of night you cannot see any sign that the sun will rise so you could say that you have faith that it will, but in the end you know that it will. It takes no faith. Faith is when you have no way to know, but you believe anyway."

"That just foolish though isn't it?"

"No, it's powerful. All the most incredible things accomplished by humanity have been accomplished on acts of faith. Even when eventually it was known instead of believed, at first it was all faith. In the end my faith will be proven as well, that all this is part of the plan, part of the Machine, but right now I just have to have faith. If I didn't than I would hesitate, or step out of my place and then it wouldn't happen the way it should."

"But if it's all part of some plan then it doesn't matter what you do does it? No matter what you do it's all just some big cosmic game."

Heart shook his head, his smile returning.

"Not at all. Have you ever cooked a stew Epiphany?"

"What?" Her brows beetled down.

"I'll assume you have," the angel said with a laugh. She nodded to confirm her status as a stewer. "When you make a stew you have a bunch of ingredients all laid out on the counter for you. That's sort of the way the Machine works. It gives you all the ingredients you need to make a stew. How you prepare those ingredients though, and how much you add of each, as well as how you season and spice the stew that's all up to you."

"So we know we're going to end up with stew, but we don't know if it'll be good or not?"

"Basically!"

"And you have faith that we're making a good stew?"

Heart nodded, his face growing serious.

"We are in a difficult place Epiphany, I won't lie, but everyone here is a good person. We are all working together and we're trying to make things right. That matters."

"I hope so."

"I have faith."

Heart gave her one last long smile and then let himself sink back down onto the pallet that had been prepared for him. Epiphany let go of the rail and walked up to join the rest of the group. They were standing in a loose circle to one side of the cart. As she approached Brendiwald looked around to make sure everyone was there.

"Are we ready?" he asked. Everyone nodded. With a nod to Stel the trip was set in motion. She flicked the reins and the cart started forward with a lurch. They waited until it had rolled past them on gently squeaking wheels and then fell in behind it. Stel kept the horses reined in so that the people on foot could keep up with her. They set a brisk pace, but not so fast that they couldn't keep it up all night. The plan was to travel through the night and the start of the next day.

Epiphany sidled up next to Gerold.

"I just had a strange conversation," she told him.

"Oh? There have been a lot of those lately."

She couldn't help but laugh.

"That's more of the truth than I like to think about, but I just had a chat with an angel about faith. I guess I wouldn't have thought an angel would need a lot of faith."

"Once upon a time we didn't." Epiphany hadn't heard Reaper walk up behind them and she jumped when he spoke.

"I'm sorry, I didn't mean to scare you," he said with a slight incline of his head.

"What you do mean angels didn't need faith?" Gerold asked, waving away the apology.

"Before the Word fell to the Lie angels didn't operate on faith, we simply knew, or at least we thought we did.

That was probably part of the problem. We thought we knew, so when things started to go wrong we didn't know what to do. It was different from what we 'knew'. A lot of good angels still serve the Word because they can't allow themselves to believe that what they 'know' isn't true."

"That's terrible," Epiphany said.

"Yes it is," Reaper's face darkened. "I've had to kill friends over 'knowing'. It was hard every time."

"I'm so sorry!" Epiphany felt such a weight of sorrow for the angels and the war they had been caught up in against their will.

"I serve a purpose. No matter what the Word says that purpose does not change. No matter what I've had to do I just remind myself that I serve a purpose. It is enough."

"So faith is hard for an angel?" Gerold interjected.

"It is," Reaper admitted. "We are not designed for questions and when you have no questions you have no need for belief. That's why you humans have always been so important, far more important than us. You question, you doubt, you change, you believe. We can really only aspire to that."

"You sound like you really admire humans," Epiphany suggested.

"Some of us do," Reaper said with a thin smile.

"Some don't," Gerold offered the obvious follow-up. "Like your twin?"

"He never particularly cared for humans, but since the War started he has come to really hate them. He thinks you're pathetic with all your fears and doubts. He never understood that was what made you strong."

"It doesn't make me feel strong," Epiphany said, wrapping her arms around herself, all the moments of terror in the last week coming back to her in a wash. Reaper's hand was like an anchor on her shoulder, drawing her to a place of stillness in the raging ocean of fear.

"You can only have courage when you're afraid," he told her. "If you're simply not afraid that is not real courage, it is just ignorance. The amazing thing about humans is that given all the odds, all the chances, you will still go for something because you believe it is the right thing to do and strangely enough despite all those things you often succeed. Your kind is blessed by the Machine."

"Do you think we'll win?" The talk of impossible odds brought Epiphany back to that fundamental question that wouldn't leave her mind.

"I guess that depends on what you mean by winning."

Reaper offered no further explanation. He took two long strides and leapt up to perch on the edge of the wagon. He leaned in close and said something that made his siblings laugh.

"They're a strange family," Epiphany told Gerold.

"There are a lot of strange things lately," he shot back.

"Yes there are, but I think we're headed the right direction."

"You mean going to see the Prophet?" he asked.

"Yes, that too, but more than that. I think meeting all these people; I think coming together now, with the Grail; I think facing this War head on; I think all of it is the right direction."

"How can you know that?" Gerold asked, shooting her a sidelong glance.

"I can't," she told him, her eyes straying to Heart, laughing with his brother and sister. "I can't know it, but I have faith."

26

"I HAVE DISPATCHED Tsayyadiel with your orders Lord," Enoch said. He knelt on the hard stone floor with his forehead pressed to the ground and his hands splayed out to his sides, palms flat against the stone as well. There was no response and the quiet stretched out beyond a pause and into a silence. Enoch lifted his head slightly.

The Word stood where he often stood, in front of one of the wide windows in the high tower room where he held audience. His calloused hands were resting on the sill and his gaze was lost to the swirling nothing beyond the Keep of the Throne. Enoch could see the thick white beard that ran down the Word's chest bobbing slightly as his master chewed his lower lip.

"You seem troubled my Lord," Enoch offered.

The Word turned pale gray eyes to regard him where he lingered prostrate on the floor.

"Get up Enoch," the Word said. His voice was soft, but it carried with perfect clarity over the distance.

The angel gathered himself up off the floor and brushed his white robes back into place. The Word motioned him forward with a wave of his hand. Enoch walked across the throne room to stand beside his Lord who gestured for him to look out the window. Enoch did as he was bid.

Beyond the unshuttered window was the formless black of the Void. It was featureless and flat and seemed to press in on the confines of the window as if it could seep into the room and devour all within. Enoch had never been fond of looking into the Void, but he was fain to deny his Lord's command so he stood and regarded the blackness in silence.

"What do you see Enoch?" the Word asked.

"I see nothing my Lord," the angel replied. "I see the blackness of the Void."

"And what do you think I see?"

Enoch was startled by the question.

"I do not know my Lord. I admit that I have often wondered if you can see something in the Void the rest of us cannot. I have wondered if there is some motion, or some pattern that you are studying when you stand at your window."

The Word smiled. Deep lines of care etched the corners of his eyes.

"No Enoch, there is no hidden form to the Void. I do not stare out this window because I see something that is there. I stare out this window because I see the possibility. What I see out there Enoch is the end of all of this."

"So you think Tsayyadiel will succeed?"

"No." The Word shook his head, white hair whispering around his shoulders.

"He may," the Word quickly added. "He is determined and vicious enough to succeed where all others have failed, but he also underestimates what is stacked against him."

"You seem unconcerned Lord. They have the Grail and could storm the Gates at any time."

"This is true," the Word conceded. He took Enoch by the shoulder and gestured into the Void again. "And if they came to destroy us this is where they would come. They would lay themselves before our gates and try to strike us down. Do you think that Gate is the only thing standing between me and defeat Enoch?"

"No ... no of course not my Lord."

The Word smiled again.

"No, of course not. The Bearer has returned yes?"

"Yes my Lord."

"And now Tsayyadiel believes the Bearer will go to the Prophet?"

"Yes my Lord." Enoch didn't understand the line of questioning. The Word knew this, so why did he ask.

"The Prophet has been in hiding a long time," the Word said. "He has eluded us at every turn, but now he might show himself. Our deadliest agent may get a chance at him. What if he fails though?"

"My Lord?"

"What would the Prophet do if Tsayyadiel failed to kill him?"

"He would marshal his forces and come here my Lord."

"Yes. Yes he would."

"I don't understand my Lord," Enoch admitted.

"I know you don't, but that is because you have not had all the information my son. Why do you think we were seeking the Bearer and the Grail?"

"So that the Prophet couldn't use the Grail against us; couldn't use it to reopen the Gates."

"No." The Word shook his head again. Enoch let his eyes fall to the floor, feeling chastised. "The greatest threat that traitor has ever posed to me has not been that he will come back here, but that he will stay there. I didn't have him killed the first time because he was trying to storm the walls and take the Throne. He was there, on earth, teaching his precious humans all the lessons he though they needed to hear, and that is exactly what he has been doing ever since. The Grail was hard to find, but the Prophet was impossible."

"Now that the Bearer is moving again it will force the Prophet's hand," Enoch said, raising his head as a measure of understanding came to him.

"Indeed. He won't be able to cut one of his servants loose, and now that they're on the run he'll feel compelled to act. The only act he has left is to come here and make his play for the Throne. Everything else would be nothing but stalling."

"So no matter what happens with Tsayyadiel..." Enoch ventured.

"It will be the end of the Prophet. Either our angel will succeed, or he will drive the traitor and his motley band right into my arms. This will end with him kneeling before the Walls Enoch, mark my words. That is what I see when I look out this window."

Enoch looked out into the endless black and really saw it for the first time. It didn't seem ominous and encroaching; empty and terrible. The Void seemed open. It seemed full of possibilities.

"Now my son," the Word said, gesturing into the expanse. "Now you understand."

Justin Phillips lives in Austin, Texas, with his wife and son, where in addition to writing he is a practicing acupuncturist and professor of Eastern Medicine.

ABSOLUTELY AMAZING eBOOKS

AbsolutelyAmazingEbooks.com

or AA-eBooks.com

www.ingramcontent.com/pod-product-compliance
Lightning Source LLC
Chambersburg PA
CBHW060952030726
47503CB00003B/838